DANCING IN IRELAND

JENNIFER SKULLY

Redwood
Valley
Publishing

DANCING IN IRELAND

A ONCE AGAIN NOVEL

Book 3

Take off to Ireland for a later in life, second chance, holiday romance to get your feet tapping...

When Rose Christopher's entire world falls apart after losing her mother, her marriage and her home within a matter of weeks, she's desperate for income and a roof over her head. So Rose takes a job as the live-in caregiver of a feisty 87-year-old widow named Agnes. Surprisingly, Agnes is a delight. Too bad the man who hired Rose seems so cold-hearted and rude.

Or is there far more to him than Rose imagines?

After his divorce, Declan Delaney claims he no longer has a heart. Except when it comes to Agnes. The successful, self-made businessman will do anything for his former grade school teacher, who inspired his lifelong love of learning, including ticking off the most important item on her bucket list—a trip to Ireland where her favorite movie *The Quiet Man* was filmed. And when he sees how Agnes and Rose bond, he knows hiring Rose was another excellent decision.

So then why is he feeling more than just professional satisfaction when it comes to Rose? And why can't he ignore the way her quiet humor, caring manner, and the promise of her sweet, kissable lips keep drawing him back again and again?

With Rose and Declan whisking her off for the trip of a lifetime, Agnes packs her matchmaker hat in her suitcase. Can she help two people with mothballed hearts learn to dance together in Ireland?

Who would have thought a trip to Ireland could bring so many second chances?

Join our newsletter and receive free books, plus learn about new releases, contests, and other freebies: http://bit.ly/SkullyNews

ACKNOWLEDGMENTS

A special thanks to Bella Andre for this fabulous idea and to both Bella and Nancy Warren for all the brainstorming on our 10-mile walks. Thank you also to my special network of friends who support and encourage me: Shelley Adina, Jenny Andersen, Linda McGinnis, Jackie Yau, Kathy Coatney, and Laurel Jacobson. As always, a huge hug of appreciation for my husband who helps my writing career flourish. But somehow I have to keep Wrigley from rubbing her face on the computer when she wants her dinner. Since it's a touchscreen, she always messes up the manuscript!

DEDICATION

This book is for all loving, dedicated, hard-working caregivers for the joy they bring to the people they help. But most especially to all the wonderful caregivers who took care of my mother over the years. For all the drives to the ocean, for ice cream, for coffee, for pizza, for breakfast at Denny's, for all the laughter and all the love. Mom was a silly sausage (I have no idea where that saying came from), and they all belonged to her silly sausage club.

To Susanna and Ana, Blue and Emerson and Aire, Lily, Janette, Jennifer, Chloe, Anthony, Iman, Sylvia, Brent, Danica, Winnie, Gabby, Niki, Denessa, Stormy, Claudia, Jovi, Jackie, Natasha, Ernesto, and to anyone I've missed. Thank you all for everything you did for Mom and for us.

"The hospital won't release Agnes until she has an adequate caregiver in place." Declan Delaney sat back in his chair and crossed his arms. "When the elderly have a fall like Agnes's, especially since this is the fourth she's had in as many months, they want to make sure the patient is protected at home. The only other alternative is to send her to a rehab facility."

Rose Christopher assessed the man behind the big desk in what she could only assume was a home office. She would have expected him to be a redhead or at least dark-haired, attesting to an Irish ancestry based on his name, but Declan Delaney was blond, his thick hair cut short, with a frosting of white at the temples. It was his electric green eyes that were Irish. He was a good-looking man—*exceptionally* good-looking—somewhere in his mid-fifties, and when he'd introduced himself, holding out his hand to shake, he'd towered over her. Rose was by no means petite at five foot seven, but he was at least six-three.

"She was very lucky she didn't break anything. When were

you planning on having her released?" Rose asked. She could start right away.

"As soon as possible. Agnes hates the hospital, and she definitely doesn't want to go to rehab. She says it's just another hospital." He tapped a key on his laptop as if he couldn't stand having the screen go to sleep while he was talking to her. "All this change is confusing for her."

"I agree, the elderly don't process change well. Is Agnes your grandmother?" He hadn't given her Agnes's last name.

"No." His voice was terse. "She's my tenant. She doesn't have any children and her husband passed away over ten years ago. She lives in one of the two flats downstairs." He waved a hand to indicate the apartment she occupied, which, facing the Victorian house, was on the right.

It was odd that he was so concerned about a tenant. "And she's not any sort of relative?"

"No," he said even more sharply. "But Agnes has lived in that apartment for close to ten years."

The house was a gorgeously renovated Victorian. Parts of San Jose were known for their beautiful old houses, and Declan Delaney's home made her drool. It was within walking distance of the Rose Garden, and the area was sometimes referred to as the Rose Garden District.

"Agnes doesn't have any family," he told her. "So she doesn't have an advocate looking out for her best interests."

"And you've taken on that role?" Why would he if they weren't related?

But he only nodded.

When she got the call from her agency for a full-time, live-in caregiver, she'd looked up the man making the request. She liked to know who her employers were. If she understood the employer, she could better understand the conditions under which she'd be working. Her agency didn't normally send live-in caregivers. They worked in shifts. Mr. Declan

Delaney wanted someone to live in, and he'd have to pay a premium for that. From her agency, Rose was the only one who'd agreed to interview.

She'd found his internet footprints all over the San Francisco Bay Area, especially San Jose. He was in real estate, owning hotels and business parks, office complexes and apartment buildings. And he lived in this magnificent Victorian, using the upper floors while renting out the first level, which he'd divided into two apartments.

In all the photos she'd found on the internet, he was all business, just as he was today, rarely smiling. There wasn't a single mention of family, so either he was extremely private or he was completely unattached. She also found no indication why this stern businessman would want to take care of an old lady. In fact, she would have thought he'd want to shunt her off to a rehab facility, maybe never to come back. Then he could rent out her apartment to someone who would most likely pay a lot more money.

But he obviously wasn't going to answer her questions. "Rather than what relation Agnes is to me, let's discuss your qualifications, Mrs. Christopher."

"It's just Rose. I'm not a Mrs. anymore." Her husband had left her after they'd been living with her mother for three years, saying he hadn't signed on to be a caretaker. Except he hadn't phrased it as nicely.

Declan Delaney didn't comment on her marital history. "I see you have a gap of five years in your work history." He waved a hand over her hastily typed resume. The people she worked for didn't normally care about her resume. If they didn't like her, all they had to do was call the agency and replace her. To date, no one had ever replaced Rose. She left because she wasn't needed anymore.

"As you can see, I've worked for several different care facilities." She leaned forward to touch the edge of the paper as if that would help him see her situation clearly. "I took family leave to care for my mother who had Alzheimer's. I felt I had the expertise to take care of her rather than putting her in a home. I was her full-time caregiver for those five years."

He glanced down at the page in front of him. "I see you started working again about nine months ago, so I assume she passed away." Something softened his green eyes as he met her gaze. "I'm sorry for your loss."

It had been a year. She'd taken three months to get herself in order before she'd signed on with the agency.

An ache tightened around her heart, even now. Sometimes the tears took her by surprise, when one of Mom's favorite songs played on the radio, or she came across a photo, or she pruned the blue hydrangeas. Rose ached about the first few years of the disease, when Mom understood that she was losing herself. First there was denial. *I'm not forgetting anything.* Then there was fear, when she lashed out. *Why are you doing this to me?* And finally the decline, when she no longer comprehended anything at all.

Rose would have let her mother go long before she actually died. That was no way to live.

"You mentioned memory loss in your application for Agnes. I've had extensive experience in memory care facilities," she told him. "And, of course, the years with my mother."

He was reading her resume again. Her life on one page. "But you're not a nurse?"

"No." She didn't bother qualifying it. She was a high school graduate, but she'd never gone to college. She could look back at the last thirty years of her life and ask why she hadn't gone to nursing school somewhere along the way. It wasn't as if she had children at home to take care of. There'd just been her husband and her. She didn't have any excuses.

Maybe it was all the years of trying to have a baby. All the miscarriages. When they finally stopped trying, there was the exhaustion. And the depression. But that was years ago, and she'd come to accept that she wouldn't be a mother.

"But if I'm not a nurse, you can see from my experience that I can handle Alzheimer's patients."

"Agnes doesn't have Alzheimer's," he said. "She's just forgetful."

It sounded like denial. "It's just one form of dementia. There are many similarities with old-age dementia. Can you describe her symptoms?"

He shrugged as if he didn't know how to quantify it. "She's forgotten pots on the stove, burned toast. I decided, for safety reasons, to turn off the electricity to the stove and range, and removed her toaster oven." He shook his head, and Rose thought she detected sadness. Or maybe it was just irritation. "She's called me because the TV remote wouldn't work. But when I come down to help, it works just fine."

Dementia wasn't just forgetting what someone told you, or repeating yourself. It wasn't just short-term memory. It was no longer being able to differentiate between the telephone receiver and the TV remote. It was thinking that someone on FaceTime was actually right there with you. It was believing that people on the TV were crowding into your room. But there were always levels to it. Agnes might not be that bad. After all, everyone forgot pots on the stove or repeated themselves a time or two.

"I've had a lot of experience with this. I can make a better assessment when I meet her." *When, not if. Stay positive.* "Can you tell me more about her physical capabilities?"

He made the smallest of shrugs, as if he didn't have the words to describe Agnes's condition. It was hard for a big strong man to understand that even something so simple as getting to the bathroom could take fifteen minutes.

5

"I'm not around her enough to judge. But as I mentioned, she's had four recent falls, all occurring in her flat. I gave her an alert button, and when I was notified, I sent someone over to check on her. This last time, she bumped her head, there was quite a bit of bleeding, and we had an ambulance take her to the hospital. Luckily she didn't break anything, but the doctors fear what's going to happen the next time." By the crease of his brow, she thought Mr. Delaney was also afraid of what might happen.

"Does she use a walker or a cane?"

"She has walkers, one for inside and one outside, but she only uses the outside one. She claims she doesn't need the help inside."

She made mental notes of his answers. "Could it be she forgets to use it rather than stubbornness?"

He laughed for the first time since she'd walked up the stairs to his office. "Oh, she's stubborn all right." Rose swore that was a fond twinkle in his eyes.

"So she's physically unstable?"

He nodded. "She doesn't even put her hands out to break the fall. She just goes straight down."

Rose smiled, not with humor but with understanding. "Has she ever broken any bones?"

"Not that I know of."

"That's probably why, because she doesn't put her arms out to break her fall, so no broken wrists or arms. But she's very lucky she hasn't broken a hip."

He snorted. "She says she bounces." His mouth lifted in a half smile. "I think it's because she doesn't have far to fall. She's only something like four foot eight." He tapped the side of his hand below his chest, indicating where her head would reach on him.

"Well, having someone with her all the time to remind her to use her walker will be a good thing. How are her spirits?"

He widened his eyes as if he couldn't fathom what Rose was talking about. "Her spirits?"

"Her mood. Is she happy or sad or upset?"

"She's fine. Except that she hates the hospital. She's been in there two days while I've been interviewing caregivers. But there's nobody—" He cut himself off as if he didn't want to say that no one had met his high expectations.

Rose pressed the issue. "But other than that, she's happy?"

His voice was terse again, as if he was tired of her questions when he should be doing the asking. "I'm not worried about her moods so much as I am about making sure she doesn't fall again. That's all I require."

He'd obviously never cared for an elderly family member.

But Rose was insistent. "I'd like to assess whether she's depressed."

He snorted. "Agnes is the least depressed person I know." He eyed her. "Except for myself."

She figured this man wouldn't know *depressed* if someone smacked him in the face with it.

"I'm wondering if she's depressed or she's just bored because she can't do all the things she used to." But he wasn't going to understand without concrete examples. "That's one of the things I noticed with my mother." She shook her head slightly, the ache in her chest returning. "It was hard for Mom to admit, but she stopped reading books because she couldn't retain the information she'd read. She couldn't even read magazines. She loved word puzzles, but she couldn't remember how to do them anymore." She pressed her lips together, her emotions rising with the prick of a tear at her eye. "So yes, she became quite depressed because she was alone and couldn't do anything without help."

Her husband had wanted Rose to put her mother in a home. But the facilities that Medicare would pay for weren't the places she wanted her mother to spend the last years of her life. Dad had died when Rose was thirty-five, cancer. And her brother lived back east. There was no one else to help. Rose had quit her job at a memory care facility to be her mother's full-time caregiver, and she and her husband moved in with Mom. The amount they saved on rent and utilities and commuting made up for the loss of income. At least that's how she sold her husband on the idea.

Rose could almost feel Declan Delaney squirm away from that info dump. "I'm sorry. All that must have been very hard on you. But I honestly don't know about Agnes's state of mind." His gaze rose to the ceiling corner behind her. "She seems happy enough."

She wondered about him. He seemed so out of touch with not just Agnes's feelings, but his own. Like the word *feeling* was enough to make him twitchy.

Rose was a caregiver. She was used to asking questions and trying to drag out information from a person who couldn't communicate well. She'd been doing it for so long it had become instinct.

She went with instinct now, even when she knew it was probably a bad idea with a man like this, especially with a job at stake. "Do you have parents?" she asked.

He was taken aback, his eyes narrowing slightly, and a tick in his jaw. "Of course I have parents." His words were clipped, as if she were asking if he'd been hatched rather than born.

Rose didn't say anything, waiting him out.

Until finally he added, "My parents are happy and healthy, in their early eighties, living down in Palm Springs. I see them every couple of months. They've even taken up golfing. My father was a plumber, and my mother ran the plumbing supply shop they owned together. Neither of them had ever golfed in their lives. So yes, I'd say they're very happy."

As if he'd actually said them, the words *so there* seemed to echo.

Living in Palm Springs, taking up golfing. She wondered if he'd made it all possible for his parents. "Then you know what happy elderly people look like," she said softly. "Is that what you see in Agnes?"

"All right." He snapped out the words. "Sometime she's a little quieter now than she used to be. I wouldn't call it unhappy. Just different."

She moved to her main point. "I think she needs to be engaged, activities that stimulate her. That's part of what a caregiver can provide. Not just taking care of physical needs and safety, but stimulation, getting out of the house, and of course, nutrition."

Declan Delaney was silent a very long, harrowing moment, his gaze hard enough to chisel right into her head. Then he said, "No one else has asked me questions like this."

"What did they ask you?"

"If they can have two days off per week, since this is a full-time, live-in job."

"That's all they ask, about the days off?"

He let the previous statement stand, as if he weren't a man used to repeating himself.

"Well then." She kept her gaze as steady on him as his was on her. "I guess I should ask whether or not I get a day off."

She'd rarely had a day off while her mother was ill. She couldn't trust her husband to do what was needed. It was a good thing Rose was strong because he'd never helped when she gave her mother a shower.

"How many days off a week do you think you'll need?"

Caregiving could be exhausting. Especially the more a patient needed, and she wouldn't know that until she spent time with Agnes. Therefore she asked for something reasonable based on the things he'd told her. "One twelve-hour period, then another half day, since I'm going to be there nights as well, and I have no idea how much interruption there'll be during that time. Is there any issue with incontinence?"

She could almost see him holding up his fingers like a crucifix warding her off. "I have no idea."

Rose allowed herself a little smile at his expense. She probably shouldn't have asked. But bodily functions were something old people had no problem talking about it. Some of them were obsessed by it. "I'm sure Agnes and I can figure that out together," she said to take the impertinence out of her question.

"One full day plus a half day seems reasonable," he said, going back to the original question. He tapped his finger on the second piece of paper he had in front of him, the one that was *not* her resume. "I have a list of questions I planned to ask you." He looked at her once more. "But you seem to have answered everything without me having to say a word."

She grinned. "Is that like saying I talk too much?"

He gave her what was probably only the second smile of the meeting. "Actually you've been very helpful." He stood. "I'll show you Agnes's flat downstairs."

Rose hoped that meant she had the job. Because listening to Declan Delaney talk about Agnes, she was beginning to like the woman without even meeting her.

2

Rose Christopher struck him as a strong, sturdy woman. From the length of her resume and the years she'd been working, he assumed her to be at least fifty, but she looked younger. She was pretty in a non-glamorized way, very little makeup, her brunette hair curly and cut short in an attractive bob, probably to keep it out of her way while she worked. She was of average height, but beneath the flowered blouse and crisp jeans, she had muscles. Caring for her mother had probably been back-breaking labor. She was exactly the kind of caregiver he wanted for Agnes, someone willing to do everything.

He held open the door leading to the interior landing. The house had been built as a single-family dwelling for a well-to-do businessman with parlor, kitchen, and dining room downstairs, bedrooms on the second floor, servants' quarters, nursery, and playroom on the third. When Rose arrived, he'd had her come up the outside stairs at the back and directly into his office, which was what once would have been the playroom. It was how he usually entered, the freestanding garage and driveway being close by.

"When I renovated the house—" He politely flourished a hand for her to proceed him out the door "—I planned for two flats downstairs, keeping the upper floors for myself."

"Do your wife and kids live here, too?"

It was a simple question requiring a simple answer. Yet he felt the inevitable wrench in his gut, and his words came out sharper than he intended. "I'm divorced. No kids."

She answered as if she hadn't heard the edge in his voice. "Me, too. Divorced with no kids. My husband didn't want to be his mother-in-law's caretaker anymore."

He expected bitterness, but her tone was light, almost as if the marriage and divorce no longer meant anything to her. He, on the other hand, offered no explanation. He didn't reply or offer sympathy for the loss of her marriage the way he had for the passing of her mother.

He led her down the stairs. "Agnes's flat occupies one half. The other tenant is a computer programmer, and we don't see much of him." He kept his hand on the banister, not because he needed to steady himself, because he loved the feel of the polished wood. He had done most of the renovation himself. The house had been a dilapidated mess that he'd seen the potential in as if it were a series of snapshots in his mind, showing the restoration and the glory of the old house brought to life again.

Instead of ushering Rose directly into Agnes's flat, he opened the front door, its oval glass etched with flowers. On the front porch, he stepped aside for Rose to follow him.

She pulled her jacket tighter around her. It was chilly out, in the low fifties, whereas last week it had been in the high sixties. That was San Jose in the middle of March, the weather extremely changeable. They hadn't had much rain yet though March was usually a rainy month.

"I installed a ramp to handle Agnes's walker," he pointed out.

Her eyes widened slightly, and he thought she only managed not to gape at the very last moment. "And you did this for a *tenant?*" she said, as if she couldn't believe.

"It was a valuable improvement," he explained. "I can rent the downstairs units as handicap accessible." But he *had* done it for Agnes. She loved the Rose Garden, which was only two blocks down the street. Although he couldn't say the last time she'd been there. "The porch needed to be redone anyway. The supports were rotting."

"Are you going to redo the garden?"

He breathed in deeply as he surveyed the unkempt yard. "It's in the plan for someday."

The bushes needed a good trim and all of last year's annual flowers should be replaced with new spring plantings. But all of that had been Agnes's job. No, not her job, but her joy. She loved working in the garden. She'd even convinced him to let his gardener go. She'd taken care of everything for years and loved it, but over the last few months, maybe even longer, it had been increasingly difficult for her to get out there. He'd built the ramp in front and another in the back, hoping to encourage her. The garden had given her such pleasure. He could have rehired the gardener, but that would have been like telling Agnes she was no longer capable. Even if it was the truth. He couldn't take away the hope that she would one day get out there again. She'd become so fond of saying, *I'm going to take care of that tomorrow.*

But he didn't explain all that to Rose Christopher. He gave her the simple answer. "Agnes liked to work in the garden, but she hasn't been able to make it out here for a few months."

He detected a glimmer in Rose's eyes as she stepped up to the porch railing and studied the ragged bushes and last year's untended flowers.

"Maybe with your help, Agnes could return to the garden," he said.

As her gaze roamed the yard, her voice was almost dreamy. "You need some blue hydrangeas out here. They'd be lovely. Blue was my mother's favorite hydrangea. Mine, too. We used to work in the garden together." Then she looked at him. "I can help Agnes out here. Absolutely." There was something in her eyes, perhaps a slight mistiness as she thought of her mother's blue hydrangeas.

"Agnes would love that. You can plant blue hydrangeas and anything else you'd like."

Inside, he unlocked the door to Agnes's flat. It opened onto what she called the parlor, the kitchen to the left, with a short hallway to the bathroom and bedroom. Typical of ladies born in the early twentieth century, the parlor was frilly, lace curtains covering the large bay window, a flower-patterned couch, an old-fashioned easy chair, tables and shelves bulging with knickknacks, doilies on every surface, a thick, oriental carpet on the hardwood floor.

Rose turned in a circle, then scuffed the edge of the carpet with her shoe. "This rug could be a terrible stumbling block. Especially since it's so thick. Fifty percent of in-home accidents with the elderly are caused by rugs on the floor."

Declan stared at her. "Did you just pull that statistic out of your..." He left the rest hanging.

She laughed, a lovely sound, sweet and soft, close to musical. "There's a statistic," she said. "But off the top of my head, I can't remember the exact number. But it's big." She pulled her phone out of her purse. "I'll look it up."

He waved her off. "You don't need to look it up. I believe you. And it's logical. Two of the times Agnes fell, she was found right by the edge of the carpet. I'll take it up before she gets home." He rolled his eyes, shaking his head. "Of course, she'll freak. The bare hardwood will drive her crazy."

Hand on her hip, Rose tipped her head. "Would it freak *you* out," she stressed, "as the apartment owner, I mean, if we put flowery stickers on the floor to simulate a pretty carpet?"

She was immediately scrolling on her phone again while his mind reeled with the idea of defacing the hardwood floors. Did she know how long he'd worked on them, sanding, staining, buffing, waxing? Obviously not.

"Look, we could even do a koi pond or a waterfall. Or a dolphin coming up out of the water. Or maybe even a scary monster climbing out of the floor." She held up her phone, and he stared aghast at the creepy image of a zombie with red eyes crawling out of a grave.

She laughed. "Just kidding." And she scrolled to another screen with what looked like linoleum tiles in different patterns and colors Declan was sure would appeal to Agnes. "We could put these on the floor in different spots, and she could feel like she had area rugs all over the place." She held the phone close to read. "It says they're easily removable, but we can test them out in unobtrusive places to make sure they don't damage the floor."

He held out his hand. "May I see?"

She gave him the phone. He looked, read, scrolled some more. Then he envisioned the tiles on the floor and Agnes's face when she saw them. And finally turned back to Rose. "That's ingenious."

She smiled as prettily as she laughed.

"I wonder how long they'll last before they start looking worn?"

Rose shrugged. "They're so cheap, I can buy extras."

He tipped his head, looking at her with narrowed eyes. "But if you're here with her, and you're making sure she uses her walker, isn't that going to be safe enough?"

She shook her head. "Rule of thumb, better safe than sorry. She'll probably be fine with the walker. But what if I'm in the kitchen making dinner and she gets up, forgetting her walker?"

Declan looked at the carpet. That's exactly what could happen. Rose Christopher might be perfection personified, but she absolutely couldn't be with Agnes every single second.

The carpet had to go.

"Speaking of the kitchen, let me show you."

Off to the left, the kitchen was large, fitting a four-person dinette in a bay window that overlooked the backyard.

"This is perfect." She turned to him, amazement twinkling in her eyes. "All the beautiful tile work and the old-fashioned porcelain sink, and that retro robin's-egg blue refrigerator.

Everything had been trimmed in blue and gray tile, countertops, backsplash, with a blue and gray checkerboard linoleum that cleaned easily. He'd installed a new white range, white cabinets, including ones with latticed glass doors for Agnes's china.

"Including the fridge, it all fits the house style. And here's the washer and dryer." He opened a door to reveal the stacked laundry unit. Then he pointed to the table in the bay window. "That was Agnes's original dining set." He'd lovingly restored it for her, recovering the chairs with fabric that matched the blue and gray of the kitchen tile.

"It's lovely. And you said you'd turned off the electricity for the appliances?"

"Yes. She has her meals delivered." He'd hired a gourmet meal service, since he was the one who'd cut off the electricity.

"It would be very helpful if we could have it back on." She added, as if she saw a grimace on his face, "I'll do all the cooking."

"I wasn't expecting you to cook. I can order meals for two."

Rose's expression turned militant, her features set. "I appreciate that. But we'll eat more nutritiously if I know what goes into the food." She softened with a smile. "I enjoy cooking. Grocery shopping can be a nice outing for us."

He gave in gracefully. "All right. I've set up a checking account for her, and I can give you the debit card to use." The account was in his name, not Agnes's, and part of his online banking profile. He could easily see what was spent.

Her eyelashes fluttered a moment as if she were about to ask a question, but all she said was, "Thank you."

A second door out of the kitchen led into the short hall outside Agnes's bedroom.

"This bedroom was originally the kitchen in the old floor plan."

It was large with two big windows for more light. He'd installed a French door for easy access to the back porch. He wasn't sure how often Agnes went out there anymore. Her world had shrunk.

"When I realized Agnes would need help when she got out of the hospital, I had two single beds brought in. I'm sure you'd prefer your own room, but—"

"No," she interrupted. "I need to be close if Agnes has to get up in the night." She crossed her arms, looked at the floor a long moment, then back up at him. "My mother could move fast. She'd be out of her bed before I knew what was happening." She gave that soft musical laugh again. "I used to put cat toys on her bed, those little plastic balls with bells inside." She held up her hand, her fingers curled to demonstrate. "They jingled as soon as she moved. Now, just in case, I bring cat bells when I'm on a job. I have a whole box of them."

He thought about what this could mean. That she'd slept in the same room with her mother. What about her husband? But those were questions he wouldn't ask. "Are you always this ingenious? Like the decals on the floor?"

She gave him a close-mouthed grin, her eyes crinkling at the corners. "The elderly can be very tricky. It's like a game with them. I've tried a lot of ways to stay one step ahead."

She obviously had. With the other applicants, he'd never gotten as far as showing them Agnes's room. They'd all been unsatisfactory. Until Rose.

"I'd like to see the bathroom."

He ushered her back into the hallway, opening the bathroom door.

"It's nice and big. Plenty of room to maneuver her walker around." She turned to the shower. "Oh, very nice, quite large. The lip isn't tall so she won't trip over it as easily."

"I installed the shower, including everything Agnes might need." He'd added a grab bar along the back wall.

Rose turned to him, her head tipped, as if she were assessing him all over again. "You realized a bathtub wouldn't work?"

"Of course. If she'd fallen getting out, she could have sued me." The thought had never entered his head when he was remodeling. He'd thought only of making things easier for Agnes.

"It's all great. But I think a handheld showerhead would be a wonderful addition, especially if she needs a lot of help." She put a finger to her lips, drawing his attention to their fullness.

"And it would be very helpful to have a shower seat. They're not expensive." Stepping into the shower itself, she ran her fingers along the grab bar. "This is great." She put a hand on the wall next to the showerhead. "But she should really have a vertical grab bar right here to get in and out." She looked around the bathroom. "And although you have a grab bar by the toilet, it would be good to have a riser with rails. She can push herself up rather than pulling on the bar."

Declan was impressed. The woman was experienced, assessing every aspect.

Stepping out of the shower, she put her shoe on the mat and moved it around the floor. "Definitely no more little rugs like this. I know her feet will probably can be cold on the tile, but we'll think of something."

Declan pointed to a switch on the wall. "The floor is heated."

She looked at him, with the slightest twitch of her lips. "Ingenious," she said softly.

And he felt... something. Though he chose not to define it.

"Order whatever you need," he said. "Charge it to the debit card and I'll make sure there's enough money in the account. I have a handyman who'll do the installations if I'm not available."

This time her look lasted longer, felt far more penetrating. Finally she said, "And she's really not a relative?"

"She's a tenant," he insisted.

"I've never heard of a landlord doing all this for a tenant."

"Agnes reminds me of my grandmother. She died when I was ten."

He didn't offer any more explanation. His parents had worked hard all their lives. They had the small plumbing supply shop his mother managed while his dad went out on calls. His grandmother had lived with them in an apartment over the shop, and she'd taken care of him. She was Agnes's age when she died, eighty-seven. After his parents retired, he'd settled them in Palm Springs, bought them a house, made sure they had everything they needed. But he'd never been able to give back to his grandmother. Somehow what he did for Agnes was almost as if he were doing it for his Gran.

Besides, he'd known Agnes since he was in grade school,

when she'd been his fourth-grade teacher. In many ways, she'd been Gran's replacement, and he loved her for that.

But Rose Christopher had no need for his history.

"That's very philanthropic of you," Rose said, a softness in her gaze he wasn't used to from other people.

"It's not philanthropy. It's duty."

"Whatever you want to call it," she said with a slight shrug. "We have an epidemic in this country of elderly people left to wither away and forgotten in care facilities."

"So you see," he said, one eyebrow raised. "It wouldn't be right to send Agnes to rehab if I have the money to pay for something better."

"That's why I couldn't send my mother to one of those places. Because I had the expertise."

It was obvious now.

Rose was the caregiver Agnes desperately needed.

3

"Shall we go to the hospital and meet Agnes?" Declan paused for one furious beat of Rose's heart. "If you have the time now."

Relief fluttered in her stomach. A live-in position taking care of an elderly lady meant she could rent out her mother's house. The income would more than cover the property taxes, insurance, and maintenance, and with a salary on top of that, she could rebuild the nest egg that had dwindled with her divorce and her mother's illness.

But she still wanted confirmation. "Do I need Agnes's approval as well?"

He gave a slight jerk of his chin. "I know what's best for Agnes. And you're it," he said with little emotion.

She was dying to do a happy dance but kept it to herself.

Declan drove, and fifteen minutes later, they were in Agnes's hospital room.

She was a tiny gnome of a woman, dwarfed by the big hospital bed. Her permed white hair was flattened on one side, color bloomed in her cheeks, and her blue eyes were bright. The bandage over the cut on her forehead didn't cover the whole bruise, which was turning from a purply red to an ugly yellow-green.

Rose had been in a lot of hospitals. This one was clean and sterile-scented, the staff efficient, and Agnes had a private room with a window overlooking a grove of trees.

Declan sat on the edge of the bed. "Agnes Hathaway, this is Rose Christopher." He made the introductions, holding Agnes's small hand in his. "Rose is going to stay with you while you get better."

Agnes waved his words away with fingers gnarled by arthritis. "You silly boy, I don't need anyone to take care of me."

His voice was gentle, unlike the no-nonsense tones he'd used with Rose. "The doctor says you can't go home until you have adequate care. If you don't have someone with you, we'll have to put you in a rehab facility."

The little lady scrunched up her face into a comical caricature of Popeye the Sailor. "It's not as if I broke a bone. I don't know what on earth I need rehab for."

"We have to do what your doctors say, Agnes."

Agnes harrumphed. "You're a controlling SOB, Declan, if I ever met one. If you were the one in this bed, you'd be telling that doctor what to do, not the other way around."

Rose laughed, even though she'd intended to stay out of the conversation until Agnes acknowledged her. The little lady was feisty, and Rose enjoyed her attitude.

Agnes looked at her. "What did you say your name was, dear?"

"This is Rose," Declan said.

Rose wondered why she wasn't thinking of him as Mr. Delaney. Which she should be, but somehow, after the tour of Agnes's apartment, he was just Declan. And she noticed Agnes had needed no prompting to remember his name. That was a good signal of her memory.

She shook Agnes's hand, the woman's fingers fragile against her palm.

"It's so nice to meet you," Rose said. "Declan has told me all about you. I'm sure we'll have a good time together while you're healing."

It was a small fib to say it would only be while Agnes recovered. If Declan got his way, Rose's stay would last a lot longer.

Beaming a wide smile, Agnes said, "I'm quite capable of taking care of myself, dear. I've been doing it for years. Sometimes my feet just get tangled up." She reached down to tap her leg.

"I'm glad to hear that. My job will be easier. I took care of my mom for a few years." She didn't say her mother had died. "She just liked to have a bit of company. We played cards and Scrabble—" At least in the beginning. "—and had a cup of tea and cookie in the afternoon." She leaned close, dropping her voice as if they were entering into a conspiracy. "We had a little nip of Baileys after dinner, too, and two pieces of chocolate each. It was lovely. Then we watched *Jeopardy* and *Wheel of Fortune*."

Agnes's eyes, which were already bright, lit up. "Oh my, those are my favorite shows. I like to watch that funny detective, too, you know, the one with the cigar."

"*Columbo*," Rose said in the same bright tone Agnes used.

"And then there's that mystery writer who's always stumbling over a murder."

"*Murder She Wrote*," Rose supplied. "Jessica Fletcher."

Agnes waved her hands in the air, her arthritic fingers opening and closing excitedly. "Yes, that's her!"

Good. Agnes remembered her favorite TV shows. Once she was back home, Rose could make a full assessment of her capabilities.

She felt Declan's eyes on her, listening to every word, taking it all in, and assessing Rose rather than Agnes.

"We can always enjoy a good movie, too," she added.

Agnes clapped her hands in raptures. "Oh yes. *The Quiet Man*, it's my favorite movie, and I haven't seen it in years, absolutely years. Could we watch that?"

"Of course, we can." Rose let enthusiasm lace her voice. "In fact, it was my mother's favorite movie, too. I have it on DVD."

Agnes put her hands to her cheeks, her mouth open in an astounded *O*. "What an amazing coincidence, my dear."

"It was my grandmother's favorite movie as well," Declan added.

Agnes slapped him lightly on the arm. "Which it should be, since your family is Irish."

"It was my great-grandparents who came over, and you know very well I've never been to Ireland."

"That's terrible," Agnes said with a gasp. "You'll need to watch *The Quiet Man* as well. Then you'll understand your roots better."

Declan laughed. It was a shockingly beautiful sound, deep but mellow. He should laugh more often. "I watched *The Quiet Man* enough times with my Gran to have all the dialogue memorized."

Agnes one-upped him. "I'll have you know that I saw *The Quiet Man* when it first came out in the theater. It was the first date with my Herbert. We fell madly in love at the same time John Wayne fell in love with Maureen O'Hara." She put her hands together and sighed dreamily.

Another good sign. Agnes remembered the actors' names. Short-term memory often went before long-term memory, and it was possible Agnes might never remember Rose's name. But she still knew her long-term references.

"I have a lot of old movies that were my mother's favorites. We can watch them all," she promised.

Agnes clapped her hands again. "Oh my, yes, the old movies are so much better than the crap they put out these days."

Rose stifled a smile at Agnes's colorful language. The word *crap* was probably the equivalent of the *F*-bomb.

Agnes shoved aside her blanket. "I need to get up," she said, pushing on Declan with her feet.

He put his hand out. "Agnes, you should really stay in bed and rest."

Agnes put a hand to the side of her mouth and whispered loudly to Rose. "I have to go to the bathroom," she mouthed as if she thought Declan couldn't hear.

"I'll call the nurse for you." Declan searched for the call button.

"I'll take you." It would be a good chance for Rose to assess how much aid Agnes needed.

"I don't need help, thank you very much. I'm perfectly capable of doing it on my own," Agnes said primly, her pert nose in the air.

"I know," Rose agreed. "But your doctor will be grumpy if he knows you got out of bed on your own. Let's make him happy by having me tag along. For appearance's sake."

Agnes harrumphed. "You're right. And that man will let me out of here faster. But those nurses are always yelling at me and telling me to use that silly button. Then they never get here fast enough." She dropped her voice again, her hand once more by the side of her mouth as if Declan wouldn't hear. "And when I have to go, I have to *go*." Her eyes twinkled. "And I have to go *now*."

Agnes was sweet, she was funny. And she was bossy. Rose liked her already.

Declan turned the car into the driveway.

He was amazed by Rose's competence, at her ability to guide Agnes, to know exactly what to say and when to say it. If you listened to Agnes, you wouldn't know she had any memory deficit at all. She'd seemed perfectly normal.

"I can pick her up from the hospital," Rose said with clipped efficiency. The doctor had come in just before they left and agreed to release Agnes tomorrow.

Declan's immediate response was to decline Rose's offer. Agnes was his responsibility. Yet in the last hour, he'd given her over to Rose. As it should be. He could return to work without worry, especially as he was currently overseeing the renovation of a new acquisition.

Yet guilt squeezed his chest.

He wasn't a man used to guilt or overthinking an issue. He made a decision, then acted on it. There wasn't all this ruminating.

Except about Agnes.

She'd come into his life just when he'd lost his own adored Gran, and Agnes filled that huge hole in his life. She'd been there exactly when he needed her, an angry, lonely, grieving ten-year-old craving a grandmother's love. She'd stayed in his heart ever since.

He couldn't do for Agnes what Rose could do. When they'd disappeared into the bathroom, he'd been relieved. If that's what Agnes needed, he was happy to hand off the responsibility. He would cover her bills, make sure the house account had a balance so Rose could buy whatever Agnes needed. Though Agnes had Medicare, it didn't cover everything, and he'd had the foresight to buy supplemental insurance for her. Any remaining expenses not covered, he paid.

It was so much easier to throw money at a problem.

There was silence in the car for a few moments, then Rose said, "If you have no objection, I'll move in today. I can put all my belongings away and make sure everything is ready for Agnes tomorrow. Then do a little grocery shopping to stock up."

He didn't object and reached to his inside pocket for his wallet. "Here's the debit card for whatever you need." He had online access and could check that withdrawals weren't excessive and purchases weren't from sites Agnes had no reason to use. "Do you need help moving?"

Rose smiled. He wasn't sure why he liked her smile. She was a good-looking woman, but nothing extraordinary. Her curly brunette bob had only a few strands of gray, and her eyes were the comforting color of maple syrup. Her smile warmed him, and her scent, something fruity, oranges, mangoes maybe, was a tantalizing perfume in the confines of the car.

He was obviously turning into a softy after all his dealings with Agnes. Especially as Rose was rescuing him from tasks he had no inclination for.

"Thank you for the offer. But I can handle it myself."

She'd taken care of her mother for five years. She was a capable woman. Even if her scent was tantalizing. "Do you live in an apartment? Do you need to sublet?" In his line of work, he could handle that for her.

"I'm still in my mother's house. She left it to me. But with this job, I'll look for a renter so it doesn't sit idle."

"I'll put my property manager in touch with you to help."

He liked sitting in the car with her. It was quiet, almost intimate. Better than his office. As if they were equals, not employer and employee, nor interviewer and interviewee.

"I'd appreciate that. I was wondering how to go about it."

"I'll give them your cell phone number, if that's okay with you?" It had been on her resume.

"Thank you."

Then, as if she suddenly realized they'd been sitting in the car far too long, she put her hand on the door. "I'll go home to pack a few things." She laughed softly, the smile lighting up her eyes. "Especially my mom's favorite DVDs for Agnes to watch." Her lips parted in a question. He couldn't say why he kept looking at her lips as if they were completely fascinating. "She has a DVD player, right?"

He nodded. "Just don't bring *The Quiet Man*, or Agnes will watch it every night. And she'll try to get me down there to watch it, too." He wondered if that was a smile on his mouth. With all he dealt with on a daily basis, sometimes he thought he'd even forgotten how.

But Rose made him want to smile. The wattage of her smile was high enough to light up the interior of the car even though they were sitting in daylight.

"It would be a terrible thing not to bring *The Quiet Man*." She pursed her lips, giving him a mock glare. "Why, she fell in love with her husband the first time she saw that movie."

"Herbert wasn't her husband. I have no idea who Herbert was. Her husband's name was Marvin."

"Oh, a mystery. It will be something for us to talk about as I pry out all her naughty secrets." Her cheeks turned pink, as if she heard the flirty tone of her voice, the seduction in her words, and felt the temptation in her gaze. She went on briskly. "Thank you for the debit card. May I have a key to the house and Agnes's apartment?"

He handed over the keyring. "I'll sign the agency contract and email it in."

"We're set then." She climbed out of the car, bending down once more, her hand on the top of the door. "Thank you again for the opportunity. She's a lovely lady and I'll take very good care of her."

Then she was gone.

He couldn't say why he remained in the car a few moments more. It certainly wasn't just to breathe in her lingering scent.

Because he'd damn well learned that any kind of too-familiar relationship between an employer and his employee would only end badly.

❀

"IT LOOKS LIKE YOU'RE SETTLING IN." DECLAN STOOD IN Agnes's frilly parlor.

That's probably what this room had been when the house was originally built, the front parlor used only for guests. A tall man, Declan seemed to fill up the space.

It was late afternoon, and Rose was arranging her mother's favorite DVDs on the shelf beneath the TV. "I didn't need to bring much. Once Agnes is settled, she and I can take a trip home to pick up anything else I need. It's not far, and it'll be a nice outing for her."

"She's missed her outings the last few months. She used to stroll to the Rose Garden, but she's done that less and less. Even if she doesn't want to admit her limitations, she knows them."

On her knees, she looked up at him. "How do you know when she goes out? Aren't you at work?" The DVDs organized, she pushed herself to her feet.

"When I'm in my office upstairs—" He pointed up. "—I can see her comings and goings. More and more often, she's been asking me to run out and get her a few things. Before she had a wheeled basket, and she'd walk to get her groceries."

"You're observant." She liked that he downgraded what he did for Agnes. And he did far more than any landlord would. "I was about to have dinner. Would you like to stay?"

He shook his head, his hands deep in his pockets. "No." Then he nodded belatedly. "Thank you."

He probably didn't want to fraternize with the help. She wondered if living upstairs he'd be checking on her, just the way he checked on Agnes, making sure she did what she was supposed to.

"Let me show you the things I put on order for the bathroom and the rest of the house. I set up my computer on the kitchen table." There wasn't a good desk area, probably because Agnes hadn't needed it. She'd seen no sign of a computer or even an iPad, and she had to phone Declan for the Wi-Fi password.

He had a very nice phone voice.

"You don't let any grass grow under your feet." He followed her into the kitchen.

"I can't afford to since Agnes will be home tomorrow. And look who's talking." She glanced at him over her shoulder. "You already had the rugs removed." She belatedly realized how overly familiar she sounded.

He didn't mention that. "You were right. It's a safety issue."

He'd probably looked up the statistic she'd quoted. She took the chair in front of the computer. "I've asked for one-day shipping. It's not exorbitant, but it's worth it, since you're going to have your handyman install it all as soon as possible."

"That's fine. I accept your judgement."

She wasn't sure if he was giving her his trust, or letting her know he'd be watching her. She turned the computer toward him, and he finally sat.

"Most of what I purchased is for the bathroom. But even though I'm here making sure she uses her walker, we need more grab bars around the apartment." She watched him study the list in her cart. He had a nice profile, a strong jawline, an aristocratic nose.

She hadn't pushed the Buy button yet. "This is the cheapest place I could find."

"I thought it all would be more expensive."

She felt ridiculously proud of herself for finding the best prices.

"Everything will be here tomorrow?" he asked.

She nodded. "Except the decals. I found some at the hardware store that'll be perfect. I'd like to have them down before Agnes comes home tomorrow."

He appraised her a long moment as if he couldn't believe how fast she'd moved. "Good. I'll contact Joe and schedule the installation of everything else, hopefully for tomorrow. I'll have him turn on the electricity to all the kitchen appliances as well."

"That would be great."

He shifted to pull a folded paper out of his front pocket and slid it across the table. "It's the number for the property management company I work with. I don't own it," he said as if he wanted her to know he wouldn't make money off her. "They're good, and their fees are reasonable. They'll find a tenant for your house, and they know the rents in the area. They can collect the rent for you, pay taxes, handle service calls for the property. Some people feel it's easier if they don't have to handle any complaints. But that's up to you."

"It would be a lot easier. I don't want to hassle with a water heater on the fritz or a light switch that needs replacing."

"There are insurance policies you can buy to cover all the appliances and necessary repairs. If the house needs a lot of maintenance, it can save you money."

"Well, everything is old. I haven't done a lot of replacements." She wondered how her brother was going to feel if he knew she was renting out the house and possibly making a profit on it. "Will this all be confidential?"

"If you want it to be. Why?"

Of course he'd ask why. "I inherited the house from my mother, and my brother was upset. He thought he should've gotten half of it, that I coerced my mother into leaving it to me while I was taking care of her." She shrugged, feeling a little ashamed. "But my mother changed the will herself, before she got really bad. She said I deserved it since I was her caregiver."

"I'm sorry about your brother. But you deserve the house. Being a caregiver is a big job."

She didn't say how difficult it could be, especially if it was your relative. The dynamics were different than when you worked for someone with whom you had no ties. She clasped her hands beneath the table, hunching her shoulders. "He sent money in the beginning to help out. So he thought he deserved more. Her estate didn't amount to much except for the house."

"You don't need to explain. It's not my business." Of course. He was only interested in things that had to do with Agnes.

"Anyway, I don't want to tell him about the rental."

"Understood." He nodded. "I don't have any family except my mom and dad, but I'm sure when parents pass on, there can be infighting."

"I don't mean my brother's a bad guy." She had a big mouth. While Declan said very little about himself.

Her stomach growled, loudly, and she put her hand over it to cover the sound.

"I'm keeping you from your dinner." He stood.

"Are you sure you won't stay?" She smiled. "It's just a sandwich. Since the electricity is off to the appliances."

She expected him to laugh, or at least smile, even a half smile, but his features remained deadpan. "Thanks, but I've got work. And I'll turn on the electricity. No need to wait for Joe."

"Thank you."

He left before she could walk him to the door.

She really had talked too much and scared the man off.

❧ 4 ❧

"**O**h my goodness. I'm so glad to be home." Agnes flopped into her chair in the front parlor as if she'd been gone months instead of days.

The gears of hospital administration ground slowly. Rose had arrived at nine-thirty, when Agnes was *supposed* to be released. It had taken another two hours. Declan had dropped by, wanting to see her home, but it took so long, he couldn't wait. There were release forms and instruction forms, and the doctor wanted to examine Agnes one more time. He'd confirmed for Rose that Agnes had not been diagnosed with Alzheimer's.

But at last, they were home. Agnes sighed in appreciation, her arms draped over the sides of the chair, hands dangling, feet propped on a short footstool with a pretty needlepoint cover.

Then Agnes gasped. "Are these all new carpets?" She pointed at the decals, mostly flower patterns, that Rose had spent hours last night placing precisely on the floor.

Rose stood back and waved her hand. "Aren't they pretty?" She didn't call them decals as she scuffed her shoe over a rectangular set that covered the bare area in the middle of the parlor. There were more in the hall, outside the kitchen, and in the bedroom. "And they're flat on the floor so they won't trip you or your walker."

"Oh my," Agnes whispered in wonder. "They're lovely." Then she waved a hand at the packages by the front door. "And what's all that?"

Rose sat in the chair beside Agnes, thankful for making it through the carpet issue without a problem. "Some things I ordered for the house."

Declan had moved the boxes inside when they'd been delivered, texting Rose that his handyman would be by in the afternoon to install everything.

Agnes clapped her hands. "Oh my. Prezzies. What did we get?" She was as bright as a child on her birthday.

Rose had to smile. There'd been moments when her mother was just as cheerful. But those times had grown fewer and fewer as the disease progressed. Watching Agnes now made her both sad and glad, nostalgic but hopeful. She could do all the things for Agnes that she hadn't been able to do for her mother. Agnes was nowhere near as far gone as her mother had been. Maybe she never would be. Rose could only pray.

"I wouldn't call them presents," Rose said. "They're things to help you around the house, like a bench seat in the shower. And one of those handheld showerheads that come off the wall. And some more grab bars." She didn't mention the toilet riser. The elderly could be sensitive about the extra help they didn't think they needed. Luckily, when Rose had helped Agnes to the bathroom yesterday, she found her capable of handling that activity on her own. The more autonomy and capability an elderly person had, the happier they felt with themselves.

"Do I need all that?" Her voice bewildered, Agnes's eyes went wide.

"They'll be a help to me. What would Declan say if I let you fall in the shower?"

Agnes rolled her lips between her teeth then puffed them back out. "Well dear, I must admit, I didn't take a shower as often as I should. That showerhead was so high my hair got wet even with the shower cap on." She patted her short, permed curls. "And it was a bit difficult to wash while I was holding onto that rail so I didn't slip."

Agnes's explanation was remarkable. Rose wouldn't have thought the little lady could remember that much, let alone articulate it.

Rose smiled. "I'll be there to help. Even if it's just to steady you." She pointed at the packages. "Declan is sending someone by to install everything this afternoon." Then she rubbed her stomach. "I'm a bit peckish." That had been a favorite saying of her mother's. "Would you like a sandwich for lunch?"

"That sounds lovely. Thank you." Agnes's eyes twinkled. "Do we have any potato chips?"

When Rose packed up the foodstuff from her fridge and kitchen, there'd been an open bag of potato chips. "I do."

At the sunny kitchen table, Agnes nibbled her ham and cheese like a bird, tearing off tiny pieces and putting them in her mouth. She pulled off all the crusts, too, and Rose made a mental note to cut them off in future.

After cleaning away the plates, she asked, "Would you like a nap?"

"Oh no, dear. I'd like to go to the Rose Garden."

Declan had said Agnes loved the garden, but that in the past few months, she hadn't ventured there often.

"That's a wonderful idea. Let's do it." It would give her a chance to evaluate Agnes's stamina and her capabilities with the walker. "I wonder if the garden is named after me. Since my name is Rose."

"I remember your name, dear," Agnes said, raising her nose at Rose's not-so-subtle reminder.

Fifteen minutes later, they headed down the ramp outside the house.

"Declan built this just for me. Isn't he the sweetest boy?" Agnes looked back for Rose's reaction.

"That was very nice of him."

With the walker to steady her, Agnes was nimble and quick. But once they arrived at the Rose Garden, she needed to rest, remembering to lock the hand brakes before she turned around to sit on the seat of her walker like a stool.

"Isn't the garden absolutely beautiful?" The smile on Agnes's face was like a beam of sunshine.

"It's gorgeous," Rose agreed. The roses were in full bloom, the pathways swept clean, and the beds free of weeds.

"In my younger days, I came out here to help weed. It's such a relaxing place." She looked at Rose. "Then I started working in Declan's garden." She smiled. "He had a useless gardener. I knew I could do so much better. A bit every day and it's done in no time." Maybe she thought she *still* worked in the garden. "It's become quite a disgrace since they put me in the hospital." Her brows drew together with indignation. "I need to get out there to tidy up."

"Perhaps I can work with you. I enjoy being in the garden."

"Gardens help you to see the little things. To appreciate how things flourish." Agnes smiled wistfully. "I try to get Declan to come out and help me but he's such a busy businessman," she quipped. "But you have to stop and smell the roses." Her eyes sparkled. "Don't you agree?"

"Totally." She patted Agnes's hand. "Do you feel ready to walk through the garden and smell the roses?"

Agnes's back went ramrod straight as if Rose had maligned her. "Of course I'm ready," she said, pushing herself off the walker.

Rose didn't help, and the little lady handled the process well, remembering to click off the brakes. With her walker, Agnes was quite steady.

They strolled the gravel paths. An elderly woman, perhaps ten years younger than Agnes, raised her head, her hair pulled up in a bun and secured with a net. Resting on a kneepad, she sat back on her haunches, pulling off her gloves, the bucket beside her full to the brim with weeds. "Agnes, darling, it's been ages."

"It's so good to see you." Agnes's words trailed off, her eyes turning glassy as if she couldn't remember the woman's name. "I had a fall, and they put me in the hospital. It's been ages and ages since I've been out here."

She'd been in the hospital only a very few days.

"I'm so glad you're better. I hope to see you out here more often." The woman looked at Rose. "Is this your daughter?"

"She's my friend." A frown wrinkled Agnes's brow, and Rose understood the problem.

She held out her hand. "I'm Rose. I'm staying with Agnes, helping her out for a bit."

Agnes burst out with, "Yes, she's Rose, like the Rose Garden."

Rose smiled. "Rose like the rose garden." She hoped Agnes would begin to remember by association. Agnes could remember to use the brakes on her walker and how it had felt to try showering with that too-tall showerhead, but names escaped her, even if she denied it.

The woman shook Rose's hand without rising off the ground. "I'm Sylvia. So nice to meet you."

She probably assumed Rose was a caregiver, and Rose was

sure Agnes wouldn't want her to explain further. She'd feel like a child needing a nanny.

"We'll make a point of it," Rose assured Sylvia.

They waved goodbye and continued their stroll. It was a lovely garden, a lovely walk, a lovely meeting with Sylvia, and when they got back to the house, Declan's handyman began installing the new equipment after Rose had shown him where everything should go.

They ended their outing with a cup of tea.

"Do we have a cookie?" Agnes's eyes lit up.

"Of course." Though there hadn't been much in Agnes's cupboards, there was no shortage of cookies. "Shall we take it to the back porch?"

"That would be marvelous."

The porch was decked out with a cafe table and two padded chairs. The opposite side of the porch, which belonged to the other tenant, was bare, no furniture, not even a deck chair.

"I never even see him," Agnes said, following Rose's gaze. Then she frowned, "But with the state of this garden, who can blame him?"

Rose wondered how long it had been since Agnes had touched it. The backyard was a shambles, even worse than the front, with overrun pathways, out-of-control shrubs, and weed-infested flowerbeds.

"Since Joe is still working inside, why don't we weed in the garden?" she suggested. "Since you're still supposed to take it easy, you can talk to me while I work." She wasn't letting Agnes down on her knees to pull weeds, not today, and probably not ever.

"That would be delightful, dear." Agnes waved her hand. "My gardening tools must be around somewhere."

Declan had built a ramp in the back as well, and Rose

found a big garden box along the side of the house where she uncovered a kneeling pad, gloves, and tools.

"I don't even know where to start." Together she and Agnes surveyed the tangle of unkempt bushes, shrubs, weeds, and overgrown flowers. If she looked hard enough, she could make out stone paths, and poking its head above the jumble was a cupid that could be part of a fountain.

"Just one square at a time, dear."

Setting the kneepad on the path, Rose picked a square of garden. "We'll start at the edge, and work our way inward."

Beneath the shade of a tree, Agnes had turned her walker around and seated herself like she had in the Rose Garden. "I'm sorry I can't help you, dear." She sighed heavily. "Honestly, I feel as if I let Declan down."

Resting her gloved hands on her knees, Rose turned to Agnes. "Why do you feel bad?"

The little lady hunched in the walker seat. "I was the one who told him to get rid of the gardener. And now look at this mess." She spread her hands, encompassing the tangle of yard.

Rose was surprised Agnes remembered. "He could've brought his gardener back. He's certainly got enough money." She waved a hand across the façade of the renovated house. "I don't think he even notices the garden." It wasn't true, but she wouldn't say that Declan couldn't bear to offend Agnes by rehiring the gardener.

"But I made a promise to him. And I broke it."

Rose caressed Agnes's hand. "You didn't break any promises." Then she smiled. "As my mother would say, don't be a silly sausage."

Agnes laughed, the lines on her face deepening. "What on earth does that mean?"

Rose allowed herself an inner smile. "It was an old expression of my mother's. It actually makes me very happy to call you a silly sausage."

Agnes commented cheekily, "I'm not a silly sausage. You're a silly sausage."

"Then we're part of the silly sausage club."

They laughed together. It was such a lovely feeling, like having a small piece of her mother back, the woman she could talk to and play cards with and who always beat her at Scrabble. She could pretend Agnes was her mother. There was a special kind of joy in that.

"But Declan's garden problems are still because of me."

If Rose thought the laughter had made Agnes forget, she was wrong. Agnes might have trouble remembering names, yet her guilt clung to her as if it were wrapped around her like a vine.

"It's not your fault," Rose singsonged.

The lilt didn't work. "I don't like to burden him. He's had such a hard life."

"Do you know how many apartment buildings, office complexes, and parking garages Declan owns?"

She shrugged. "Not really. But his life has still been difficult. His parents came from humble beginnings, and Declan worked very hard to get them where they are. He went straight to work right out of high school, and handed over every nickel he earned to help the household."

Rose stared at her aghast. "Did he tell you that?" She couldn't imagine Declan Delaney revealing so much about himself. But then he'd known Agnes for ten years.

She shook her head. "I was Declan's fourth-grade teacher. His mother and I have been friends ever since."

Really, Rose wanted to say. Declan had known Agnes far longer than ten years. So why did he insist on saying she was *just* his tenant?

Agnes went on with the story while Rose pulled weeds, filling the bucket beside her.

"He was very smart, too, working construction, learning everything he could. Then he started buying a little thing here and fixing it up. And with the proceeds, he'd buy something else over there and fix that up, too. His mother is very proud of him."

"I'm sure she is," Rose agreed. She wondered if she should stop Agnes right now. This really wasn't any of her business.

But she kept pulling weeds, and Agnes kept talking. "He didn't go to college, but he's very, very smart. I think he sometimes feels a little inferior because he doesn't have a college education. But you'd never know he doesn't."

Rose marveled again at the strength of Agnes's long-term memory. Long before she passed, Rose's mother had lost the capacity for meaningful conversation. Even though a part of her knew she shouldn't let Agnes reveal all Declan's secrets, Rose loved listening. She loved the camaraderie of real conversation, especially after realizing just how long it had been. Most of her patients had been closer to her mother's level.

"College isn't always end-all, be-all," Rose said. "I don't have a college education." But then she didn't own all the businesses that Declan did.

Agnes sighed. "He might've been happy except for that horrible wife of his."

Here was something she shouldn't listen to. "Agnes, I don't think—"

But Agnes went right on. "She married him for his money. You know she worked for him."

"No, I didn't." But she did remember his reaction when she'd asked if he had a wife and kids living with him. There'd been something dark and sad in that look.

Even as she knew she should stop Agnes, she didn't.

"She was his secretary." Agnes screwed up her nose as if the word had nasty connotations. "And she was a gold digger if there ever was one. She had her eye on him right from the beginning."

You shouldn't listen, you shouldn't listen, Rose repeated to herself. But she kept on listening.

"She was only twenty-five and he was forty. And she was gorgeous just like a gold digger should be. What man could resist that temptation? But he should've had an affair with her." She shook her head, the sun glistening on her white hair. "He never should've married her."

Rose couldn't help laughing. "I've never met an eighty-seven-year-old lady who thinks like that."

Agnes snorted. "That's because you've never met anyone like me, dear."

They'd only been together for a day, and Rose already appreciated that.

"Anyway, Declan wanted to have children right away." She winked. "He wasn't getting any younger." Then she rolled her eyes like a teenage girl. "Only it didn't happen." She finally took a breath and lowered her voice to a loud whisper. "Sadly, it was his fault. The mumps. He had them when he was a teenage boy."

"The mumps?" Rose asked.

"Yes, the mumps." Agnes nodded her head as if she'd said something profound. "It's quite rare," she revealed with a dire tone. "But sometimes the mumps can keep those little swimmers from swimming."

Rose burst out with a laugh she couldn't contain. "I can't believe you just said that."

Agnes tittered. "I think it's a nice way of saying..." She let the words trail off.

It was better than saying he was sterile.

"He wanted to adopt. But she didn't. At least that's the way Declan's mother tells it."

Rose felt another shiver of guilt for drinking in the gossip. Yet she was fascinated.

"He never would have left her," Agnes declared. "Declan is honorable that way. But then she had an affair with a man Declan worked with. When she got pregnant, she was so unashamed about it. The man had more money than Declan at that time. But boy, did she learn what a mistake she'd made when that awful man's business tanked."

Rose loved the contemporary terms coming out of the elderly lady's mouth. She'd bet Agnes knew how to cuss, too.

"Declan's worth so much more now, and she's crying her crocodile tears."

Rose couldn't help laughing again. "I really shouldn't let you tell me all this."

Agnes fluttered her eyelashes. "You should know who you're working for."

"I work for you," Rose said.

Agnes gave her a look. "You're my friend, but you work for Declan." Her words touched Rose. "I love that boy like a son," she went on. "His mother is gracious to share him with me. And I know my pension doesn't pay for you."

Rose wondered right then if Agnes had faked her inability to use the TV remote. She certainly seemed on the ball right now. Maybe she'd just wanted Declan to spend time with her.

5

Rose continued weeding as they talked. "I feel sorry for Declan. You're right. He's had a bad time."

Agnes sighed, her lips turning down in a frown. "He really wanted children. But not all of us are blessed." She tipped her head. "You never had children?"

"I had several miscarriages." Rose shrugged. After all the years, it was no longer the painful memory it had been. "I'll tell you a terrible secret," she said in the same loud whisper Agnes used. "My husband and I had to get married the summer after we graduated from high school because I was going to have a baby."

Agnes waved a hand. "That wasn't a terrible thing in your day. That would have been after the sexual revolution." She gave a little snort. "Nobody really cared about babies out of wedlock. Not like in my day. Girls had to pretend the baby was premature. But God forbid—" She rolled her eyes dramatically, even her head getting in on the action. "—if the father left before he married you."

"Well, we got married. And it did feel like a horrible scandal at the time. My parents were not happy." Earlier, Rose had told Agnes both her parents had passed. They'd wanted her to go to nursing school. She'd been working in a nursing home even then. She liked elderly people. "Sadly, though, I had a miscarriage." She could have gone to nursing school after that, but her father had refused to help her pay for it, even though he'd been ready to do so before she got pregnant. He'd said that since she was married, she was now her husband's responsibility.

"I'm so sorry," Agnes said, her lip quivering in sympathy.

"We tried again. But I could never carry a baby past the first three months. Please don't ask me how many miscarriages." It had been five. She sank into depression for a while, and though the memory didn't hurt the way it had, she still didn't like to dredge it up.

"You never wanted to adopt?"

"We didn't have a lot of money. I don't think we'd have qualified. So it was just me and my husband."

"But now you're divorced."

Rose dipped her head. "Did Declan tell you that?"

Agnes pointed at her finger. "No ring." Then she put her hand over her mouth. "Not a widow, are you? I'm so sorry."

"No. It was divorce."

"Because you didn't have children?"

Rose shook her head, piling more weeds in the bucket, filling it almost to the top. She'd done far more than a square foot. "It's hard to say exactly what happened." She hadn't wanted to admit it, but things were going wrong even before they moved in with her mother. "He was a mechanic, and he worked in this little shop for a dear old man I adored, Emmett was his name. And Emmett told my husband Kevin that he'd get the shop when he passed on. And Kevin stuck with him because he thought he'd own the shop one day."

"But he didn't?"

"No." Rose sighed. "Emmett died quite unexpectedly, a

heart attack right there in the shop. And the next thing my husband knew, Emmett's son told him that he was selling out. Kevin said it was supposed to be his." It had been a terrible time. "But Emmett never made a will giving Kevin the shop. And Kevin had put money into the business, too, when they had a bad month, which seemed to be often. But they never wrote anything down, no legal agreement. And the son refused to pay back that money. He didn't believe Kevin. It was all a mess. And Kevin was out of a job, too."

"I'm so sorry," Agnes commiserated. "That's terrible. Some people are so selfish."

"Kevin was so upset. He had a hard time finding another job, and the longer it took, the more he drank. Then he couldn't keep a job when he finally got it. We were already living with my mother, and—" Rose let out a long exhale.

"Everything went to hell," Agnes said for her.

The statement was excruciating enough to surprise a laugh out of Rose. "Exactly." When Kevin left, saying that he was sick of taking care of an old lady who should have died years ago, Rose hadn't missed the arguments or his drinking or his passive-aggressive barbs. That was three years ago, and she no longer missed him. She missed her mother far more.

"It's a tale as old as time," Agnes said. "Men."

"Men," Rose agreed. And since she'd made her tell-all, she had no qualms asking Agnes. "What about you? Why no kids?"

"I had a son. He died a few hours after he was born. They used forceps for a difficult birth back then, and I always believed they squished his head."

Rose sucked in a breath, and despite the dirt on her glove, she reached over to put her hand on Agnes's knee. "I'm so sorry. That must be the worst thing in the world."

"It is. He would have been a beautiful boy." Agnes sniffed, then she looked at Rose. "It's no worse than your miscar-

47

riages. People think that because it's not a baby that you've been able to hold in your arms, that it shouldn't hurt as much."

"Thank you for understanding. People seem to think that miscarriages don't have the same effect, but they do. Although carrying a baby full-term then losing him right after he's born is a terrible thing to bear."

Agnes nodded over their shared pain. "I couldn't have any children after that. But Marvin and I bumped along just fine after we got over the trauma. He passed more than ten years ago." She puffed out a breath, widened her eyes. "Can you believe it's been that long? He was a good man." She gave Rose a twinkling smile. "But he wasn't my first love." Rose could see she was gearing up for a good story.

"The boy you went to see *The Quiet Man* with?"

Agnes wore a dreamy smile. "Herbert was so handsome. He was strong and smart and funny. He kept me in stitches." She leaned forward to whisper. "Shall I tell you a big secret?"

Rose nodded. "I'll keep your secrets if you keep mine."

"I gave him my virginity. That was before any of that sexual revolution stuff." She slapped her hand in the air as if to say the sexual revolution was nothing compared to what she'd done. "He was going off to war, the Korean War, and we weren't sure we'd ever see each other again. It was wonderful and amazing." She sighed, a far-off look in her eyes, living that memory, falling in love with Herbert all over again. "But he didn't come back."

"Oh, Agnes, I'm so sorry." Her heart broke for the poor woman and the tragedies she'd lived through.

Agnes sighed. "It was all a long time ago. It was war. During World War Two, there were so many who didn't come back. Then the Korean War was only five years later. It was almost like we got used to loss. I'm sure that sounds strange to you." She looked at Rose. "And none of that means I didn't

48

love Marvin. He was a good man and we were very compatible. But there's really nothing like your first love, is there?" She put her hands together, her eyes closed in blissful recollection.

"I think it's amazing that you can still feel good about the memories even though it didn't end well."

Agnes wrinkled her nose. "What's the point in dwelling on the bad? Just remember the good."

She was so right. Rose had married her first and only love. And maybe that was the problem, that with all the years together, all the loss, all the disappointment, all the hardship, and all the tragedy, love had died.

But she liked seeing Agnes in her happy place, and she said, "My first love was more like puppy love. I was in the eighth grade. His name was Dirk Trammell."

"What a lovely name. It sounds very rich."

Her bucket full, Rose said, "I thought so. But he ended up going out with another girl." She slapped her hands on her thighs. "And I need to empty my bucket." When she returned and was once again kneeling, she waved her hand like a magic wand. "Look at how much we cleared. At least six square feet." She smiled at Agnes. "See how much work can be done while we're talking."

"It's amazing," Agnes said. "But I need to use the facilities."

"Let's check if Joe is done."

"We'll have to throw him out if he's not." Agnes smiled impishly. "Because I really have to go wee-wee."

Rose laughed. "Oh, you silly sausage. We'll just have to kick him out." She got to her feet, her knees creaking after she'd been down on the ground so long.

They'd been together only a short time, but Rose was completely taken with Agnes. She liked her forthrightness, her ability to laugh at herself, her sunny disposition despite the tragedies she'd experienced in her life. They were going to have a lot of fun together.

Joe was packing up his tools, and all the equipment Rose had purchased was installed.

"Thank you so much," Rose said. "And so fast." She looked at the placement of the grab bars, the handheld shower, the bench. "It's perfect."

A quiet man, Joe merely nodded before carrying out his toolbox.

With Joe gone, Agnes used the bathroom. She didn't say a thing about the toilet riser except, "Oh my, that's so easy." With a smile, she added, "I'm a little tired. Would you mind if I rest?"

"Of course not." Rose hadn't suggested it, wanting to give Agnes the leeway to decide on her own. But now she helped Agnes remove her shoes and laid a blanket over her.

"You should still work in the garden, dear. I'll be fine." Agnes waved her away.

Rose debated a moment, then decided Agnes would be all right. She pointed to the monitor—she'd brought it from home—on the bedside table. "Here's a walkie-talkie. If you need anything, you can talk to me." She picked up the other monitor and showed it to Agnes.

"Do I have to press a button?" Agnes said, a frown appearing on her brow.

Rose smiled. "Just talk and I can hear you." It was a baby monitor, but for Agnes it was much better to call it an old-fashioned walkie-talkie.

While Agnes napped, she could work another hour in the garden.

Outside, she knelt on the pad, pushed a button, and spoke into the walkie-talkie. "Can you hear me, Agnes?"

Agnes's laugh came through loud and clear and bright. "Yes, dear, I can hear you. This is marvelous."

"You call me when you're ready to get up and I'll come in."

"I'll be fine, dear. You don't need to leave your gardening."

This was where things could get difficult, with Agnes believing she didn't need any help. "Agnes, I know you don't *need* me," she said with emphasis, "but I would feel better if you called me when you're ready to get up. Then I can start dinner."

"All right, dear. It's my responsibility to make you feel useful." Agnes followed that up with another lovely laugh.

Rose laughed, too. She'd left the walker by the side of the bed so Agnes couldn't walk around it. Everything would be fine. She muted her receiver so her work in the garden wouldn't disturb Agnes's sleep.

She'd used a baby monitor with her mother, in addition to the neat trick with the bells on the bed, because sometimes Mom had been quiet as a mouse. Over the next few days, she'd judge whether Agnes needed the bells, too.

In the meantime, she relished her work in the garden. When she was taking care of her mother, gardening had been her relaxation. She loved watching the progress as all the weeds and the dead flowers were cleared away. She loved planting, fertilizing, watching the flowers bloom, pruning when they needed it. She loved figuring out how to make her blue hydrangeas stay blue or training a camellia to grow into a tree. She never spent much, looking for plants at Costco where they were cheap, or annuals when they were on sale, or even making her own cuttings. Sitting on the back deck in the evening and gazing out over a pretty garden with all its beautiful blooms one of life's delights.

Agnes was right, if you tended things, they would flourish. Her mother had loved being out in the garden with her, and though she was like a withering bloom at the end of summer rather than a new flower fresh in spring, her mother had loved the garden.

For Agnes, Rose wanted to keep her happy and active and flourishing for as long as possible.

DECLAN PULLED HIS CAR INTO THE DRIVEWAY. IT HAD BEEN a long day. He'd hoped to get back much earlier to see how Agnes had settled in, but as usual, time got away from him. He worked from home when he could, but there were always sites to visit and outside business to conduct.

He would have jogged up the steps to his flat, but he wondered if Agnes might be sleeping, so he took the treads lightly.

He was halfway up when he saw Rose down in the garden, her cap of curly brunette hair shining in the sun. He couldn't see Agnes. Maybe she was in the shade, close enough for Rose to watch her.

Setting his briefcase by the door, he headed back down. But Agnes wasn't anywhere that he could see. His heart began to pound as if he'd found her crumpled at the foot of the stairs.

Why the hell wasn't Rose keeping an eye on her? That's why he'd hired the woman. It was crazy, and he stomped along the gravel path.

Rose sat back on her haunches, shading her pretty amber eyes to look up at him. Then she smiled, actually smiled.

"Where the hell is Agnes?" He towered over her, fisted hands mashed on his hips.

She pointed around him to the house. "We've had a lovely day, with a nice lunch, a stroll through the Rose Garden. Joe was installing all the equipment when we got back so we worked in the garden until he was done. Then

Agnes felt she needed a nap." Her voice was calm and sweet and rational.

And that pissed him off.

"All that sounds perfectly lovely." His voice was unnecessarily snide. "But if Agnes is in the house, why are you out here?"

"Actually," she said, without even a hint of snideness. "I'm assessing how much help she needs."

"I told you how much help she needed." His back teeth were grinding. "I told you she can't even figure out how to turn her TV on and off. She forgets to use her walker. And you had me hire a man to install benches and grab bars and toilet risers. I'm paying you to take care of her, not to work in the garden."

She didn't bother to stand. As if what he said wasn't worth acknowledging. He was forced to add, "She could fall out of bed."

Rose reached down to the object beside her, something that resembled a transistor radio. But who the hell used transistor radios anymore? They wore earphones or a Bluetooth.

She held it up, and the device emitted a sound resembling a delicate snore. "She's still sleeping. It's a baby monitor." Agnes was snoring, for God's sake. "I can hear everything," Rose assured him. "And I can be there in two seconds. Plus her walker is right by the bed. She can't get by it without using it. I brought the monitor with me from home. It was an invaluable tool with my mom. It will be for Agnes, too."

Somewhere during the soft, soothing tones and her reassuring words, his anger evaporated. For a moment he couldn't say a word.

"You don't have to worry about a thing," she said, smiling widely.

He felt like a chastised child. But Agnes was special, and a knot of tension and worry and fear had twisted his guts since

53

she'd gone into the hospital. No, far longer than that, when she started to decline, when he noticed that she forgot things more often, left the stove on, setting off the smoke alarm. The knot grew tighter even as he tried desperately to pick it loose. Now he'd taken it out on Rose, despite the fact that she was the one person who could care for Agnes and ease the tension tearing him up inside.

He managed to say, "I'm sorry. I shouldn't have—"

Even before he finished, she was saying, "You've been worrying over this problem like a dog gnawing a bone that has no meat left. Now you can let it go. We're in this together, and we've got Agnes covered."

She sounded like she cared. Christ, she sounded like his mother. Which was even worse.

She stood then, rising slowly, peeling the gloves off her fingers. Then she put her hand on his arm. "Joe did a brilliant job." She spoke to him in that soft, soothing voice, like he was a jumper she was trying to talk off a ledge. "And she loved the decals, didn't utter a word of complaint about the rugs having been removed. Thank you for being so good about all the changes and the expense."

"You don't have to thank me. I did it for Agnes." He wanted to shake off her touch, mostly because it felt too good. He didn't want anything about Rose to feel good.

He realized she was gently leading him back to the porch and the two chairs at the café table. But he refused to sit. "I'm glad everything's going well. I'll leave you to your duties." It was a subtle reminder. To both of them. He was the employer. And she had a job to do.

He started up the stairs to the briefcase he'd left outside his door.

"You said she was just a tenant," she called out to him softly as she stood at the bottom of the stairs watching him.

"But she's your mother's friend. And she was your fourth-grade teacher. You've known Agnes since you were a boy."

He turned. He didn't owe her an explanation, but he gave her one anyway. "I never said I'd known her only since she became my tenant."

She smiled, not even noticing the rebuke. "That's why the apartment is so special, why you took such care renovating it. Because Agnes was moving in."

"I did it because it increased the rental value."

"You just aren't going to give yourself any credit, are you?"

"I have no idea what you mean."

She just smiled. And that's why he hadn't told her. Because she'd think he was a nice guy, when he truly wasn't.

He opened his door, closing it behind him before she could start talking again.

He liked it when Rose talked.

That's why it was better not to listen. She was the employee. And he needed to keep her playing that role. Especially when it was so easy to forget.

Hadn't he learned his lesson?

6

"Let's call Declan and invite him to dinner." Agnes smiled gleefully. "I want to show him all my new stuff."

They were in the kitchen, Agnes seated at the table while Rose cooked chicken pesto pasta.

"What stuff?" Rose asked. They hadn't even gone shopping yet, and she'd brought all the ingredients for dinner from her own fridge.

"The bars in my shower. And that wonderful new bench for me to sit on. And the showerhead." Agnes waved a hand imperiously. "Go on, give him a call."

Rose hesitated. Declan had snapped like a lion ready to bite off her head when he found her alone in the garden. He'd apologized when she showed him the baby monitor, but Rose still felt like she'd stepped over some invisible line she hadn't known was there.

"Oh, dear," Agnes singsonged. Rose still wasn't sure if Agnes remembered her name.

"I didn't make enough to feed three of us." It sounded like a good excuse.

"The amount of pasta you dumped in the pot will feed an army. Call Declan so I won't have to eat leftovers for three nights in a row."

Rose gave in, pulling her cell phone out of her back pocket. She already had Declan on speed dial. He was her employer, after all.

When he answered with a gruff, "Delaney here," she said, "It's Rose. Agnes would like you to come to dinner. It's chicken pesto pasta. You probably don't like pesto, do you?" she challenged, hoping he'd say no.

Agnes called out, "Tell him I want him to see all my new stuff."

"Agnes says—" she started, and he cut her off with, "I heard."

"So?" That sounded a bit rude, and she added, "Would you like to come?"

"I can't come for dinner. But I'll come down to see Agnes's stuff."

Rose looked at Agnes. "He can't have dinner, but he wants to see your toilet riser." She wanted to laugh, but the effect was better if she said it straight-faced.

Agnes gasped. "Is that what it is?"

"Yes." She turned her attention back to Declan. "Agnes would love to show you her toilet riser. Please come whenever you like. And the offer of dinner still stands."

Agnes called out, "You're a poophead if you don't eat with us."

Just in case he hadn't heard, Rose repeated, "She says you're a party pooper."

She didn't know why she was jerking him around, except that he'd been such a bear out in the garden.

He sighed. "All right."

He sounded so ungracious, she had to smile. "Dinner will be ready in ten minutes."

He added, to her surprise, "Thank you. I'd appreciate a home-cooked meal." His voice was tight, as if she were twisting his arm. "Can I bring some wine to go with the meal?"

She shouldn't. But she did. "I like champagne."

At last, he gave a barely there chuckle. "You're pushy. I'll be there in ten minutes."

She heard dead air as he hung up, and she turned to Agnes. "Are you satisfied?"

Agnes's face beamed with the brightest smile. "Yes, I am, you silly sausage."

Rose was inordinately happy that Agnes remembered the silly sausage club.

Ten minutes later, on the dot, Declan was at the door. He'd changed from his suit into neatly pressed slacks and a polo shirt. He was freshly shaved and his short blond hair recently combed as if he'd prepared for a date. Why did she have to find that distinguished hint of silver at his temples so appealing?

He held out a bottle of champagne, the label facing away from her.

Rose took it, not looking, holding it close to her chest. "Thank you. You really didn't have to."

There was a slight uptick of his mouth before he said dryly, "I thought it was an order."

"You're my employer. I can never order you around." She smiled and turned on her heel, leading him into the kitchen.

Agnes had laid out placemats, napkins, and utensils, and Rose set the champagne on the table. The garlic bread in its basket scented the air with an aroma delicious enough to make Rose's mouth water.

"Declan, dear boy." Agnes clapped her hands when she saw him. "Let's eat first because Rose worked so hard."

Rose noted that Agnes had remembered her name this time. Maybe it was the Rose Garden link that did it.

"Then we can look at all the new things in my bathroom." Her smile was wide and delighted, as if she were talking about a new dress or a china figurine.

"I can hardly wait," Declan said dryly, slowly blinking his too attractive green eyes as if he were trying to telegraph a message.

Agnes patted the seat next to her. "You sit here." Which left the chair opposite him for Rose.

Declan leaned over to kiss Agnes's cheek. "I'm so glad you're home. It's been very quiet around here without you."

Agnes tittered like a happy bird while Rose dished out pasta and set a steaming plate in front of her.

"Oh my." Agnes closed her eyes, breathing in the scent. "That smells so good. You must be the best cook ever, dear."

Rose brought plates for Declan and herself.

"Isn't this the most delicious thing you've ever smelled?" Agnes twirled a tiny bit of pasta and chicken on her fork and put it in her mouth daintily. Closing her eyes, she groaned, making appreciative noises. "Oh my," she said dreamily. "Best ever."

Rose laughed. "You're going a little overboard, Agnes."

Agnes patted Declan's hand. "Try it."

Declan did as ordered, his expression changing as he chewed, a nod of his head, his eyes widening, then a smile. "I never doubt Agnes. This is absolutely delicious."

"Schmoozer," Rose said.

Declan laughed. A real laugh as delicious as the chicken pesto pasta.

Rose had to turn away, and the champagne was a good excuse as she peeled off the foil. "Oh my God." She gasped, holding up the bottle, her mouth hanging open. "This is Dom Perignon."

He raised one overbearing eyebrow. "You asked for champagne."

"But—" She didn't know what to say. She'd completely embarrassed herself. "I didn't mean." She'd only been teasing him. She hadn't been angling for a hundred-dollar bottle of champagne.

"If I'm going to drink champagne, I want good champagne." He stood. "Shall I pop the cork?"

He'd popped her cork all right.

"I'm not sure we even have champagne glasses." She looked at Agnes, who merely shrugged. Rose began opening cupboard doors. "Ah, there we are." On the top shelf of the corner cabinet. "I'm afraid I can't reach."

Declan reached around her, taking down three glasses, his body heat arcing across the scant inches between them. Then he popped the cork, without spilling a drop, and poured expertly. Rose carried the glasses to the table.

"Ooh, champagne," Agnes cooed as the sparkling wine fizzed in her flute. She raised her glass. "Here's to a wonderful adventure." They clinked glasses over the garlic bread in the middle of the table.

Dinner was pleasant, the conversation covering everything Rose and Agnes had done that day. Declan was complimentary about the meal, and Agnes was excited that there weren't any leftovers. "When I was a girl, my mother made a big pot of stew or a huge casserole, and we all had to eat it for days and days and days." She squeezed her eyes shut, her lips pinched, her nose wrinkled. "I hate leftovers."

"I'll keep that in mind," Rose said. "But perhaps we can make three meals, then have three days of leftovers, so you don't feel like it's the same thing day after day."

"That sounds a bit better," Agnes chirped.

"And we're not wasting our leftovers either."

Declan merely nodded, as if he had any say at all. He

didn't smile much, his face wasn't particularly expressive, and he never seem to get animated about anything. Except the first taste of her pesto pasta.

She wondered if he'd felt that spark as his body almost brushed hers when he'd reached for the champagne glasses. But that was probably all her. She had to do her utmost to keep her mind off sparks. The problem was that Rose had only ever been with one man. Too consumed with her mother's care, she hadn't dated after Kevin left. The months since she'd lost her mother had been about settling the estate, arguing with her brother over the house, and finding a job. Dating had been the last thing on her mind.

But Declan Delaney reminded her what it was like to be a woman. To have desires and needs.

When they were done, Rose cleared the plates, saying, "I didn't plan anything for dessert, but I saw some canned pears that will do."

"I don't have time for dessert." Declan pushed his chair back and stood. "You and Agnes should share the pears."

Agnes bounced to her feet, which for her was more a laborious push out of her chair. "But you have to see all my new things in the bathroom."

"Of course," Declan said. "I wouldn't miss that."

Rose pulled the chair away so Agnes could get out while Declan brought the walker. She continued to be amazed over how much Agnes remembered. Maybe it was excitement and enthusiasm firing up her memory banks.

She led them down the short hall to her bedroom. "Look at these flowery little rugs." She pointed at the decals. "And I can't even trip over them."

"Ingenious," Declan said looking at Rose with almost a smile.

Then Agnes proudly flourished a hand when she entered the bathroom, like a queen showing off her crown jewels.

"And this is my thingy that I hang onto when I get in." Agnes wrapped her fingers around the grab bar. "And I've got that bench if I get tired when I'm taking a shower."

Her long-term memory was intact, but Agnes sometimes had trouble with the names of things, so the grab bar became a "thingy." But Rose found words sometimes escaped her, too.

Agnes sat on the closed toilet seat. "And this is my new throne," she said, beaming at Declan.

The seat had rails along the side to help Agnes push herself up, and the riser itself added four inches of height, so she didn't have to plop down, so to speak, when she sat.

"Isn't it all amazing?" she asked, her eyes alight as she looked up at Declan.

Rose wanted to guffaw, because yet again they were talking about bodily functions. She detected a slight reddening of Declan's cheeks, but also a slight curve on his lips.

"I'm astounded," he said deadpan.

Rose stepped forward, grabbing the tool sitting at the back of the toilet. "And here's your royal scepter."

Agnes's eyes twinkled, and her smile stretched out the wrinkles of her mouth. "My dear, it's perfect." She grabbed the handle. "Take a picture, take a picture."

Rose fished her phone out of her pocket, snapping a picture of Agnes holding a toilet plunger as if it were a royal scepter. "All you need now is a crown."

Behind her, she was sure she heard a snicker.

DECLAN BENT DOWN TO KISS AGNES'S CHEEK AS SHE SAT IN her customary parlor chair.

"No, no," he said at the third entreaty to stay. "I have to work, so I must skip fruit and a movie."

"You're never going to stay healthy if you don't eat fruit," Agnes grumbled. But really, it was all about getting him to stay.

That's why he'd found Rose for her. Rose would keep her company and do everything Agnes needed, especially the things Declan couldn't do.

Even more, Rose would make Agnes laugh. Like she had in the bathroom holding her royal plunger. Even he'd laughed.

He'd done his duty and found the perfect companion for Agnes.

Walking to the door, he turned back, his hand on the knob, only to find Rose right there, showing him out like a proper hostess.

It was impolite not to say something. "Thank you. The meal was delicious."

He'd found a good cook for Agnes as well as an intelligent, friendly, humorous woman to take care of her every need. "The installations in the bathroom will make her very safe. Thank you."

"You're welcome, but you paid for it all."

"But you knew exactly what to get. And how to lay down the decals so she actually thinks there are rugs on her floors."

It sounded like some sort of mutual admiration society, which made his brain segue to his anger this afternoon. It had been totally uncalled for. "I apologize again for the way I reacted in the garden."

"What did you do, Declan?" Agnes called out. He forgot that even at her age, she had excellent hearing.

"He simply said—" Rose looked over her shoulder at Agnes. "—that weeding the garden was your job, and I shouldn't take the pleasure away from you."

Agnes laughed. She was such a happy lady. Sometimes, after a long day, he visited her just for a sip of good cheer.

Was she depressed, Rose had wanted to know. He would never call Agnes depressed.

"I know gardening is your favorite job," he added, backing Rose's assertion while she covered for him.

Agnes put a hand to her chest and, in the regal tone of a queen on her throne with scepter in hand, she said, "My dear Declan, at this time of my life, I do believe I much prefer watching other people do the weeding."

They all laughed, and he realized he'd laughed more tonight than he had in a long time. There was that moment in the bathroom when Rose handed Agnes the plunger. And there was now. But then Agnes could usually drag a smile or two out of him.

He stepped into the hallway, only to have Rose follow him. When he'd divided the downstairs into two units, he'd kept the main stairs leading up to the second floor and his flat, as well as a hallway to the back of the house and a door that opened onto the outside porch. It left a large space for the foyer, and he didn't have to stand so close to Rose. Yet he remembered that burst of heat as he'd reached for the champagne glasses.

"You don't have to apologize again," Rose said, holding the door of Agnes's flat slightly closed to muffle their voices

"All right then, I'll just thank you for dinner."

"You don't have to keep thanking me for dinner either." She smiled. Had he noticed yesterday what a pretty smile she had? "I promise not to let Agnes call you every night, forcing you to come down to dinner."

It was on the tip of his tongue to say he didn't mind, but then he recognized it was too dangerous to come down here every night with Rose always around.

"I'll check on you both every once in a while." Then he quickly modified it. "Not checking up on *you*, but just to see how Agnes is doing."

"She'll love that. You're her favorite person, you know."

Silence ticked between them for two seconds. He felt suddenly as if it were the end of the night when you stood at the door with a date unsure whether she wanted you to kiss her.

But any thoughts about kissing were totally inappropriate. And a bad idea. Really bad. He knew exactly how *that* could turn out. Never get involved with an employee was his motto.

Especially if she was as appealing as Rose Christopher.

He inclined his head, said, "Good night," and headed up the stairs.

Yet Rose's citrusy scent clung to him, giving him untoward thoughts, until he was forced to take a shower to wash her off.

The only problem was that standing naked in the shower made him think even more about Rose.

7

Over the next few weeks, Agnes filled up the empty spot Rose's mother had left behind. No one could replace her mother, but Rose felt joy she hadn't known since the last time Mom recognized her.

Agnes was bright and active, talkative and fun-loving. They laughed all the time, they called each other silly sausages, and together they were the silly sausage club.

The property management company Declan recommended found a renter for Rose's house, and for three days, she and Agnes had cleaned out all the personal belongings, taking them to storage or dropping off what Rose didn't want at a local thrift store. Agnes watched and talked and made Rose laugh. The house would go furnished to a young family with two children. After moving her mother's good Sunday china and collectibles to the storage unit, there was nothing irreplaceable left in the house. All her mother's favorite movies were shelved at Agnes's, and they were slowly working their way through the DVDs.

As Agnes's bruise and cut faded, they settled into a routine, strolling in the Rose Garden every morning, shopping if it was needed, then playing Scrabble or cards or even adult coloring books, which Agnes loved, crowing that she could still color within the lines. She'd made up a game of picking a relatively long word out of the dictionary then making as many words as possible out of those letters.

With all games, Rose was better able to assess Agnes's capabilities. Sometimes she needed help with the next card to play or a hint on a Scrabble word. She needed reminders to use her walker, and she definitely needed help with showering and dressing. The TV remote was occasionally a problem, but other times Agnes worked it without trouble. Sometimes her fingers hurt, and Rose rubbed in cream. Or her neck was stiff, and Rose applied a patch. They read Reader's Digest together, and Agnes was fairly good with the articles. But she had trouble with books because she couldn't always remember every detail of what they'd read the day before. She had some diminished capacity, to be expected at the age of eighty-seven, but she was nowhere near the state her mother had been when Rose moved in.

Her conclusion was that Agnes would have done well in an assisted living facility where aides were in and out to check on her. But living entirely on her own definitely put Agnes at risk.

Rose had never had the chance to help her mother this way, keeping her brain working with all the activities. If Rose could keep Agnes engaged, hopefully her functionality would decrease at a slower rate, employing the old adage, use it or lose it.

Often in the afternoons, Rose worked in the garden and they had lovely conversations about anything from what it was like to be born during the Great Depression and live through the Second World War to when Agnes heard her first Beatles song.

While Agnes napped, Rose gardened or cleaned or did

laundry or made shopping lists or ordered whatever they needed online.

Sometimes she called her brother. They were still at odds over the share of the house he thought he deserved, and the phone calls were brief and tense. But Rose couldn't let Bernie go. He was the only family she had left, and she hoped eventually he'd understand how much she'd given up to take care of their mother.

Agnes claimed she never slept, just closed her eyes, despite the delicate snores Rose could hear. Then they watched Dr. Phil or Judge Judy. Agnes loved grumbling over the bizarre things Dr. Phil's guests did and the crazy conflicts of the claimants Judge Judy had in her courtroom. They both enjoyed a cup of tea and a cookie or two, no more because Agnes didn't want to get fat.

"Old ladies always get fat." Agnes patted her belly. "I refuse to let that happen. But I do like my cookie in the afternoon and my chocolate and drop of Irish cream in the evening."

For dinner, they settled into the routine Rose had suggested, three nights of new meals, then three nights of leftovers.

Sometimes Declan dropped in during the evening to see how Agnes was doing.

He didn't stay for a movie, but Rose usually followed him to the door. And he would say things like, "Agnes is doing well. You're doing a good job. Thank you." Always complimentary but somehow aloof.

She tried not to think of him as a man but as her employer.

Yet it was as if her middle-aged body had suddenly come to life. She'd even had an intimate dream or two about him.

It was during one of those evenings as Rose prepared dinner and Agnes sat in her usual spot in the kitchen's bay window that Agnes said, "Are you making extra for Declan?"

Sautéing the mushrooms, Rose said over her shoulder, "We didn't invite him to dinner."

Agnes turned militant. "Then we need to invite him. I want to watch *The Quiet Man* tonight. And it was his grandmother's favorite movie so he should watch, too."

"He's seen it many times."

Agnes huffed. "He can watch it for me. It was your mother's favorite movie. And my favorite movie. He has to come."

Rose shook her spatula at Agnes, then swiped a paper towel across the floor where a drop of oil had landed. "That's extortion."

Agnes smiled like a cheeky child. "Of course it's extortion. How else am I going to get him down here?"

"He comes down to see you almost every night."

"But he doesn't stay," Agnes moaned pitifully. "He doesn't have dinner or a drink. He doesn't sit in front of the TV and watch a wonderful movie with us. And I want all of that." She pounded her little fist on the table. With anyone else, the utensils would have jumped, but Agnes made barely a thump. She rose out of her chair, stiffly pushing herself up with her fists on the table. "If you won't call him, I will."

Rose gave in. "All right, I'll call."

She'd made stroganoff with nonfat sour cream, serving it over rice instead of noodles, broccoli on the side. The meat and onions had been in the slow cooker all day. Setting aside the spatula, she pulled her phone out of her back pocket, and sent Agnes a cross-eyed glare as she punched his number.

He answered with, "Is something wrong?"

She didn't call him unless she needed something.

"Agnes is getting pushy. She wants you to come to dinner then watch *The Quiet Man* with us." She heard the deep groan across the airwaves.

"Do I have to watch that movie again?" he whined adorably like a little boy.

"I'll put her on and you can talk her out of it."

"When that woman decides something, she can't be talked out of it."

"I agree."

"What are you making?"

"What difference does it make?"

"It makes a difference to the wine I bring. You don't think I can watch *The Quiet Man* again without fortification, do you?"

"We like champagne better than wine."

"I don't have any more Dom Perignon."

"Bring the cheap stuff."

He snorted. "I never drink cheap stuff."

"I *always* drink cheap stuff. All you need is a sugar cube soaked in bitters, and you turn even the cheapest champagne into a cocktail."

"I wouldn't deign to destroy a good champagne by adding bitters in a sugar cube," he stated like a stuffy aristocrat.

"That's why I buy cheap champagne. It tastes better than using the good stuff."

"You'll have to make do with what I have."

"I'll enjoy whatever you bring."

"What time do you want me?" Then, as if he'd suddenly heard the potential sexual innuendo, he coughed. "I mean, when should I come?" Which wasn't any better and possibly a lot worse.

"Half an hour." She let him off the hook by *not* saying that she wanted to come first.

Oh my, as Agnes would say, she was bad.

DECLAN ARRIVED WITH A BOUQUET OF FLOWERS AND A bottle of very good champagne. Rose had seen it at Costco, and it wasn't cheap. She certainly wouldn't add a bitters-soaked sugar cube.

The meal was delicious, if she did say so herself, and Agnes chattered nonstop, with neither Rose nor Declan saying much more than a polite *yes, no, thank you,* or *please, pass the rice.* She and Declan didn't exchange conversation at all.

She wanted to tell him it hadn't been a sexual innuendo, but that would add the word *sex* into their conversation.

After dinner, Agnes settled in her chair with a bowl of canned peaches, and Rose primed the movie.

"I've seen it so many times I have all the lines memorized," Declan told Agnes.

"Good. You can say them right along with me."

"Ag-neess," he said, a long slur on the second syllable. "There aren't enough chairs." He pointed to the two comfortable wingback chairs that Rose and Agnes used in the evenings.

"There's a comfy chair in the bedroom. Bring that in."

"I'll get it," Rose offered.

Declan probably hoped Agnes had forgotten about that chair. But when you wanted her to forget something, she never did.

"I'll get it," he gave in.

They shifted all the chairs so he would have a good view.

While Agnes said all the good lines right along with the actors, Declan kept his mouth shut. Halfway through the movie, Rose served more champagne and Agnes's chocolate.

At a particularly funny moment, Agnes pointed at Declan. "You just smiled."

"I never said it wasn't a good movie. I just like to watch something where I don't know the ending."

"They didn't do alternate endings back then," Rose said.

Declan snorted. "Right. They actually had to make a decision about what was the best ending for a movie."

"I wish they'd had an alternate ending for *I Am Legend* where the dog doesn't die." Rose sighed wistfully.

"You should watch *Omega Man* with Charlton Heston," Agnes said. "It was a much better version. And no dogs were killed in the making of that movie. Only people."

Both Rose and Declan stared at Agnes. Then Declan said, "Isn't *I Am Legend* a zombie movie?"

"They're not really zombies," Rose said. "Not quite vampires either."

"In the actual book, they were definitely vampires," Agnes said.

Rose and Declan could only gape. It was amazing the things Agnes remembered, and even more amazing that she'd read a vampire book.

Then Agnes pouted. "We're missing the movie. He's going to drag her back to her brother."

"Plot spoiler," Declan said.

Rose turned, a hand on her hip. "I thought you remembered the whole movie."

"I remember every scintillating moment," he drawled, finishing with a big grin.

Wow! Declan Delaney's grin was a sight to behold.

Agnes clapped wildly as the movie ended, though, because of her arthritis, her palms barely met. "Best movie ever," she said, her smile so big it took up her whole face.

Declan rubbed his hands down his thighs and made to rise. "Well, ladies," he began.

But he got no further as Agnes said, "I have to make my dying wish."

Declan immediately plopped back in the chair. "You aren't dying, Agnes."

Agnes pursed her lips and said quite primly, "I could pop off at any moment."

"I certainly hope not," Rose answered with horror. The thought gave her palpitations.

Agnes flapped her hand. "It's not my deathbed wish. It's my bucket list. Where people write down all the things they have to do before they die." She explained as if she'd coined the phrase herself.

"I know what a bucket list is." Declan's tone was dry as an autumn leaf.

"First on my list is a visit to the little town in Ireland where they filmed *The Quiet Man*."

Absolute silence reigned. Declan and Rose exchanged a look. Then, while Declan opened his mouth, Rose beat him to it. "Are you sure you want to take a ten-hour plane ride?"

"Is it really ten hours?" Agnes's eyes went round with wonder.

The tension eased in Rose's body. "Ten hours in a tiny seat, with tiny bathrooms that you have to stand in line to use."

Not that Rose had ever made a transatlantic flight, but she and her mother had flown back east to visit Bernie.

"Well then," Agnes said, "you have to go with me."

Rose stared, mouth hanging open.

"Rose doesn't have a passport," Declan said as if he were sure she'd never traveled abroad.

She didn't like the way Declan made the assumption, as if she'd never had enough money. Even if it was true. "I have a passport," she said with a hint of defiance.

Declan gave her a look. And she realized her mistake when Agnes crowed, "That's wonderful."

"Mom and I thought we'd take a trip to the south of France where it was lovely and warm. But we never used the passports," she admitted.

Agnes understood what she wasn't saying. "She became too sick?"

Rose couldn't handle taking care of her mother on the trip, navigating the airport, getting her mother to the bathroom on the plane, not to mention herding her through the countryside. There was the money issue, too. But what she said was, "It gets harder for the elderly to travel."

Agnes didn't grasp Rose's point. "This will be like the trip you and your mother never got to take." She beamed. "Except it would be Ireland instead of France. And maybe colder and rainier." Even that thought didn't daunt Agnes's enthusiasm.

"I really don't think—"

Agnes cut her off with a beseeching, woebegone look. "Please, please, please," she said like a little girl, her hands together in prayer.

Declan took over. "Agnes, it isn't practical."

"Of course it's not practical. But at my age, you don't have to worry about being practical. Haven't you heard that saying, 'Live like you only have two years left?'"

"Uh, no," Declan had to admit.

Rose was astounded at Agnes's memory of a profound proverb.

Then again, Agnes might have made it up herself.

"If," Declan said, "we all lived like we only had two years left, we'd chuck our responsibilities and fly off to visit the wonders of the world like Machu Picchu, the Great Wall of China, and the pyramids at Giza."

Agnes's eyes lit up like sparklers on the Fourth of July. "Is that what you'd do, Declan?" Then she snorted. "You'd never chuck your job. But even so, you could take off two or three weeks to visit those places."

Declan pokerfaced her. "I didn't say *I* wanted to go. I said that's what *other* people might do."

Fall in love, Rose thought, that's what she'd do. It was so clear in her mind, as if it lay just below the surface of her consciousness. Of course, it wasn't possible. Taking care of Agnes, she didn't even meet men. Except Declan. And he didn't count.

"Well," Agnes said, punctuated with a little harrumph at the end. "If I only have two years to live, then I want to walk in the footsteps of *The Quiet Man*."

"It's not like what happened in the movie was a historical event," Declan pointed out. "The town isn't real."

"But they filmed it in Ireland," Agnes insisted. "Even if they made up the name of the town. And that's where I want to go." She shot Declan a sly look Rose was sure he didn't notice. "You need to escort us."

Declan snorted. Loudly. "Didn't you just hear that I'm not ready to chuck my job or my *huuge* responsibilities." He drew out the word, forcing the point home.

"What would your mother say if she heard you were sending off two defenseless women—one of them as old as dirt, by the way— all alone to a foreign country?"

Declan opened and closed his mouth.

"You look like a fish, Declan."

Rose yawned, the only thing she could do to shut down the conversation before those two came to blows. Hopefully by tomorrow, Agnes would forget about her bucket list. "Oh my goodness. It's past our bedtime." She covered her mouth as the fake yawn became a real one.

Declan grabbed the excuse like a lifeline. "I've kept you ladies up far later than usual."

It wasn't that late, but Rose didn't correct him.

Agnes was infected by a smaller and daintier contagious yawn. "I know what you two are thinking. You're hoping I'll forget by the morning. But I won't." She waved her hand imperiously and asked for her walker. "Good night."

Rose feared they were in for a long battle.

8

True to her word, Agnes hadn't forgotten by the morning. Still seated at the kitchen table after breakfast, she pestered Rose to look up *The Quiet Man* on her computer. Perhaps Rose shouldn't fuel the little lady's fantasy, but she typed "filming *The Quiet Man*."

"You see." Agnes squealed with delight. On the screen was a statue of Maureen O'Hara and John Wayne straight from a scene out of the movie.

"What does it say? I can't see that far," Agnes groused. "The letters are so small." Her eyesight was fairly good and Rose surmised she wanted a synopsis without the work of actually reading.

"It was filmed in a little town called Cong. And there's a museum there."

Agnes was less than excited. "That's a lot of words on the page for just a town name and a museum." She thinned her lips.

Rose didn't sigh. And she couldn't lie, even though she knew Declan would frown on her for looking it up.

Well," she began. "The museum is a replica of the cottage

76

they lived in. And there are tours of the places they used in the film. And buggy rides like the one in which John Wayne courted Maureen O'Hara. And the bar they all frequented." There were statues and stores and mementos. The little town had turned *The Quiet Man* into quite an industry. "And there's a beautiful castle nearby that's become a hotel."

Agnes put her hands to her cheeks. "Oh my. There's so much to see. You have to get Declan to see how important this is." Her gaze on Rose was piercing. "Maybe you should sleep with him. Then you can talk him into anything."

"Agnes," Rose burst out. "Do not tell me you ever slept with a man just to get something you wanted."

Agnes's cheeks didn't even burn. She tapped her temple. "You know I have a terrible memory, dear. I can't even remember your name. So how am I supposed remember what I did years and years ago in my youth?"

Rose snorted. "I'm beginning to believe you have selective memory issues. I bet you know exactly how to turn on your own TV, don't you?"

Agnes shook her head solemnly. "I have good days and bad days," she said, admitting nothing.

Rose would give it a few more days and hope Agnes forgot about the little town of Cong in County Mayo, Ireland where they filmed *The Quiet Man*.

And if Agnes didn't forget, Rose would dump the whole problem in Declan's lap.

Let him be the bad guy.

AGNES DID NOT FORGET.

Not the next day, nor the day after. Every day, she worked on Rose. Today it was in the middle of tea and cookies and *Dr. Phil*. "I've got a little nest egg we can use."

Rose doubted she had a nest egg. Then again, maybe she did since Declan paid for everything. He probably didn't even charge Agnes rent.

She tried the you're-too-old approach. "It's such a long, long way, Agnes. Older people can get blood clots in the legs because they can't move around. My brother once got a clot, and it went all the way to his lungs. He was lucky to survive."

She'd only read about that on the internet, and she hated the lie. But these were desperate times.

"We need Declan's opinion." Agnes rapped her knuckles on the arm of her chair.

"Declan's not going to say it's a great idea any more than I will."

Agnes's eyes twinkled devilishly. "Let's make a very special dinner and butter him up."

"That's sneaky." Rose narrowed her eyes, though she wanted to laugh.

Agnes beamed one of her outrageous smiles. Kids and old people were adorable.

"All right." How could she fight that smile? "What shall we make for dinner?"

After much discussion over lasagna or chicken cordon bleu or beef stew, they decided on shrimp scampi.

Declan graciously accepted the invitation and arrived with another bottle of delicious champagne.

Agnes started in on him when the first shrimp went into his mouth. "Isn't this the best shrimp scampi you've ever had?" she asked before even tasting her own.

He croaked out, "Delicious."

"Rose is the absolute best cook ever." Agnes was laying it on way too thick. "She's also very smart on the computer. She can find anything. She found out all about the little town where *A Quiet Man* was filmed."

Without even raising his head, he shot Rose with a red-hot-and-ready-to-explode look.

She shrugged, trying to indicate it hadn't been her idea.

But Agnes wasn't done. "There are so many things to see, statues and museums and the old bar, and you can take ride in this very same cart that John Wayne and Maureen O'Hara went courting in." None of them used the actual characters names, only the actors.

"And—" Agnes went in for the kill. "—there's a gorgeous castle that, can you believe it, is a hotel." Her voice dropped to a reverent whisper.

"And you found all this out for Agnes on the internet?" His whole face got in on the glower he sent Rose.

"She works for me," Agnes said. "She has to do whatever I tell her."

"I thought Rose worked for me," he said with a distinct click of his teeth as he bit down on half the words.

It went on like that the entire dinner and into dessert and out into the parlor where Agnes conned Declan into playing cards.

She was all Ireland, all *The Quiet Man*, all the time.

Until Declan said, "Agnes, you're eighty-seven-years old. Traveling to Ireland is the dumbest idea—"

It was Rose's turn to glower at him, and he cut off his rant, starting again. "It's not a good idea for an eighty-seven-year-old woman to take such a long trip."

Agnes, after all the cajoling and buttering up and hands together in prayer, actually sobered. "But even old people need a dream. Or their spirit dies."

A tear tickled the back of Rose's eye.

"I know," Declan said very softly. "But I think another dream might be more easily attainable."

Agnes slowly, sadly shook her head. "I don't think so. And

this time I won't forget. I know you and Rose keep hoping I will, but I won't."

Rose's heart ached. She remembered the times her mother became lucid enough to realize all of the faculties she was losing. The fear, even terror, in her eyes. The tears. She heard the echo of her mother's voice. *I just don't feel like I'm myself anymore*.

Agnes closed her eyes a moment, and when she opened them again, she muttered, "I'm tired. I'd like to go to bed early. Is that okay, Rose?"

"Of course. I'll help you."

As Agnes readied for bed, there wasn't another word about Ireland or *The Quiet Man*.

She tucked Agnes in as if she were a child, kissing her cheek. Since it was too early for bed, she took the baby monitor back out to the parlor.

She was surprised to find Declan still seated in the chair. He'd cleared away the cards, but he hadn't left.

He poured them each another glass of champagne, and looking at the baby monitor in her hand, he said, "Since you have that, let's sit on the porch and talk."

It was a question, but it wasn't an order, and Rose grabbed her sweater before following him. With the small café table between them as they sat, Rose put the baby monitor down.

"She can't hear us?" he asked.

She shook her head. "It's muted on this end. But I can hear when she needs me."

He stared across the front garden, turning the stem of his glass between his fingers. "She might be playing me. I wouldn't put it past her. But I can't ignore her either."

"You're not saying you want her to go to Ireland?" Her heart gave a little flip.

He sighed, took a sip, and spoke to the night, not looking at her. "I hear what she's saying. If you don't have a dream, you don't have anything to strive for." Finally he turned his head, his eyes dark in the gloom. "And I can give this to her.

"She says she has a nest egg."

He nodded. "It's not enough for this, especially not a five-star hotel in a castle." He focused on a street light as if he were seeing so much more. "Sitting in a coach seat isn't going to cut it. She has to be able to move around, be comfortable, get to the bathroom. She needs first class."

She couldn't believe they were actually talking about making this dream come true. "I'd buy some of those compression socks for her."

He puffed out a breath that could have been a laugh. "Don't tell me this is what you planned all along?"

She shrugged. "Honestly, I don't know. The truth is that sometimes the elderly can be a pain in the butt."

Declan outright laughed. "Go ahead and say it like it is."

She grinned. "Agnes is very good. She does pretty much whatever I ask her to. But there's the walker and the bathroom and all the logistics that people our age don't think about."

She thought hope lit in his eyes. "So you want me to squash it?"

Rose shook her head. There might be difficulties, but the trip *could* be done. "Even at eighty-seven, you can't just lay down and die. You have to do the things you want to. And Agnes has a lot more function than I'd ever dreamed possible from what you first said. She surprises me all the time. I don't want to be the one to squash her dream if it's at all possible to make it happen." She looked at him, a long, steady look. "You tell me, is it possible?"

He picked up the champagne, took a gulp rather than a sip, and finally said, "It's possible."

"But you'll be the one who has to pay for it."

His laugh was little more than a snort. "I have a bit in

savings."

Rose almost choked on her champagne. She knew about his real estate. It was an empire.

"I can afford two flights to Ireland and a suite in the castle hotel."

She wagged her finger at him. "Oh no. Agnes wants you to go, too. You'll need to take two weeks off."

He gave a hard shake of his head. "Not possible. I've got too much going on here."

She was telling her boss what to do, which was a bad idea. But she'd already started and couldn't stop now. "I bet you can do just about everything over the phone and online and in video meetings. You don't have to be physically here."

He didn't fire her. And she could hear his mind working.

He downed the rest of his champagne, set his glass on the table, and said, "I could probably swing it. For Agnes."

She shouldn't have felt a thrill. But in the intimate darkness of the front porch, she couldn't help it.

When Declan moved, he moved fast.

He bought three first-class tickets. When Rose argued about the extra cost and said she could sit in coach, coming up whenever Agnes needed her, Declan stared at her, his eyes saying, *"Are you crazy?"*

When Agnes fussed that her hair needed a perm before the trip, Declan sent them off to the salon. Rose had her hair cut, too.

When Agnes said they needed new clothes for the trip, Declan sent them to the mall where Agnes bought three new dresses, because she was of a generation that dressed up to travel. Of course all the dresses were far too long, and Rose sat up late into the evenings hemming them.

"You're so good to me," Agnes said when she saw them hanging in her closet.

"That's because you're so sweet," Rose replied.

In a matter of two months, she'd come to adore Agnes. Agnes didn't replace her mother, no one ever could. But it warmed her heart that she could do all the things with Agnes that her mother had no longer been capable of. Like making a trip to Ireland.

"Oh, I'm just a bundle of nerves," Agnes said the day they were to leave as Rose packed their bags for the early evening flight.

Mid-May in Ireland could still be cool and sometimes rainy, so she packed layers of clothing for most eventualities, including raincoats and umbrellas, even scarves, hats, and gloves.

"What if I have to go to the bathroom on the plane?" Agnes whispered in her too loud voice, as if Declan were in the parlor and could hear everything. He, however, was attending to last-minute business.

"I'll be there to help you. Declan and I will take care of everything."

"Declan?" Agnes squeaked. "He can't take me to the bathroom."

Rose laughed. "I meant making sure the trip goes smoothly. When was the last time you flew anywhere?"

"I once flew to London. It was our trip of a lifetime. And it was a good thing we did it then because he died only a year later." Rose knew their story. Marvin had been an accountant for a small manufacturing company, working until he was in his seventies. His death had been quick, a heart attack. They hadn't even known he had a heart problem. "After that, there didn't seem to be much sense in traveling."

No wonder Agnes wanted Declan to go on this trip.

"But why did you renew your passport?"

Agnes sat up straighter in the chair. "What if I met a gentleman friend who wanted to take me to a fabulous foreign locale for a holiday?"

Rose stifled a smile. Well, of course, a gentleman friend. Agnes was ever optimistic.

As their departure time for the airport drew closer, Agnes clapped her hands and declared, "I want to wear my pretty pink skirt and blouse. And you have to wear that lovely blue top you bought."

Rose wore jeans to go with the lovely blue top. She owned only three dresses, one of which she'd purchased for her mother's funeral. She packed another of the dresses, in case she had need of it.

"All right. But you should you take a nap."

Agnes fluttered her hands. "I'm too excited for that now. I'll nap on the plane."

Over the next couple of hours, Agnes had Rose packing and unpacking and repacking and checking to make sure they had everything. Declan returned an hour before their departure to the airport to throw his bag together.

When it was time to go, a big town car arrived. It was a relief to relax in the backseat.

Agnes was still fluttering. "What if I've forgotten something?"

"We can buy anything in Ireland," Declan declared. "We're not trekking into the Amazon jungle."

Agnes flapped her hand at him. "You're a man. You bring two changes of clothing and think that's all you need."

Declan grinned. "That *is* all I need."

A wheelchair was waiting for Agnes at the airport, and she'd harrumphed. "I can use my walker. I don't need a wheelchair."

"There's a special line for wheelchairs which gets us through security faster," Declan informed her. "That's the

84

only reason for the wheelchair." What he didn't mention was that Agnes might have a problem waiting in the long security line if her legs began to ache. It was no way to start out the trip.

Rose doublechecked that Agnes's walker was tagged properly with their luggage. And with Agnes in the wheelchair, they were preboarded.

"Now," Agnes began in a non-nonsense voice she'd probably used on Declan when he was in the fourth grade, "I'll tell everyone that you're my son and daughter-in-law. I don't want to go through the rigmarole of explaining."

Rose didn't say a word while Declan shook his head. "We don't have to explain to anyone. Rose doesn't need to be my wife."

Agnes shook her finger at him. "Just do what I tell you."

"You certainly act like my mother," Declan grumbled, but his smile peeked through.

When the flight attendant stopped by to see if there was anything they needed, Agnes said, "This is my son Declan and my daughter-in-law, Rose. And I'm Agnes."

With enviable dark curls and a polite smile, the flight attendant shook Agnes's hand. "It's so nice to meet you. I'm Catherine."

"Oh my." Agnes clapped her hands. "You have such a pretty accent."

Most of the flight attendants had Irish accents, and Rose wondered if it was a job requirement.

"Oh my, will you look at all this," Agnes enthused. The seats were wide and comfortable with lots of leg room, a video screen the size of a laptop, and a side console that was big enough to double as a desk. Rose was excited, too.

Declan sat across the aisle. "What do you think of you first transatlantic flight?" he asked Rose, remembering that she'd never used her passport.

"I'm spoiled. If I go to Europe again, I don't how I'll fly without having my own berth."

Not that Rose would ever go to Europe again. This was her trip of a lifetime. Get paid to go Ireland, how could you beat that?

All she had to do was take care of Agnes and enjoy herself.

THEY WERE SERVED CHAMPAGNE BEFORE THE FLIGHT EVEN took off. As they sipped, Rose and Agnes giggled like schoolgirls on a field trip.

Declan spread workpapers on the console but couldn't concentrate. The ladies chattered and laughed as if every step of the journey was something new and amazing they'd never forget.

Once he decided to make this trip, he'd been determined. His admin booked the flights, the hotels, the car rental. He made sure Rose was added to the car as a driver for days when he couldn't accompany them. And there would be many with the amount of work hanging over him.

But as he watched their delight, he felt how right this trip was. How good for Agnes. How good Rose was for Agnes. She'd come to life again with Rose.

She was happy and lively, enjoying life, walking to the Rose Garden, going to the shops, all the things she'd stopped doing. With Rose, she had that freedom again. He watched them now across the aisle, giggling and whispering and making plans.

And Declan felt... good. It was the only word for it. He felt good that he was doing this thing for Agnes. He felt good that he'd brought Rose into Agnes's life.

Into *their* lives.

9

Rose sat back in her seat, her fingers linked with Agnes's on the console. A slight sense of vertigo twirled her around as the plane's engines roared in her ears and the force of their acceleration pushed her back against her seat. It was exhilarating, the feeling of weightlessness as the tires left the ground and they were flying up, up, up. Agnes breathed out a little *weeee* as if they were on a roller coaster.

This was the trip she would have taken with her mother, flying off to Ireland instead of France, a completely different kind of destination. Yet it filled a need inside her, touched a hidden spot that whispered she hadn't done right by her mother. This trip, being with Agnes, it felt as if her wound could start to heal.

The flight attendant brought menus once they'd reached cruising altitude and the seatbelt sign had been turned off. Agnes read, her nose scrunched as she pointed at the picture of the steak. "It's probably going to be as tough as old shoe leather."

"It's gourmet," Declan said from across the aisle. "Nothing but first class for you, Agnes."

"Schmoozer." Agnes harrumphed, but Rose heard the laugh and saw the gleam in the little lady's eyes as she added like an excited child, "Get the fish, and we can try out each other's meals and compare."

Rose glanced at Declan, smiling, but his gaze was once again glued to the laptop screen.

In short order, the flight attendant delivered their meals along with a second glass of champagne. "Oh my." Agnes groaned with her first bite of steak. "It really is gourmet," she whispered in her usual loud voice.

"I told you so," Declan said." He'd ordered the trout almondine like Rose.

"When did he turn into such an I-told-you-so?" Agnes groused.

Declan chuckled. "Don't get tipsy."

"Killjoy," Agnes muttered.

"I'm looking out for your best interests."

"I've got Rose to look after my best interests."

Rose loved the grumpy banter, the enjoyment threaded through their words, the gleam in Agnes's eyes. It was going to be a good trip.

"Taste my steak." Agnes cut off a chunk and put it on Rose's plate. They dined on real plates with real silverware and real glasses, nothing plastic.

"Take some of my trout, it's amazing." They were supposed to share anyway.

They made identical groans and moans of pleasure, and Rose turned to find Declan's eyes on her.

He raised his glass of Irish whiskey. "Here's to first class."

After dinner, they had two bottles of Bailey's each, because, as Agnes said, "There's barely a drop in one of these teeny tiny things."

They settled in to find a movie they could watch together just like they did at home. It struck her that she'd begun to think of Agnes's flat as her home.

She'd begun to think of Agnes herself as home.

She helped Agnes scroll through her screen menu and found several classic movies, many Agnes had seen and didn't want to see again. "I don't remember what happened," Agnes admitted, "but I remember it wasn't very good."

Rose pulled up the listing of TV shows, hoping they'd find something interesting.

Agnes tapped the screen. "That one."

"*The Walking Dead?*" Rose's voice arched with disbelief. "It's a zombie show."

Agnes rolled her eyes dramatically. "The title says it all, dear."

Rose laughed at Agnes's sarcasm. "Don't you want to watch something nice?"

"Would you prefer *Dr. Phil?*" Declan drawled without looking up from his laptop, obviously listening to every word.

She thought about all the *Dr. Phil* episodes they'd watched. "All right," she said, "*The Walking Dead.*" They binged three episodes with a couple of trips to the bathroom in between.

"Well," Agnes said. "That was quite a lot of lopped-off heads."

She stifled a laugh, especially with Agnes's serious tone.

"But I do like the sheriff. He's quite a hottie."

Rose laughed out loud, and even Declan took his eyes off the computer.

"Well, he is," Agnes muttered. Then she yawned.

"Maybe we should go to sleep," Rose suggested.

Agnes shook her head, her curls bobbing. "Let's keep watching. I really can't sleep sitting up like this."

Rose didn't point out that Agnes often fell asleep sitting up in her chair. "Your seat turns into a bed."

Agnes stared wide-eyed. "Really?"

Declan added, "Really. And if you sleep, you won't feel the jet lag so badly when we get there."

"But I want to watch more of *The Walking Dead*. And that sheriff." Agnes pouted.

Rose patted her hand. "We can binge the rest on streaming when we're home."

"The world has become an amazing place." Agnes stared at the little TV screen as if a genie might pop out of it. "Who could ever have imagined that we wouldn't have to wait a whole week for the next episode? And no commercials either."

After one more visit to the bathroom, they settled in. The last thing Rose remembered was Declan's whispered, "Good night."

WITH THE TIME CHANGE, THEY ARRIVED IN DUBLIN IN THE early afternoon and were met at the gate with a wheelchair for Agnes. The business of customs and luggage all seemed miraculously easy, and soon they were in the rental car, Rose and Agnes seated in the back as if Declan were chauffeuring them.

"I booked a Dublin hotel for a couple of nights." Declan looked in the rearview mirror. "I thought we'd need a rest before we drive to Cong."

The wet streets teemed with double-decker buses and bicycles and a street car that looked like a bullet train. There were modern buildings of glass and chrome, and older buildings of red brick. Off the thoroughfares, the streets were narrow and cobblestoned, some of them only for walkers and closed to cars, many of the buildings with brightly painted facades.

Agnes pointed and oohed and aahed at the spires of churches, the beauty of some old government building, or a marvelous bridge over the river.

Rose gave their hotel a five-star rating, its marble lobby dotted with comfortable chairs where she and Agnes waited while Declan checked them in. The rugs were intricately woven and sumptuous beneath their feet. Despite the people rolling suitcases to and fro, the noise was level low, as if everyone respected the ambience.

The elevators were manned, and a bellboy was tasked with bringing their luggage.

"Oh my," Agnes enthused as they entered their suite, just as she had over the first bite of steak on the plane.

An elegant sofa with matching chairs filled the center of the room, thick carpets covered the hardwood floors, and a small dining table for four sat by the bay window. Declan's bedroom was on the left, its massive king-size bed draped in a thick down comforter. Agnes and Rose's room was decadent with two fourposter double beds, a café table and two chairs by the window, and an incredible view of the River Liffey.

Declan had gone top-of-the-line all the way. Rose almost felt guilty.

But Agnes clapped in delight. "This is marvelous, Declan." She held her hands out to him. "Are you sure I have enough in savings?" Her usual loud whisper was suddenly soft.

Declan squeezed her fingers. "Absolutely. I check your balance every day."

"Thank you, thank you." She spoke with such feeling that Rose's heart melted.

She would never reveal that Declan was paying for it all.

"Take a rest," Declan suggested. "Then we'll go out for dinner."

"Oh no." Agnes looked at him, her mouth a round *O* of astonishment. "I can't waste a single minute on sleep. We have to see everything."

But Declan was insistent. "We have another whole day in Dublin."

Rose had scoured the internet for all the best sights to see before leaving for Cong and County Mayo.

"Agnes, we really should rest." Yet she understood Agnes's need. She could feel time ticking away, and she was just as excited to get started. But she wasn't eighty-seven.

"Please, please, please." Agnes put her hands together, her gaze beseeching.

Rose felt herself weaken. "We did sleep most of the flight. But are you sure you're not tired?"

Agnes shook her head, her curls, which had flattened during the flight, springing to life. "I can totally do this." Agnes really did watch too much teenage TV.

Although *The Walking Dead* wasn't any better.

Rose looked at Declan. "We could visit the gardens. Do a little walking."

He stared her down, his gaze dubious.

He finally gave in to Agnes's eagerness. "All right. I'll make some work calls while you're out."

"Oh no, you don't," Agnes said, her hands going militantly to her walker. "This is a vacation. You have to come with us.

He breathed in deeply, his nostrils flaring. "It's a working vacation. And I've got *work*."

"Are you really going to let two defenseless women out in Dublin all on their own?" Agnes gave him her best stern teacher look. "What would your mother say?"

While Rose reminded him, "You got a lot of work done on the plane while we watched *The Walking Dead*." She leaned closer and dropped her voice. "Plus, due to the time change, it'll be easier to get hold of people this evening after we've gone to bed."

The tiniest of smiles lifted the corner of his mouth, as if he knew the two of them were playing him.

"All right." He shook his finger at Agnes. "But you can't pull this trick the entire time we're here."

Agnes shook her head solemnly. "Of course not, Declan."

But with that telltale gleam in her eyes, Agnes intended to pull this trick as often as she could get away with it.

THOUGH IT HAD RAINED EARLIER—DECLAN READ ONLINE that it could rain nearly every day in spring—the afternoon sunshine had come out for their walk in a nearby park. May was obviously a perfect time of year, with everything in bloom. Water droplets glistened on the flower petals. Old and young strolled the paths, sometimes hand in hand, families with kids running ahead.

Agnes claimed she wasn't overtired, although she sat a few times on the seat of her walker. "I want to take in this marvelous view," she'd say.

Leaving the park, they wandered pretty streets of houses with brightly painted doors in all the colors of the rainbow, their flowerboxes overflowing. The sidewalks were filled with women and strollers, elderly ladies with dogs, old men leaning on canes. Everyone was out walking, as if the sun drew everyone outside.

They found a path along the river. Rose and Agnes chattered about everything they saw, Agnes telling Rose to take a picture of this or that. He couldn't count the number of photos Rose racked up on her phone. He'd offered to get her international service, but she'd said she had no one she needed to call back home.

They stopped for tea and a treat, and the afternoon was surprisingly relaxing. Declan couldn't remember the last time he'd relaxed. It wasn't a word in his vocabulary. He remembered vacations he'd taken with his wife, always rushing to make sure they didn't miss an important sight. Despite himself, he'd been exhausted. Squiring an elderly lady was entirely different.

And a holiday with Rose was tantalizing.

He'd give himself this one day.

Too much time with Rose, even with Agnes between them, wasn't advisable. He knew all about fraternizing with an employee. And it never worked out well.

Rose had been waiting for Agnes to crash, but she didn't. After a cup of tea and a pastry, she was reenergized.

But as dinnertime approached, Declan herded them toward the hotel. "Let's have dinner in the hotel restaurant."

Agnes wasn't having any of it. "I want to go to that bar."

"What bar?"

She waved a hand imperiously. "The one Rose and I looked up online. Very famous. Everyone goes there."

"The Temple Bar," Rose reminded her.

"I'm sure we can have dinner at that bar." Agnes was insistent.

Declan called a taxi, and the driver knew exactly where to go. Getting Agnes's walker in the trunk took some finesse, and by the time they'd retrieved it and stood on the sidewalk outside the iconic Temple Bar, Agnes was aghast at the crowd.

"I can leave my walker out here," she said, with both Declan and Rose answering her at the same time. "Oh no, you can't."

"Let me go inside and see if they have handicap seating," Declan suggested. "Maybe that'll get us in faster."

"I'm not handicapped," Agnes snapped.

Declan modified his words. "I'll see if they have seating for elderly ladies." Returning only moments later, his features were grim. "It's a long wait."

"How long?" Rose asked.

"An hour and a half."

"I might expire of starvation." Agnes made a horrible face, something akin to a gargoyle, setting Rose off in peals of laughter—which Declan almost joined.

Finally Rose managed, "I bet we can find another pub."

"It won't be as famous," Agnes grumbled.

"Even better, we can find a pub that only the locals go to. This place is all tourists."

That seemed to satisfy Agnes. "You've got a point."

There was no shortage of pubs in Dublin. They found one a couple of blocks away, with a long wood bar and scuffed hardwood floors. Thankfully there were booths and not just barstools that Agnes could never sit on. There were still tourists, but Rose made out quite a few Irish accents despite the noise and the music.

Their waitress, her curly hair a remarkable coppery red, had a lovely Irish lilt as she set down their menus. "What can I get for you?"

Agnes tapped the table with both hands. "I want that special stuff everybody drinks in Ireland."

The girl frowned. She couldn't have been much more than twenty-one. "Um," was as far as she got.

"Are you talking about Guinness?" Declan interpreted.

"I don't know," Agnes shrugged. "I just want what everyone drinks over here."

"You're not going to like Guinness." Declan tried to steer her away.

But Agnes was not to be steered. "I won't know until I try." She gave a militant jut of her chin.

Declan shrugged. Everyone gave into Agnes. "All right, three Guinness."

Rose held up her hand. "Not for me. I'll stick with water."

While the waitress scurried off to fill their drink orders, they poured over the menus.

"Fish and chips," Agnes said without reading.

Declan set down his menu. "You can get that at home. Maybe you should try something else."

Agnes snorted loudly, though the pub was so noisy no one could have heard. "That's what everyone in Ireland eats at a pub. I want to see if they're better than what we have."

"Well, here's an Irish specialty." Declan shoved his menu at Agnes. "Bangers and mash."

"Bangers and mash?" Agnes shivered and made another gargoyle face. "That sounds gross."

Both Declan and Rose curbed a laugh. "How about bubble and squeak?" Rose suggested.

Agnes grimaced, asking, "Is that made of squeaking mice?"

"It's cabbage and potatoes fried together." Rose pointed at the menu description.

Agnes shook her head until her curls bounced. "Fish and chips."

"I'll have to get the bangers and mash since you won't," Declan declared.

Their waitress arrived with two mugs of foamy Guinness plus Rose's water, then walked away with orders for bangers and mash, fish and chips, and Irish stew for Rose. It was far too much food, Rose was sure.

When the girl was gone, Agnes rubbed her hands together. "I'm excited, excited, excited. We're here, we're here, we're here. I can't believe it, this is miraculous." She turned quickly to Rose. "Do you think the quiet man came here, maybe ate that... what was it you called it, Declan?"

"Bangers and mash."

"I wonder if John Wayne ate bangers and mash or bubble and squeak." She was on the edge of her seat squirming like a child, her feet barely touching the floor.

"It's all very exciting to imagine." Rose wanted to join in Agnes's enthusiasm.

"I'm so glad you ladies are thrilled." Declan picked up his mug of dark Guinness. "Cheers." He downed a gulp.

The mug was too big for Agnes, but at least it had a handle. "Bottoms up."

When she lifted it, Rose put her hand under in case Agnes dropped the mug. The little lady put it down after an amazingly long drink, her lip foamy.

"How is it?" Declan drawled, probably sure Agnes would spit it out.

But she smiled wide and said, "That's the most terribly bitter stuff I've ever tasted."

They all laughed, and Agnes didn't touch another drop, drinking water instead.

Their meals arrived piping hot. Rose's Irish stew was delicious, made with lamb rather than beef.

"That's sausages and mashed potatoes." Agnes pointed at Declan's bangers and mash.

He spread his hands. "See, you could have eaten that, something more Irish."

She pointed at her fish and chips. "They're so much better than anything I've ever tasted back home." She beamed as she ate chips drenched in malt vinegar.

Bickering and bantering back and forth, they were like a family. Agnes and Declan had somehow become her family. Even if it lasted only during this trip, Rose felt needed and wanted... and happy.

10

A gnes lost her energy five minutes after dinner. The long day getting ready, the flight, the excitement, and the afternoon walk all caught up to her.

Declan called a taxi. Agnes was so tired, Rose thought she might not be able to wheel her walker to the room. But they made it.

And finally, the little lady was in bed, the covers pulled to her chin like a child. She was asleep the moment her head hit the pillow. Rose wasn't even close to tired yet after sleeping on the plane.

With the baby monitor in hand, she grabbed her e-reader and tiptoed from the room to a chorus of Agnes's gentle snores.

She was surprised to find Declan seated on the sofa rather than having retired to his room. His laptop was open on the coffee table, and he'd poured a short glass full of ice cubes and amber liquid.

"Sit." He flourished a hand at the chair opposite him. "I didn't want to open your champagne until you came out."

She hadn't expected him to wait for her or to order champagne. She'd expected he'd closet himself in his room to make his calls. When she and Agnes had peeked inside, there was a big desk that would be far more comfortable than the coffee table.

"Did you get that out of minibar?"

He grinned. Was he grinning more than usual? "I raided the minibar."

"Aren't they humongously expensive?"

"It's my treat." He twisted the top off and poured expertly, tilting the flute for minimum foam. "No arguments. We'll stop at a store on the way to Cong and buy champagne for the rest of the trip."

A thrill coursed through her, a sudden feeling of cama-raderie accompanied by a sweet tingle that *he* was the man pouring her champagne. And a frisson of fear about what he thought of her. "Thank you, but you make it sound like I drink all the time."

He handed her the glass, picked up his own drink, and clinked with hers. "I've never seen you do anything to access. But Agnes enjoys a tipple, and you love your champagne. A glass in the evening won't hurt anyone."

"Thank you." Then she added, "I'm surprised you're not tapping away on your computer or making phone calls."

He stretched out his arm, his sleeve riding up so he could see his watch. "There's plenty of time. I wanted to talk to you first."

Oh God. *Talk*. She felt like a new med tech pulled into the head nurse's office and couldn't help saying, "Is something wrong?" Her voice trembled slightly, and she wished she had more control over herself.

But Declan said, "Nothing's wrong. I want to thank you."

"For what?" She sipped her champagne before she could start babbling nonsense.

"For all the changes you've brought about in Agnes." He

settled back on the sofa, propping his foot on his knee and holding it there with a hand on his ankle. He'd removed his shoes and wore only socks. And the room suddenly seemed intimate.

"Thank you, but I just do my job."

He shook his head. "You've done far more than your job. She's happy, she's active, she's engaged with the world again. I didn't notice her decline in such a real way until I see the changes in her now." He waved a hand in the air. "Yes, I hired you because she was forgetting things, and she definitely needed help. But watching the two of you together, I realized how isolated she'd become before you arrived. She stopped going out, stopped working in the garden. I have a terrible feeling that she just sat in front of the TV all day. I don't think she even read. But now she's bright, lively, and laughing often."

"She's a delightful woman to be with."

"But what you do for her is above and beyond." He was so earnest, his green eyes deep, penetrating.

She was warmed by his praise. "I appreciate you telling me. But you don't have to thank me. I love Agnes." She hadn't thought of it in words, but she did love Agnes. She was more than just a replacement for her mother. Agnes was special.

He pointed a finger at her. "I'd hoped to find someone who would care for Agnes like this, but I didn't truly believe it was possible."

His eyes seemed misty with emotion, but it couldn't be. He was an understated man, his emotions buried deep.

"You make things flourish and grow, Rose." Then he quickly added, "I never thanked you for the garden. Both the front and the back are stunning. You have a green thumb. You even uncovered the cupid fountain. I'd forgotten it was out there."

"I love gardening." This was something she didn't have to

feel self-conscious about. "When my mother was ill and things got overwhelming, the garden was my salvation. I studied what plants were best for our soil and climate, how to fertilize everything, the best time to prune." She smiled. "You might even say it became an obsession."

"I'm sure the garden at your house must be beautiful."

She laughed softly. "It is, if I do say so myself. And here's a secret. I asked the property managers to let me be the gardener."

He huffed out a breath that sounded like a laugh. "You're amazing."

The word sent a thrill up and down her spine. "I can't let the garden go to rack and ruin if the tenants don't take care of it. And I'm too thrifty to hire a gardener."

"I assume the company agreed."

She nodded. "Agnes and I go there a couple of times a week to keep it in shape. There's not a lot to it as long as I keep the weeds under control. The renters work during the day and they don't even know I've been there."

"That's what I appreciate about you." Declan swirled the ice cubes in his glass. "It's the way you involve her in everything. You want to work in the garden, and you take her with you. You need to shop, and she goes along."

"I don't leave her alone. Except for a ten-minute walk around the block while she's napping. She never even wakes up. With Agnes I don't need to use the cat bells I told you about. Not even at night."

He shook his head. "You don't need to explain about taking a short walk. I apologize again for that day I yelled at you. But please don't say it's just your job to take care of her the way you do. What you do is special." He put a hand to his chest. "I care about Agnes very much, and it does my heart good to see what you do for her."

Tears pricked her eyes. "You're going to make me cry. Stop it."

They both laughed, an intimate laugh, as if they were sharing something secret and special. She pushed for a bit more. "I'm dying to hear the whole story about you and Agnes when she was your teacher."

He had such an attractive smile when he actually used it. With his silver-frosted blond hair and those captivating green eyes, the smile was like whipped cream on a sundae. Was it really just his wife who had turned him into a sober, somber man? Or perhaps it was the weight of responsibility from a young age. Agnes had said his parents struggled, and Declan had done his best to take care of them as soon as he could.

"You know she was my fourth-grade teacher. I thought she was ancient and horrible. But of course, Agnes would only have been about forty. And the truth is that I was a little terror."

"No," she scoffed. She couldn't imagine him as a terror. He was so disciplined.

He nodded gravely. "A holy terror, if you listened to the school principal."

"What did you do?"

He was relaxed, slumping into the sofa, his features softer. She wondered if this was the Declan he really wanted to be. "I set fire to a trashcan in the cafeteria and almost burned down the school."

She didn't mean to, but she burst out with a laugh. "No way."

He nodded. "I was afraid they'd try to send me to one of those military camps or schools for delinquents. They did suspend me, but Agnes went to bat for me. She visited my parents and said I was a very smart child." He snorted a laugh, but Rose knew the assessment was accurate. "She declared she'd take me in hand, especially after school hours, and make sure I didn't get into any more trouble. I believe I told you my dad was a plumber and my folks had a plumbing supply store that my mom mostly ran. And I was alone a lot after my grandmother died. They both worked long hours and things were tight. Plumbers weren't paid exorbitant prices like they are now."

That was certainly true. Now, just getting a plumber to the house cost a couple of hundred dollars, and that was before they even did anything. "But why did you try to burn down the school?"

He put a hand to his forehead, shook his head, his lips curved in a thoughtful smile. "It was a hot day and me and the guys just wanted to go out to the park and swim in the pond. And they dared me to set off the smoke alarm so we'd all get out of school the rest of the day. I was supposed to stomp out the fire as soon as the alarm went off. But I was stupid and there was a window right next to the trashcan and the curtain caught on fire. Back then they weren't so conscious about fire safety. The curtains started to go up before the fire alarm even went off." He laughed again. "Some fire alarm, right?" Shaking his head, he went on with his story. "I tried slapping out the fire and when that didn't work, I got scared and ran. But everyone knew I'd done it, and they all talked."

"Tattletales."

"Yeah, right? And they were the ones who got the day off and went to the pond to swim." He gave her such an honest-to-goodness little boy look. It was cheeky and mischievous and endearing.

Her heart turned over in her chest. "I'm utterly shocked," she said, managing not to smile.

He made a wry face. "The principal wasn't. She claimed I'd always had it in me. That I was a hoodlum."

"But you listened to Agnes?"

He smiled, his face soft with memory. "She was some sort of kid whisperer. I wasn't the only one she saved over the years. She kept me busy, tutored me when I needed it. And I realized I wasn't as dumb as I thought."

"I see now why Agnes has a special place in your heart."

"Yeah. And she and my mom became good friends."

"So when she lost her husband, you brought her here to live with you."

"I would have moved her to Palm Springs to be near my folks, but she didn't want to leave the area. I bought the house with the idea that she could move in on the ground floor and I'd be around to look after her."

"That's astonishing."

The man had so much more depth than she'd imagined. He truly cared, even if in the beginning she believed he was all business without a single caring bone in his body. And he was modest, too, saying only that Agnes was a tenant, never taking credit for the wonderful things he'd done. To buy a house and renovate it just so he could provide a home for Agnes? It was unbelievable.

She liked him even more than she had.

And far more than she should.

DECLAN LEFT ROSE ALONE TO READ HER BOOK AND WENT to his room to make his phone calls. He'd made it through more than one of them when jet lag finally caught up with him, and now he lay on the edge of sleep, his mind wandering. And it wandered to Rose, going to places he shouldn't go. Like wondering how soft and smooth her skin was, how her kiss would taste, how silky her short brunette curls would feel against his fingers.

Something about Rose inspired confidences. Declan

wasn't a touchy-feely man who displayed all his emotions. But she inspired him to reveal things he normally wouldn't.

The atmosphere in the suite had become too intimate, her champagne, his whiskey, her soft voice and gentle questions, encouraging him to reveal his past.

They were here for Agnes. Only Agnes. He'd promised himself he would make her last years comfortable, enjoyable, and carefree. He wasn't here to have sex with her caregiver.

Yet that was exactly where his mind was heading.

It would become a nightmare in the future if he and Rose actually had sex. Because inevitably the relationship would end. Employer-employee relations always ended badly. Then he'd have to search out another caregiver for Agnes. But no one would measure up to Rose.

The only option was to avoid intimate, late-night conversations.

⚜

THEY'D HAD SUCH A LOVELY TALK LAST NIGHT. DECLAN had told her that funny story—well, not exactly funny, just interesting and revealing—about his youthful folly and how he'd met Agnes.

It showed so much about him. Rose could see him as a vulnerable boy who wasn't sure of himself, a kid who wanted to fit in and did what his friends told him to. She wondered if that's why he was now such a responsible man. He'd turned himself around because Agnes had been good to him.

They'd crossed a line, not a bad one but a good one, where they understood each other better, could even be called friends.

Yet this morning, he flatly refused to go sightseeing with them, had even been curt about it. Agnes had pouted and cajoled, but it hadn't worked. She'd ordered and demanded. That didn't work either.

"I don't know what's wrong with that boy," she said as she wheeled her walker around the walkways, flowerbeds, and green lawns of Saint Patrick's Cathedral. It had rained in the night, but the morning was dry and even sunny, and Rose snapped pictures of the amazing gothic edifice and towering spire.

"I have no idea." She was as dumbfounded as Agnes.

"He's so on again, off again," Agnes complained. "Let's sit here. It's a lovely shady spot." Agnes could walk quite a long time, provided she took these little rests. Turning, she sat on the seat of her walker, while Rose took the bench.

Inside, the cathedral had been all vaulted ceilings, elaborate archways, intricately tiled floors, carved seats for the choir, and stained-glass windows. The brass eagle lectern made her heart beat faster as she imagined listening to a resounding sermon.

But Agnes had complained the chapel was too noisy with tourists, saying she preferred to be outside, observing the cathedral as if she were painting it in her mind. There were times when Agnes could be so eloquent.

"What did you to talk about after I went to bed?"

A kernel of heat blossomed in Rose's chest, as if she had something to feel guilty about. "What makes you think we talked? You went out like a light."

Agnes lowered her oversized sunglasses down her nose and looked at Rose over the rims like a motorcycle cop who wasn't buying her excuse for speeding.

Rose told her, minus how intimate it felt sitting with Declan as they drank champagne and whisky. "We talked about how the two of you met."

Agnes clapped her hands. "Oh, he likes you if he's telling you stories."

"Well, I hope he likes me. If he doesn't, I could lose my job."

"Oh piffle." Agnes waved the thought away. "He'll keep you as long as I like you." She patted Rose's hand. "And I do like you, my dear."

"I like you, too." Rose smiled. "In fact, I very much enjoy being with you."

Agnes blushed like a schoolgirl who'd been complimented by the handsomest boy in her class. "I know I can never replace your mother, but I like to think of you as a daughter."

Rose held Agnes's hand. "You ease some of the ache in my heart so I don't miss my mother quite so much."

Agnes brushed her eyes. "Oh my dear, you make me cry."

She squeezed Agnes's fingers. "You'll make me cry, too."

"Let me tell you my fondest wish. You would be perfect for Declan."

Rose laughed outright. Even as her heart leapt. "Don't hold your breath, Agnes, or you might turn blue and I'll have to call the paramedics."

Agnes tucked her chin and glowered. "Why not?"

Still smiling, Rose shook her head. "I'm your caregiver. I'm an employee."

"But in all those gothic romances, the governess always falls in love with the duke while she's looking after his children."

She laughed, her hand covering her mouth. "I'm not a governess in a Gothic romance novel." Even if she'd loved all those stories as a teenager. "I'm a middle-aged divorcee. And I don't have the time or the desire for romance."

"You should, my dear," Agnes teased.

She caught a glimmer of something in Agnes's eyes. "Do not tell me you planned this trip so you could matchmake for us."

"Of course I didn't." Agnes pressed her lips together

primly, as if Rose had lost her mind. "This trip is my bucket list."

Rose thought of that night they'd talked about their bucket lists. The only item on her list had popped into her head like magic. She wanted to fall in love.

But Declan was a totally inappropriate candidate. Even worse, he was dangerous. He could fire her. She'd have to leave Agnes. They'd only been together a couple of months, but losing Agnes would be like losing her mother again. She couldn't take the double blow. No romance was worth that.

She had to nip Agnes's matchmaking plans in the bud. "I just don't have feelings like that for Declan."

"But you think he's handsome."

A squirrel ran up to Agnes's chair, as if he were asking for an acorn or a bit of bread. Agnes chattered back at the little creature, and Rose was grateful for the diversion.

Because she found Declan terribly attractive. If he'd tried to kiss her last night, she'd have let him. But she was middle-aged, and he obviously liked younger women since he'd married one. He was rich, and he needed a beautiful model or a socialite to grace his arm.

He could never want her.

Changing the subject, Rose consulted her list of sights for today. "On to Ha'penny Bridge. It's a mile. Shall we get a taxi?"

Agnes scowled. "I can walk a mile. With a couple of rest stops." Her eyes twinkled. "But I'd rather have tea and crumpets."

"I'm not sure they have crumpets in Ireland. Aren't they British?"

But they found a teahouse that served them, and there wasn't another word about Declan or matchmaking. Agnes could always be distracted by goodies.

11

There was no intimate conversation over champagne that night after Agnes went to bed. Rather than go out to the sitting room, Rose lay in the dark with her e-reader, pushing through a few chapters and putting herself to sleep.

In the morning, after breakfast, they headed to the town of Cong where much of *The Quiet Man* was filmed. The car was big and comfortable, and Agnes sat in front next to Declan so she could see the scenery. Without stopping, it would have been three hours on the motorway. But they stopped, a lot, and had lunch at a quaint pub along the way. It rained off and on, but by the time they made it to their accommodation, the old castle hotel, the sun was shining.

Declan had planned to drive through the village itself, but Agnes said she wanted to wait and savor the surprise when they could spend more time.

"Oh my," Agnes said as they turned into the long drive bordered by a manicured hedgerow that opened onto a magnificent view of Burkefurd Castle.

It was definitely an "oh my" moment. The castle walls

were rimmed by hydrangeas gloriously in bloom, pink, blue, and white. Pink versus blue needed a different soil composition to get the desired color, so someone had taken painstaking care of the bushes. The green lawns were bisected by paths and flowerbeds. The castle itself was of weathered grey stone and huge latticed windows that looked much newer than the stone. The turrets on all four corners had slit-size windows that, in ancient times, would have been used by archers to defend the castle. They were joined by battlements all along the top where soldiers would have patrolled, watching for an enemy bent on scaling the castle walls.

Agnes clapped her hands. "I'm flabbergasted." She pinched Declan's arm. "Is this real?"

"It's real, Agnes," he answered with less enthusiasm. But then no one could match Agnes's gusto.

Declan circled the central fountain and pulled up to the stone front steps polished to a shine. A bellboy immediately appeared and Declan retrieved Agnes's walker from the trunk while Rose helped her out of the car.

"Oh my, isn't this magnificent? Like something right out of *Downton Abbey*."

"Or maybe *Anne of the Thousand Days*." Rose suggested the old movie about Henry VIII and Anne Boleyn. Although this castle looked older, perhaps even from early medieval times.

"There you go," Declan said as Agnes gratefully grabbed the walker handles.

"Our ramp is right over there," the bellboy said, a rugged young man with a handsome face. "Can I help you up there?" he asked politely.

Rose shook her head. "Thanks, we can manage."

They left Declan and the bellboy with the luggage. Obviously a much newer addition, the ramp was nevertheless made of the same polished stone as the steps.

Since the day was so nice, the tall double front doors stood open, and a portly gentleman with a ruddy complexion greeted them in the foyer. "Welcome to Burkefurd Castle." His accent was British rather than Irish.

Agnes said regally, "Thank you, good sir, my son will be checking us in. My daughter-in-law and I would like to look around your sumptuous lobby."

"Of course, madam, please make yourself comfortable," he said in a cultured tone that matched Agnes's imperiousness.

Rose barely stifled a laugh, but she didn't bother to hide the smile. "Son and daughter-in-law," she said softly as they strolled away. "That was supposed to be a joke."

Agnes harrumphed. "What am I supposed to call you? You don't expect me to admit I need someone to look after me." She stopped, gazing all around, up to the mezzanine and the glittering chandelier above them. "Declan sure didn't book us into a dump." She used her usual loud whisper, and Rose glanced over her shoulder to find the concierge smiling indulgently.

Indeed, this was no dump. The carpet was plush beneath her shoes, an intricate pattern of blues and pinks and yellows against a red background. Pastel chairs and delicate tables were scattered about for weary travelers. The walls were of walnut paneling as was the railing around the mezzanine level. Delicate figurines decorated tables and filled up tall, elegant, lighted cabinets. A suit of armor guarded a hallway that led deeper into the castle, and ornate lion andirons flanked a crackling fireplace. Paintings hung on the walls, men and women in old-fashioned dress, perhaps portraits of people who'd once lived here.

As Declan entered, the portly gentleman welcomed him. "Our valet will park your car, sir, and your luggage will be taken up to your room as soon as you've checked in."

"Thank you."

There must have been a separate entrance because the bellboy never appeared with their luggage cart.

The man tapped a tablet in his hands. "Your name, sir?"

With no formal registration desk, the man simply typed in Declan's details, took his passport and credit card, then slipped through an unobtrusive door Rose hadn't noticed.

Agnes had been uncharacteristically quiet. The little lady was agog at the opulent surroundings.

She met Rose's gaze. "It's all I could have dreamed of. Marvin and I stayed in a bed and breakfast in London, which was very nice but nothing like this." Her eyes were misty, either with memory or gratitude.

She waved Declan over and took his hand. "Come down here," she beckoned, and he bent to her. Agnes kissed his cheek, whispered, this time in a soft, endearing voice, "Thank you, my boy."

Declan kissed the back of her hand just as the concierge returned with the passport and credit card.

"We're so pleased to have you," the man said. "Your room is on the third floor overlooking our rose garden. Here are your keys." He handed over a cardboard carrier, and Rose was disappointed they had key cards instead of old-fashioned locks.

"Your luggage should be in your room when you arrive," he went on. "The elevators are right down this hallway." He pointed past the suit of armor. "Breakfast is complementary in our dining room which is right through there." He indicated the double glass doors at the end of the lobby. "We're open from six-thirty to nine-thirty. We also serve luncheon and dinner."

He turned up the wattage of his smile. "And please don't hesitate to call for anything you need."

They'd installed modern conveniences like elevators. "I'm so excited," Agnes repeated for perhaps the fourth time as she wheeled her walker around in the elevator car and faced forward, ready to rush out the moment the door opened. "It's beyond my imagination. When can we see all the sights in the village? The museum is supposedly a replica of White O' Morn Cottage." Rose had shown her pictures of the town and all *The Quiet Man* points of interest over and over.

Declan glanced at his watch. "Tomorrow. Let's get settled today and take a stroll around the gardens." He paused and Rose knew he was mentally adding time for Agnes's nap. "Then we'll have dinner here."

"Marvelous." Agnes's eyes glittered like precious jewels.

The elevator lurched slightly to a stop and Agnes practically burst out the door like a racehorse dashing from the gate.

Declan, moving more slowly, looked at the packet of key cards for the room number and headed them in the right direction. The hallway was painted in pastel blue, the carpet thick and luxurious, decorated in small, dark blue flowers against a lighter blue background. Alcoves held glass cabinets filled with vases and ornaments, or a bust on a pedestal, while landscape paintings hung on the walls.

As Declan opened the door and ushered them in, Agnes moaned with pleasure.

The hardwood floors were painted white and covered with the same blue rug as the hallway. The walls were the palest blue and the furniture delicate while still appearing comfortable. The dining area occupied one corner while the other corner held a bar with coffee maker and small refrigerator. Sofas and matching chairs with a coffee table were front and center, behind which French doors opened onto a balcony overlooking the rose garden, a maze of tall, clipped hedges, a glass conservatory, the sprawling lawns of the castle, and beyond all that, woodlands that stretched for miles.

Agnes's hands flew to her mouth. "This is so unbelievable." She looked once again at Declan, tears brimming in her eyes as she held her hands out to him. "You've always been so good to me. You sent Marvin and I on that trip to London."

Rose should have known Declan would do something like that.

"Then buying the Rose Garden house because you knew I loved it." She sniffed loudly. "And now this."

Declan looked at Rose, his cheeks red as if he were embarrassed.

"Thank you, my dear, dear boy. I know my meager savings didn't pay for all this, no matter what you said."

Declan cupped her papery cheek. "I only helped a little, and I know you would have been fine with something smaller, but I wanted to stay in the best. Since that was all about me, I'm paying for it."

But he'd done it all for Agnes.

AGNES SETTLED DOWN FOR A HALF-HOUR NAP. THE FULL-size, canopied beds were low to the floor, the room was decorated in the same pale blue tones, and the bathroom was handicap-equipped, with two pretty pedestal sinks, one lower than the other and dabbed in light blue flowers that matched the floor tile.

The only thing missing was a jetted tub like the one in Declan's room, which Rose had drooled over when she and Agnes toured through his half of the suite.

The bellboy had delivered their luggage, and Rose quietly unpacked while Agnes napped.

"Dear," Agnes whispered loudly.

"Sleep," Rose whispered back.

"But I have to ask you something," Agnes pleaded.

"You can ask me when you get up." She put Agnes's nighties and lingerie in a drawer.

"But what if I forget?"

"If it's really important, you won't forget."

Agnes had the uncanny ability to remember what she wanted and forget what she chose to. There was no doubt that living alone was difficult. Left to do her own cooking, she would eventually burn the house down, having forgotten whatever was on the stove. But it wasn't Alzheimer's. It was old age.

"It's very important. And I won't get to sleep unless I ask."

Rose gave a weary sigh, hiding her smile behind it. "All right, ask. But then you need to sleep."

Agnes looked at her with unblinking eyes. "Will you stay with me until the very end?"

The question stabbed her heart and brought the ache of tears behind her eyes. She sat next to Agnes, taking her hand. "I'm going to be right here with you for as long as you need me."

Agnes smiled, and finally closed her eyes. In a few moments her breathing evened out and her lips parted to emit a ladylike snore.

Rose didn't let go of her hand for a very long time.

"I haven't been swimming in years and years," Agnes said.

While Agnes was napping, Declan had taken a brief tour of the castle to stretch his legs. And he'd found the pool.

"We're doing it now." With a lot of pulling and tugging, Rose finally got Agnes into her bathing suit.

Rose hadn't been in a swimsuit for years and years either. But what was a vacation if you didn't pack a swimsuit?

"This is going to be good for us." Even if she was self-conscious. "I can swim and do exercises in the pool."

"I will, too." Agnes patted her hair. "Just don't splash and get my hair wet."

"No worries."

"And I don't like the water in my face."

"I won't push you under," Rose assured her.

Finding two fluffy robes in the bathroom, they wrapped themselves up for the walk down to the indoor pool which could be used all year round, even on cold or rainy Irish days.

They hadn't made it out for a stroll yet. Life moved slowly with Agnes, and Rose liked it that way. Though her feet clamored for a long walk in the castle's beautiful gardens.

That was her biggest problem. Sometimes she craved a strenuous hike, but with the frequency that Agnes needed help, she could never be gone for long. Her exercise consisted of isometrics, her work in the garden, and fast but brief walks around the neighborhood. Not that she was complaining. Agnes was so much better than some of the patients she'd cared for. She hadn't grown crotchety with age but was sweet and happy and cooperative.

They stepped into the suite's common area to find Declan in his swim trunks.

"You're coming with us." Agnes clapped her hands in childish delight.

Rose said, "You're coming with us," her voice low and a little panicked.

She'd thought he'd use the time to work.

She wasn't exactly ashamed of her body. But she wasn't twenty-five-years old either.

And this was Declan, who looked far too sexy in swim gear and a towel slung around his shoulders.

"Agnes convinced me. I haven't been swimming in years and I'd like to do a few laps."

The afternoon was sunny and a few degrees above normal. They'd had fabulous weather so far, especially since she'd read that May could be rainy and overcast. Big sliding glass doors brought the garden and lawns inside the pool area, and they laid their towels on three adjoining loungers. They hadn't come at the height of that tourist season, and there was only one swimmer in the pool, while two brave sunbathers had dragged chairs to the outside deck.

As she laid her robe on a lounger, she was aware of every bulge in the one-piece swimsuit. Her stomach wasn't as flat as it used to be, and her legs felt lumpy. At least her arms were buffed from all her work.

Declan dumped his robe on the chair next to Agnes. *Yum.* The sound almost slipped from Rose's lips, but she contained herself.

Declan Delaney in board shorts was absolutely mouthwatering. She didn't stare, but oh she wanted to. Badly.

Luckily she had Agnes to concentrate on. Rose was right behind her as she wheeled her walker to the pool steps. "How am I supposed to get in there?" Agnes asked dubiously.

"Carefully," Rose said. "Wheel your walker next to the pole, and hold on as we walk in. You can take my hand, too."

The water was warm as she stepped down, one stair below Agnes.

Declan hovered in case they needed help. But once Agnes had one hand securely on the railing and the other gripping Rose's, she gained confidence, each step easier than the last. Until they were in the shallow end.

"You don't expect me to swim, do you?"

"Can you swim?" Rose asked.

"Yes." Agnes fluffed her hair. "But I don't have a bathing cap."

"We'll just walk back and forth and do some jumping and arm exercises. Doesn't that sound exciting?"

"Extremely exciting," Declan drawled.

Rose flicked water at him as he climbed into the pool. "You go swim. And don't make fun of our water exercises."

"Never." His voice was solemn but his lips curved. Then he dove under like a dolphin.

The elderly gentleman doing laps climbed out, and Declan took his position in the lane.

"Let's venture a little deeper." She led them to armpit depth, at least on Agnes. "First, we'll do arm exercises. Thrilling, right?"

"Terribly thrilling," Agnes said with enthusiasm as minimal as Declan's.

"You're such a silly sausage." But Rose persisted. "Just cup your hands and use the water as resistance."

They waved their arms back and forth through the water, then up and down. It was like using weights and felt surprisingly good. "Now let's run in place." She was the drill instructor.

"I can really do this." Agnes was now exceedingly pleased with herself.

Rose was, too. Here was a way they could get daily exercise. She'd talk to Declan about a membership at the community pool when they got home.

She glanced at him, a fine figure as he cut through the water, muscled and gorgeous, his blond hair slicked back.

"Stop drooling," Agnes said, catching Rose in her study of Declan's body.

"What are you talking about? I'm working very hard here."

Agnes just raised an eyebrow.

Declan swam laps until his arms ached. It was different than gym exercise but still a good work-out. He climbed out, toweled off, then sat on the lounge chair to watch Agnes and Rose. They splashed and laughed as they did their exercises. This was probably the best exercise Agnes could do besides walking. She was weightless in the water, and her body moved better.

He'd talk to Rose about a gym membership, a place with a pool. Agnes would love it. Rose would enjoy it, too. That look on her face was pure joy.

Agnes leaned close, whispering to Rose, something he couldn't hear over the noise collecting in the high ceiling. After a nod, they jogged to the pool steps. He was about to rise, but Rose easily helped Agnes out of the water. She grabbed their robes and threw one over Agnes's shoulders, shrugging into her own. Then they headed to the restrooms at the far end of the pool, Agnes holding steadily to her walker.

Agnes needed the facilities quite regularly. They'd made a number of stops along the way. It struck him in a way he'd never considered before that Rose was tied to Agnes. She could go out to the garden with the baby monitor at her side and for ten-minute walks around the block, but she always had to be close enough to rush to Agnes's side. She never had time completely to herself. He'd hired Rose to be there for Agnes, he'd just never considered exactly what that meant for one person to handle. She'd negotiated for days off, but she'd never used them.

He needed to find someone to spell Rose.

He knew what she'd say, that she didn't need it, especially since they relaxed in the evening with a movie. But even Superwoman needed time off.

He watched as they returned from the restroom.

She was so good with Agnes, so caring, always smiling, always keeping Agnes upbeat.

And she was beautiful, gray strands only slightly coloring her rich brunette curls. He found himself looking at the slim lines of her body. She was in shape, really good shape. Her job was a workout, not to mention all the hours she gardened. The one-piece suit fit snugly, and while she wasn't looking, he ogled her breasts. Not that he'd ever make a pass. She was his employee.

But Rose had a body that should be enjoyed. And he wanted to enjoy the sight. Looking couldn't hurt anything.

As they approached, he heard Rose ask, "Would you like a little more swim time?"

"I'm ready to lie down on that comfortable lounge chair." Agnes waved Rose away. "But you go swim, dear."

Rose settled her in the chair next to him, and Agnes patted his arm. "Declan will take care of me."

At the edge of the pool, Rose stood for one moment in front of a lane. She was extraordinary, her muscles toned, her arms like a bodybuilder, her body a perfect package. He didn't even qualify it by adding the words "for a woman her age." She was simply perfect.

Then she executed a graceful dive and came up stroking, solid, surging through the water, her short bob sleek against her head.

"She's good, isn't she?" Agnes watched the direction of his gaze.

There was no reason not to agree. "She's quite a good swimmer."

"I meant she's good with me."

He turned to Agnes. "Yes," he agreed again. "That makes me very happy."

"And she's terribly cute, too."

He chuckled at her words and the excitement animating her face. Agnes was becoming her old self again. "Cute is for teenagers. She's not a teenager."

"I'm so glad you noticed." Agnes beamed at him.

He'd fallen straight into her trap. "It's hard not to notice she's a woman."

"I'm glad you've noticed that, too."

"Agnes." He had to cut off that line of thinking right away. "Do not try to set us up. It's not going to work." But he couldn't seem to take his eyes off Rose slicing through the water.

"Why not?" Agnes asked with unequivocal sincerity. "You're about the same age. She's pretty. You're handsome. You have me in common. What else do you need?"

He wanted to laugh. He *needed* to laugh. But this was no laughing matter. "She's our employee, Agnes. It's never good to mix business and pleasure." After the divorce, Agnes should know that as well as he did.

She put her hands together, gazing at Rose's swift, strong strokes. "But it's like those Gothic romances I read when I was a girl," she said wistfully. "With a beautiful governess and the handsome Duke falling in love against their very wills."

"Oh hell," he said softly.

"I loved all those authors. Anya Seton, Phyllis Whitney, Victoria Holt, Barbara Eden."

"Wasn't she in *I Dream of Jeannie?*"

She flapped a hand at him. "You're missing my point."

"No, Agnes, you're missing *my* point. It's out of the question."

She turned to him, her smile far too knowing and actually scary. "Then why do you keep looking at her like she's a chocolate truffle you want to bite into?"

With that, Agnes slipped her sunglasses over her eyes, despite the fact that they were indoors, and lay back on her lounge chair as if she'd fallen asleep.

A chocolate truffle? No, he looked at Rose like she was a sexy, seductive, sensual woman.

He looked at Rose like he wanted her.

That first night in Dublin, as they drank their evening cocktail while Agnes slept, the atmosphere had grown quiet and intimate. He could have kissed her. He'd *thought* about kissing her. And that hadn't been the first night he'd had those thoughts. Far from it.

But it had to stop.

He watched her in the water, the beauty of her movements, a barely there splash of water as she propelled herself with powerful strokes.

He wouldn't think about kissing. He'd forget how sexy she looked in that slim swimsuit that revealed everything.

He would stop. Right now.

"What about a gym membership, Agnes?"

"Hmmm." She puffed a loud breath. "A gym?"

"A swim center where the two of you can do water exercises every day."

She grunted. "I can't do that every day."

"Every other day then."

He looked at Rose in the water, but that had nothing to do with actual *looking*. It was assessing while he made a decision about the swim center.

"Did you enjoy today?"

After a long, thoughtful moment, she said, "Yes."

"Let's get a family membership. I wouldn't mind a swim once in a while."

He felt rather than saw Agnes turn her head to look at him." You want to go, too?"

"Yes," he said, still watching Rose. "I think you'll like it."

She made an odd little sound that might have been a laugh. "Yes, Declan, I'd like that very much."

DINNER WAS LATER THAN USUAL DUE TO THEIR SWIM, AND they lingered over a dessert of café lattes, decaf, of course, and bread pudding. But it was still light by the time they finished. The sun didn't set until nine o'clock, even in May.

They were in the lobby on the way to the elevators when Agnes stopped her walker. "Rose wants to take a bath in that fabulous tub in your room. So you—" She poked Declan in the chest. "—are going to take me for a stroll in that pretty garden outside."

Rose spluttered as if she'd sucked her coffee down her windpipe. "I never said any such thing, Agnes."

Agnes, the sneak, smiled. "Of course you didn't, dear, but I saw the look in your eye. You were drooling. And since there's only a shower back in my flat, you should take advantage." She turned that sneaky smile on Declan. "Declan doesn't mind, do you, my dear boy?"

He had no idea what game she was playing. Now, if Agnes

had suggested that he accompany Rose *into* the tub, he'd know exactly what she was up to. But this ploy? He had no idea. Unless it was to make sure he had images of Rose naked in the tub when he went to bed.

And he would have images of Rose drifting through his dreams after seeing her in nothing but that swimsuit. What was a few more?

"You're welcome to use it anytime. And I'd love to show Agnes the garden."

Rose was still finding excuses. "I'd like to see the garden, too."

Agnes waved her hand airily. "You'll see that in the daytime." She leaned in as if she were about to whisper a secret. "I'd take the opportunity when you can. Who knows what will happen tomorrow?"

Agnes was good with the prophetic statements. And he imagined Rose naked in his tub. He even dreamed of joining her. Not that he would.

He shrugged as if the dangerous thought meant nothing. "Go ahead."

Rose looked at Agnes, then at him, and back to Agnes. He recognized the desire in her eyes. Not for him, but for the bath in that big tub. He wanted to be the little devil whispering on her shoulder. *Do it. You know you want to.*

As if she heard the voice, she finally smiled. "All right. I do miss my baths."

He thought of the big soaker tub back at home that he never used. Rose could have used it all along.

And he could have been imagining her there right from the beginning.

He should have slapped himself. But then they'd guess the direction of his thoughts.

"Thank you." She bent to kiss Agnes before heading to the elevator.

"She has such a spring in her step." Agnes watched her go.

He was looking at things other than the spring in her step.

"Now how do we get out to the garden, dear boy?"

Minutes later, they were strolling the gravel path through the fragrant garden.

"How does it compare to the Rose Garden back home?" he asked.

Agnes tipped her chin up and breathed in deeply. "For some reason, the roses smell sweeter here."

"Maybe it's the type they grow."

"English roses," she said. "Some are very fragrant."

Speaking of the sweet scent made him think of Rose in that big tub. Before going through the outside doors to the garden, they'd wandered the gift shop, its shelves filled with bottles of rosewater. He'd had the ridiculous notion of lying in bed, drawing in the rosewater scent of her bath, remembering, imagining, his mind getting carried away.

Thank God he hadn't bought a bottle for her. By the morning, he'd have been mad.

"Do you mind if I sit down a moment?"

"Of course not. Let's watch the sunset." The sky was turning pink.

Agnes parked her walker by a bench, and he sat next to her. "Thank you, Declan." She was unusually solemn. "I know this trip sounded like an old woman's silly fancy. But I can't tell you how much it means to me."

He covered her gnarled fingers with his. "You can have anything you want, Agnes. All you have to do is ask and it's yours. You don't have to keep thanking me."

"But I do."

He put a finger to her lips. "You don't. I'm paying you back for everything you did for me." He raised an eyebrow. "I probably would have been a juvenile delinquent without you."

She patted his knee. "You *were* a juvenile delinquent. You tried to burn down the school."

He laughed. "Thank God you stopped me."

She gazed at him with watery eyes. "I love you, Declan Delaney."

"I love you, too, Agnes Hathaway."

They sat in companionable silence, breathing in the scent of roses as the light faded. Until Declan looked at Agnes and saw her drooping chin and closed eyes.

"Why don't we go back to the room?" he suggested softly, not wanting to startle her.

"I was just resting my eyes." She stood up with his assistance. "But I might be a little tired."

He wondered if Rose would be done with her bath.

A very big part of him hoped she wasn't.

13

After draining the tub, Rose dressed in leggings and a flowing blouse. A bath had always been one of her relaxations, second only to working in the garden. She'd indulged almost every night after she'd managed to get her mother into bed. She realized now how much she'd missed the luxury.

It would have been glorious to wrap herself in the thick, fluffy robe supplied by the hotel, but Declan and Agnes would soon be returning from their garden stroll.

Yet even though she expected them, her heart skipped a beat as they entered the suite. She imagined Declan's eyes taking in the leggings, the scent of her bath all over her. She couldn't have him. But she could dream.

"The garden is marvelous." Agnes's face was aglow with the cool evening air and the exertion. She sat on the seat of her walker, wheezing as if walking from the elevator had taken the wind out of her. "It's been such a wonderful day. But I'm a little tired and I wonder if you two would mind if I went to bed." It was only an hour before Agnes's normal bedtime at home.

Rose wasn't tired. She still hadn't felt the jet lag everyone talked about.

"Of course we don't mind," Declan replied almost before Agnes finished. "Rose and I can go over tomorrow's itinerary and make sure you see absolutely everything in the village."

"And tomorrow night," Rose had to add, "we can attend a special showing of *The Quiet Man* down in the castle's theater." She'd read the hotel brochure while she lounged in the bath.

While Declan groaned, Agnes clapped her hands. "Goody!"

Once again she was asleep the moment she shut her eyes. The little lady wanted to keep going and going, but the Energizer Bunny she wasn't.

Quietly closing the bedroom door behind her, Rose half hoped, half feared Declan would be seated on the sofa, a glass of whiskey in his hand, just as he had in Dublin.

Instead, she found the balcony doors open and Declan already seated out there. She retrieved her thick cardigan and a pair of slippers to warm her feet, then went out to plan their itinerary.

"Thank you." She took her seat, reaching for the champagne he'd poured. At one of their stops along the way, he'd insisted on buying some good champagne along with Irish cream for Agnes and Irish whiskey for himself. And he wouldn't accept any payment for the champagne. She'd felt slightly unnerved yet grateful for his kindness.

After the delicious bath, she felt sated, almost boneless. Slumping in the seat, her feet on the balustrade, she sipped the champagne. "So, tomorrow," she started. "We should—"

"We should talk about your hours first."

She felt a chill, and it wasn't just the cool Irish night. "What about them?" Was he going to take Agnes away from her?

"It occurred to me that you have absolutely no time off. You're tied at the hip to Agnes."

"I have Sundays off. And the half day."

He turned his head, the light of the moon gleaming in his eyes. "And have you even taken those days off at all?"

"I want to learn Agnes's routine, her likes and dislikes. Then I can properly train anyone who's going to take care of her while I'm out." She felt a tiny shudder, as if she were about to lose something she needed badly.

"But you're always on the job, Rose."

"I relax in the evenings with Agnes, then I have time to myself after she goes to bed. Plus when she takes a nap in the afternoon. And I love to work in the garden. She's not hard to take care of. Most the time we're taking walks or shopping or playing cards or other games. It's not like work at all."

"When you're out with Agnes, you're walking her pace. Though I'm not sure Agnes even has a pace," he concluded.

"I get most of the exercise I need out in the garden."

"But out in the garden, you have the baby monitor at your side."

"Sure, but she doesn't wake up so I usually have at least an hour to myself. I'm fine with the way things are."

He shook his head adamantly. "There's got to be something illegal about having you work twenty-four hours a day."

"It's not work when it's Agnes," she insisted.

He pulled back slightly, looking down his nose at her. "Are you really telling me that sometimes when you're walking with Agnes you don't want to just break into a run?"

"Of course. Sometimes. But I can't leave Agnes behind."

"That's my point. You need time to yourself without Agnes. More than just a short walk or gardening when she's napping."

"But it's not a problem."

"You're very argumentative."

"And you're very bossy."

"That's because I'm the boss," he said, tapping his chest.

She wanted to hear a smile in his voice, but she wasn't sure it was there. Which made her sick in the pit of her stomach. Was he angling to replace her? Maybe he thought she was making Agnes too dependent on her.

"I love Agnes," she said simply, pleading in her voice.

Declan put his hand over hers where she gripped the arm of her chair. "I know you love her." The stroke of his thumb across her skin left a trail of sparks. "That's why it's important for you to take a rest sometimes. To do things you can't do with Agnes."

When she opened her mouth to argue, he rode right over her. "It doesn't have to be a full day. Maybe just a couple of hours every other day."

"But I took care of my mother twenty-four hours a day. It can be done. And Agnes is so much easier."

He squeezed her hand, and she wondered if she was only arguing so he wouldn't let go.

"I want you to answer honestly, Rose." He waited a beat for her agreement. "Didn't you ever wish for a moment to yourself while you were caring for your mother?"

She wouldn't say it aloud, but she'd resented her husband for not spelling her for even an hour a day. He absolutely refused to be alone with her mother. She sent him out for the shopping though she was dying to go herself. After he left her, the house felt like a prison. She'd ordered everything they needed online and had it delivered, including the groceries. Her only relief had been when her mother was sleeping and she could work in the garden or take a bath.

She gave Declan an inch. "It would have been nice to have a break sometimes." She sighed. "I had hospice help the last six months. They have volunteers who'll spell you for a few hours while you go out and aides who'll come in to do a sponge bath and nurses who'll help with medications or whatever you need." She closed her eyes against the pain, almost as visceral as when it was happening. "But I felt guilty leaving Mom alone with a stranger. And I only did it when I absolutely had to." She didn't say there'd been times where she had to get away, just for a little while, just to breathe. Until the guilt took over, and she rushed back. "Sometimes when I left the room, she whimpered. It broke my heart."

He leaned closer, holding her hand in both of his as he brushed a kiss across her knuckles. "I'm so sorry," he said softly, as if he were whispering endearments.

She jammed her thumb and finger to the bridge of her nose, trying to keep the tears at bay. She'd never told anyone. Not her brother. Not Agnes. Yet despite trying to hold out until she was alone, the tears finally fell.

"I'm sorry, I'm sorry," she whispered, her voice soggy.

Somehow, she couldn't quite tell how, Declan had pulled her onto his lap, wrapped his arm around her, one hand rubbing her back. "It must be the worst thing in the world," he said so gently, "to watch someone you love deteriorate like that. To have no relief. To do it all yourself."

That only made her cry harder. As if there were years of tears trapped inside that suddenly had to get out.

He crooned to her in soft words, things like, "It must've been terrible, it must've been heartbreaking, it must've made you die a little inside every day."

She absorbed every word, every caress, let them fill her up as the tears cleansed her. She clung to him as if he were a life preserver thrown over the side of a boat. And with every word he whispered, he dragged her back up out of the water, up, up, up into the light. Until finally the tears were just hiccups and sniffles.

A tissue appeared miraculously in front of her, and she

blew her nose, aware of how undignified it looked but not caring. Another tissue appeared, and she wiped her eyes.

"I'm sorry. I didn't mean to do that." She was afraid to look at him. Afraid to see the discomfort in his gaze, maybe even horror at how she'd broken down.

But Declan put his fingers under her chin and tipped her head. "You have nothing to apologize for. I can't imagine taking care of your mother for five years. I couldn't do it. Look how I handled Agnes, I called someone in to help."

"You have a job. You couldn't take all that time."

"Your mother was your job." He ran his thumb lightly under her eye, catching one last teardrop. "Now Agnes is your job. And in all good conscience, I can't let you do that same thing to yourself."

"Agnes is so much easier," she said, the words coming out on a breath.

"But don't you see how much like your mother's situation it is? You're afraid to let anyone else help you."

"I'm not afraid." As soon as the words were out, she knew them for the lie they were.

He said it for her. "You're afraid that if somebody else takes care of her, she'll like that person better, and she won't want you back. That *I* won't want you back."

He laid bare all her fears. The one constant with her mother had been that she was needed. No matter how hard it was or how combative she became, her mother had needed her. She couldn't turn Rose out.

"Agnes needs you." His voice was gently cajoling. "She will always need you. A couple of hours every day isn't going to make her forget you."

"What if something goes wrong? What if she has a fall?"

"Your helper can call you. But you're looking at the worst things, not the best. Getting out will give you relief, stretch your mind and your muscles. It will be like breathing fresh air. That's what I want for you, just a little rest."

She hiccupped the last sob she hadn't known was there.

"We need you, Rose. Agnes and I aren't going to throw you away."

She felt as transparent as a child.

He pushed a lock of hair behind her ear. Then he wrapped his fingers around her nape, his thumb against her chin, forcing her to look at him. "I've been taking advantage of you. I knew you weren't taking those days and yet I never insisted. I'm so sorry. When we get back home, together we'll find someone to help. How does that sound?"

She let the words out on a sigh. "That sounds good."

It was exercise she was lacking. Long walks. She couldn't even remember what that felt like, a hike along a trail in the park, her legs pumping, her breath coming fast. Declan was right, she needed it. As much as she loved Agnes, she needed that time to herself.

She'd gotten so used to attending her mother that she hadn't even thought about needing time. And Agnes was so much easier than her mom, like the breath of fresh air she craved.

"Thank you," she said softly.

His thumb still on her chin, his fingers still on her neck, she was still sitting in his lap.

The cool night air sizzled between them. If she said anything, the moment would evaporate.

It happened without conscious thought. She simply stopped breathing. And then she couldn't help herself. The moon would have to fall out of the sky, the sun would have to stop shining, and even then she might not have been able to stop herself.

She put her hand on the back of his neck, his hair soft against her fingertips, and she pulled him down. He could have stopped her if he wanted to. But he didn't try. Their lips met, and there was no hesitancy, no tentativeness. Instead, the kiss blossomed. He tasted of the whiskey on his lips, the taste of sin, the taste of desire. He kissed her openmouthed, tongue, lips, body heat. She wrapped her arm around his neck and anchored him to her, letting him plunder, plundering him in return.

God, oh God, when had she ever been kissed like this?

It was slow and delicious, sexy and insane. And he liked it, too. She felt him against her hip, and yes, oh yes, he liked it. He sifted her hair through his fingers, then trailed down her shoulder blade, her back, her hip, cupping her bottom, pulling her tight against him. And he groaned, a gentle sound welling up, something that could almost be explained away as a noise in the night. Yet it caressed her soul. He wanted her. It had been so long since she was desired.

He slid beneath her cardigan and the flowing blouse, found her hot skin with roughened fingertips. She moaned into his mouth as he flattened his palm against her back, his fingertips playing her spine like an instrument.

This was Declan. It was crazy. He was her boss. He could take Agnes away from her.

Rose didn't care, not right now. She shifted against him, eliciting another deep groan. She didn't pull back, didn't say a word, wouldn't ruin the moment. He wanted her. It was amazing. Even as he consumed her, she wanted to tear off his shirt, put her hands on him. But she didn't in case he stopped. With her arms around his neck, she gave him full access, permission to do anything he wanted.

The kiss pulsed between them, strong and deep, then waning, backing off, yet never ending. His hand was on the move again, slipping, sliding, and finally, she felt him palm her breast. He traced her skin, back and forth, back and forth.

When he cupped her fully in his hand, his thumb flicked across the hard pearl of her nipple.

She kept her mouth on his, tongue playing with him, keeping him occupied, keeping his thoughts on the physical and nothing else. She might have been seducing him, taking advantage of his sympathy, but she didn't care about that either.

This was her bucket list. Sort of. She wanted to fall in love, but that could be parsed into individual needs. She wanted to be desired. She wanted to touch a man intimately. She wanted him to touch her. She wanted to feel him, taste him, make love to him.

He pinched her nipple lightly, and her body contracted deep inside. She was suddenly wet. And if he did it again, she'd actually come. That's how long it had been.

That was how close he brought her with his touch.

Then he pulled back, saying, "Rose," just when she'd been about to say the words clamoring in her head. *Don't stop, please, please don't stop.*

She thought she might die.

But he shifted her, echoing her thoughts, "Don't make me stop," with utter desperation. The desperation she felt. "I need to touch you. So damn much."

She moved at the press of his hands, sliding her knees down either side of the chair, fitting her body to his.

He groaned. "God, yes, just like that." He pulled her down, rising up to rock against her.

The sensation was exquisite.

He closed his eyes, letting his head fall back against the chair, his hands on her hips holding her down, caressing her with his hard heat.

"Undo your blouse."

She would have done anything, wanting it so badly she

almost tore the buttons. Then her breasts spilled into his hands.

"You did this on purpose," he whispered, burying his nose in her cleavage. "Wore just this flimsy blouse right out of the bath to drive me crazy."

She hadn't really thought about it because she'd pulled on the cardigan to join him on the balcony. But she cupped both his hands to her. "If it makes you feel better to think I'm the one doing all the enticing, go ahead."

"Christ," he whispered, squeezing her breasts, flicking his thumbs over her. "All you have to do is smile at me and I'm enticed."

Then he put his mouth on her, licked her, made her mindless.

They were outside on the balcony, in full view of anyone down in the garden. But the lights were off behind them, and she didn't think anyone would notice what they were doing.

And so what if they did?

As he claimed her breasts, made her moan and writhe on top of him, he tunneled down between her legs, stroking her through her leggings until she trembled.

It had been so long. Forever.

Would she even remember how?

Then he whispered, "Let me inside."

She was almost too far gone to even know what he was talking about. But she wanted whatever he wanted. "Yes," she answered on her very last breath.

He tugged down her leggings just far enough to slip his hand inside.

"Oh God, oh God." She barely recognized her own voice and throwing her head back, she closed her eyes, riding the pleasure of his touch. "You can't possibly know."

Her flesh burned. Her body ached. She moved to the rhythm of his fingers as he pleasured her.

"How long has it been?"

"I don't know." In that moment, she truly thought it had been forever. But she gave him the first number that came into her head. "Three years."

Since her husband left. And probably long before that.

"I want to make it the best it's ever been."

She opened her eyes to stare at the sky above her, the stars, the moon, the beautiful night. "It's already the best," she whispered.

Then he did things to her that made her forget how to talk. She was merely sensation, her nerves firing, her cells gyrating. She held onto his shoulders and leaned as far back she could, steeping herself in pleasure. Her body moved as if she were making love to him. And maybe that's what this was.

Heat washed through her body. Then it was as if every sensation existed only where he touched her, doing all those delicious things. Her whole being shot right down to that spot, and when the explosion hit, it was like the Apollo rocket blasting off in a plume of fiery smoke, the flames licking her. Until she was sky high, gasping, crying, writhing, gritting her teeth, tears leaking from her eyes.

Never ever. Not like this.

His arms were around her, holding her tight, his hard body rising against her, stroking her, stoking her fire all over again. She wanted to tear off her leggings and take him. Under the night sky. Above the garden. Beneath the moon. In the stars.

Then Agnes's walkie-talkie squawked. Agnes was talking to herself. "Let's go, let's go, let's go.

Oh God. Agnes was getting out of bed. And Rose had been so enmeshed in sensation she hadn't heard the first stirrings.

She flew off Declan's lap, almost falling into the balustrade, his hands steadying her at the last moment.

She couldn't look at him. She couldn't say anything. She could only rush through the suite to the room she shared with Agnes, buttoning up as she ran, straightening her leggings, her body flushed with sex, her face colored with embarrassment.

It took only a matter of moments to crush the glory of being in his arms.

❧ 14 ❧

Declan hadn't known he could come this close to losing it simply by touching a woman, by feeling her jettison in his arms.

But this was Rose. And she was special.

If Agnes was matchmaking, she'd picked the wrong moment to get out of bed.

He didn't regret kissing her, or touching her. But he knew the dangers, both for her and for him. He'd broken the rule he'd lived by since his divorce. He'd fraternized with an employee. Yet he was past giving a damn about his rules anymore. Not after he'd kissed her and held her in his arms.

And he wanted more. He suspected she wanted more.

It couldn't end well.

But that didn't stop him from palming himself, feeling the heat, the hardness. And knowing it wasn't over yet.

It was the same part of him that had said a very similar thing the last time he'd let a woman get under his skin.

Yet now that he'd tasted her, it wasn't enough. She hadn't been with a man in three years. Maybe she didn't have the itch after her husband left. Declan had to admit the older he got the fewer itches he had, and it had been a while. Maybe five or six months. That could be what was happening to them. They were starving.

He had friends he could call, women who liked their itch scratched. But his gut knew this wasn't just an itch for sex, but for Rose in particular.

She hadn't finished her champagne. He hadn't finished his whiskey. He took a sip now, the fiery liquid burning down his throat the way she had made him burn.

If Agnes hadn't interrupted them, he'd have taken Rose right here on the balcony. He hadn't cared about the night or the garden or who might hear them. He hadn't cared from the moment he put his hands on her.

But he didn't want a few stolen hours while Agnes slept, with the possibility of another squawk on the baby monitor interrupting them.

He wanted a whole night with Rose. If a whole night could actually satisfy him.

It was ill-advised, maybe even idiotic. It would end, and probably badly. He was an arrogant asshole for wanting more.

But he'd tasted her. And she was exquisite. He had to have her.

It was just a matter of when.

Despite the fact that it was only May, that the tourist season hadn't truly begun and the Irish weather was still cool, the small town of Cong teemed with tourists, the average age about seventy. Obviously Cong wasn't a young person's hotspot.

But Agnes was entranced.

They were exceptionally lucky with a sunny day, white clouds scudding across the sky. But they carried their umbrellas as they waited in the line outside the museum, having read and heard about the changeable weather.

Declan leaned close and whispered in Rose's ear. "How can they have a museum for a couple who never existed in a town that doesn't even have the same name they used in the movie?"

She elbowed him. "Don't spoil it for Agnes."

Declan zipped his lips.

He hadn't mentioned what they'd done last night on the balcony. He didn't even seem embarrassed. She'd anticipated that he'd go into avoidance mode, that he might even have begged off today's jaunt. But if anything, he was more attentive. When he leaned close and whispered things in her ear, he made her a little crazy. Or a *lot* crazy. And somehow the guilt she'd felt last night when Agnes's voice squawked over the baby monitor seemed to melt away.

But not the worry. She wanted to talk to him about what happened. She wanted to know if she'd still have a job when they got home. If she'd still have Agnes.

Yet despite Declan's attention, he'd managed not to be alone with her for even a moment. Not that they'd had a chance to be alone.

Maybe pretending it hadn't happened was better. There was nothing to be embarrassed about. Right?

"Why don't you two ladies wait on the picnic bench over there while I get our tour tickets," he offered.

"Oh, my dear boy." Agnes put her hands together in prayer. "That would be marvelous." She wheeled her walker over to a picnic bench where several other elderly people were waiting. Turning her walker, she sat on the seat, waiting patiently for Rose to join her.

Rose said to Declan, "Thank you. We can visit the museum after the tour." The website said the walking tour was about an hour.

Declan laughed again. "Seriously, what can they possibly have in the museum that Agnes needs to see?"

She laughed with him, because he didn't usually laugh. It made her feel giddy. "It's made up like White O' Morn Cottage from the movie. And they have the bicycle built for two that John Wayne and Maureen O'Hara rode."

"We *must* see the bicycle built for two." Was that a cheeky smile? "I'll love it because Agnes loves it."

She swung her arm, indicating the queue. "A lot of people love it. My mother would have loved it."

He passed a hand over his face, his features suddenly sober. "I won't make fun. I promise. Not even when we take the pony ride and the driver tells me not to play patty-cake with you in the backseat."

She burst out in helpless laughter. "Agnes will slap your hand if you try anything. And it was patty-fingers, not patty-cake."

Declan leaned close to whisper, "You mean like the way I played patty-fingers with you last night?"

Her heart was suddenly racing.

When he was standing tall and straight again, there was the glint of mischief in his eyes. He left her with her pulse thrumming and her skin hot.

She sat on the bench next to Agnes. "Are you sure you don't want the car tour instead of the walking tour?"

"I can walk. The internet said it's not that far. Driving wouldn't be the same." Agnes eyed her with a gleam. "Declan is certainly chipper this morning."

Chipper was right, and after that last comment, maybe even amorous. She still felt the answering thump of her heart. "He's excited because you're excited."

Agnes batted her eyelashes as if she knew Rose was lying. "Really, dear?"

There was no way Agnes had heard anything last night.

She was fishing. Or maybe she was playing patty-fingers with Rose's mind.

Declan was back in fifteen minutes. "We're in luck, I got the last three tickets for the next tour." He rolled his eyes. "The lady very sweetly told me that we should have booked online." He held up his other hand like a magician pulling a rabbit out of his hat. "And I got three tickets to high tea at the Royal Arms."

Agnes lit up with a smile. "Goody!"

Rose was delighted. Declan was getting into the spirit, doing everything he could to make this the best for Agnes. She'd thought he'd stay at the castle, working all the time.

Then she wondered if it was all about Agnes. Or if maybe it had something to do with last night, that he wanted to spend time with her. Her pulse picked up all over again.

A craggy-faced gentleman called out with a lovely Irish lilt. "We're ready for the eleven-thirty tour." Those seated at the picnic benches rose to join him.

There weren't just American tourists. She heard French, German, Spanish, and Japanese.

The gentleman put his fingertips together. "The tour will last about an hour. We'll see Pat Cohan's Bar, the dying man's house, the Reverend Playfair's house, plus sites for the courting scenes, the fights, and..." He paused dramatically. "The statue of Sean Thornton with Kate in his arms." He smiled, his white eyebrows rising almost to his white hair. "All your favorite scenes from the movie." He held up a little recorder. "We've got French, Italian, Spanish, German, Chinese, and Japanese translations for those who need it."

Some of the tour patrons were putting in the earphones to listen. She couldn't believe the movie was so international.

Agnes slipped her fingers through Rose's, squeezing. "I'm thrilled, my dear." Then she pulled on Declan's arm until he bent down for her to kiss him on the cheek. "Thank you."

He kissed her hand in return.

Agnes was delighted with each step. "Oh, do you remember that scene?" she said to the British lady next to her. And the white-haired woman put her hand to her chest. "Oh my, yes, it was one of my favorites."

Their elderly tour guide knew almost every line, quoting just the right thing at just the spot, outside Pat Cohan's Bar or by the Reverend's home or by the red door of the dying man's house.

It brought joy to her heart, witnessing Agnes's enthusiasm.

To a Japanese woman, Agnes said, "We're going to see the movie tonight at our hotel. They have a theater." Her eyes were round with amazement,

The regal, gray-haired lady was as animated as Agnes. "You must be staying at Burkefurd Castle." Her accented English was excellent. "We're there, too, and we saw the movie last night. I wanted to see it again before we did the tour."

"I watched it just before we left home."

Agnes made friends everywhere.

"Take lots of pictures, dear," she instructed Rose. "I want to remember everything."

The tour finally ended at the statue of John Wayne and Maureen O'Hara.

Beside Rose, Declan murmured, "That scene where he's dragging her across the field? It might be domestic abuse."

She elbowed him again. "Some things are sacred. Do not let Agnes hear you abuse her favorite movie."

"I promise I won't drag you anywhere." He winked at her. "I'll make absolutely sure you want to come willingly."

She almost let her jaw drop. Did he mean? He couldn't mean... But he did. And that was definitely a flash of desire in his eyes.

"Dear?" Agnes waved at her. "Could we have Declan take a picture of the two of us right here?" She stood by the statute, hands on her walker.

He didn't touch her. But Rose felt his hands on her. She felt his mouth all over her.

What did he have planned for tonight?

AFTER THEIR SPECTACULAR JAUNT IN THE PONY CART, where Declan tried to play patty-fingers even though their driver had given him a stern warning beforehand, they arrived at the Royal Arms.

High tea was the ultimate experience. The tearoom was filled with mostly old ladies and a few gentlemen, everyone dressed up in their Sunday best. Rose felt conspicuous in her jeans, especially when they were served on bone china as pretty as her mother's.

"What's the pattern called?" Agnes made Rose turn over her saucer to see.

"*Old Country Roses* by Royal Albert."

"That's my favorite pattern," Agnes said. "I have a set of six teacups and lunch plates." She patted Rose's hand. "We should use them. We can make our own high tea at home." Her eyes were bright with delight.

After their tea was served, their waitress brought several sandwiches on thin bread, all the crusts cut off, just the way Agnes liked.

"We've got cucumber and cream cheese. Egg. Cheese and tomato. Ham and brie. Chicken with cranberry." The girl, a pretty twentysomething, pointed to each tier of the tray. "And the open-faced rounds are salmon and cucumber on rye." She refilled their cups from a porcelain teapot, leaving it on the table covered by a tea cozy. "Enjoy." She waltzed away.

"They all have such lovely Irish accents," Agnes said.

"This is Ireland," Declan said. "We're the ones with the accent."

Agnes giggled. "I never thought of it that way."

"We're never going to eat all this," Rose said, taking a couple of finger sandwiches on her plate.

But they did. And enjoyed every bite.

Next, they were served scones with clotted cream and lemon curd.

Agnes wrinkled her nose, luckily *after* the waitress left their table. "The names of these things sound terrible. *Curd* and *clotted*." She took a bite, savored. "Why on earth would you give something so delicious such a horrible name?"

Rose and Declan shared a smile.

This was how she wanted to be if she made it to Agnes's age. Happy, never grumpy, enjoying every moment she had left.

The table was cleared and a fresh pot of tea came accompanied by a cake stand brimming with fancy sweets, macaroons, Viennese whirls, petit fours, tiny cups of chocolate mousse, bite-size strawberry shortcakes, slices of Victoria sponge cake.

"I'm going to float away after all this tea." Agnes patted her stomach.

On a trip to the restroom, Rose leaned down to whisper in Declan's ear as she passed. "I think it's time for us to have a rest."

"Especially if Agnes wants to watch the movie tonight," he agreed.

On the way back to the castle, Declan took them a roundabout way, touring a little more, and passing by Squire Danaher's house from the movie, delighting Agnes once again.

"Thank you, thank you, thank you." Agnes bounced on her seat. "This has been an awesome day."

How Rose wished she could have brought this kind of joy to her mother. She should have taken Mom to interesting places, museums, the zoo, a day in the city. But then her mother's condition had been so much more debilitated than Agnes's.

She made a pledge that when they got home, she would do fun things with Agnes, like high tea in San Francisco or a drive along the coast for fish and chips at a pub. She would create so much joy in Agnes's life.

If Declan didn't fire her after what they'd done last night.

When they returned to the room, she suggested a nap before dinner.

"I don't need dinner after everything we ate." Agnes groaned dramatically. "But I could rest my eyes a few minutes. We did so much today."

"And there's so much more to come," Rose assured her.

She closed the bedroom door quietly once Agnes's breathing evened out.

The living room was empty, and Declan's door was closed. He must be making phone calls to his office. Housekeeping had delivered a carafe of fresh lemonade, and she carried a glass out to the balcony. Slipping her shoes off, she propped her feet against the balustrade.

With the baby monitor on the table and her e-reader in her hand, she settled in for an hour of reading.

This was what she'd been trying to tell Declan, that Agnes didn't need her every moment. But he was right, too, that she couldn't leave for long periods of time, couldn't drive to the county park for a hike. She was always on call.

Though she'd opened her e-reader, it lay in her lap as she relaxed into the chair. She could almost smell the things they'd done last night, the aroma of sex still in her head, his scent, masculine, sexy, musky with desire.

What did his sexual innuendos this morning mean? And

why was he locked away in his room? Maybe he regretted the heated looks he'd given her. She thought endlessly about last night, recalling every word, every touch. Had she seduced him? Or had it been mutual? Maybe he thought she'd played the sympathy card by bursting into tears.

She was just so inexperienced. She didn't know how men thought or what they wanted. Especially a man like Declan.

She had no idea how long she'd been mulling it over until the suite's outer door opened. Declan hadn't been in his room at all. She felt stymied. Should she ignore him, pretend she hadn't heard him enter? What was the etiquette? She was like a sixteen-year-old girl worrying because she'd gone to second base with a boy and wasn't sure if he'd dump her the next day.

She didn't hear his bedroom door open, and she could make out footsteps shifting from the carpet to the hardwood floor by the terrace doors.

Declan set a gift basket in her lap.

"What's this?" She flattened out the pink cellophane, trying to see through.

Declan dropped into the chair beside her. "For your bath."

Her stomach rolled, either with excitement or terror. "Can I open it?"

She looked at him just as he gave her a heart-melting smile. "Of course."

Her fingers trembled as she untied the bow. When had she last received a gift? At least as long ago as the last time she'd had sex.

The cellophane crackled as she tore it away, and she gasped at the delights inside.

Looking at him, she couldn't read the gleam in his eyes. She drew out the luxuries buried in the basket. First a bottle of champagne, then rosewater bath salts. She opened the lid and closed her eyes to breathe in the aroma.

"That smells amazing." She held it out for him to sniff.

He smelled the salts, his gaze on her, as if he were sending her a message. His intensity made her heart beat faster, heated her skin, and she had to look away.

Concentrating on the basket, she found a jar of dried rose petals, rose-scented candles, a box of petit fours, white chocolate truffles shaped like roses, and rose-shaped soap. "This is amazing. Where did you find all this?" It was all so perfect.

"The gift shop." The slight curve of his mouth said how happy he was with himself.

Each thing he chose touched her heart, as if he'd picked them out because he *knew* her.

He shrugged. "Agnes told me to do it."

That wasn't the whole truth. He'd done it for her.

"We discussed it last night in the garden."

Last night while she'd been naked in his bath, before he'd kissed her, before she'd kissed him, before he'd touched her and rocked her world.

"I can't tell you how much it means. Thank you."

"It's just a small token of appreciation. You do so much for Agnes."

She didn't want the gifts to be a thank-you for what she did for Agnes. She wanted it to be all about her. "I'm going to treasure it all. And I want to use that tub again tonight after dinner, if you'll let me."

His eyes glittered. Last night it had been moonlight, now it was sunbeams. "I was hoping you would."

She reassembled the basket, pulled up the cellophane, tied the bow, set it down beside her. "Thank you," she said again.

"Rose." That was all he said. Just her name.

She didn't prompt him, didn't say anything at all, afraid the use of her name heralded something bad.

"About last night."

Oh, it was something bad. He regretted it, they could

never do it again, it was a mistake, he was sorry, he didn't mean to hurt her, but...

"I want you."

She felt her heart open like a flower in the morning sunlight.

Then he broke her down again. "I don't want whatever happens between us to get in the way of what you and Agnes have. What I mean is, when it's over, I don't want you to leave her."

Did it have to be over?

But she knew it did.

Declan went on driving the nails deeper. "I don't want to hurt you. I don't want to make it impossible for you to stay. I want this to be good for us. Not bad."

He was a man. He thought differently. He could have sex without emotion.

But could she?

"I don't want to get hurt either. And I want to make sure I'll still be here for Agnes." She pursed her lips a moment before she blew out a long breath. Then she told him what she needed to make this good for her. "And I want to pretend it's not just a business deal."

❦ 15 ❦

"**I** sound like an asshole, don't I."

"Yeah, you kinda do." Rose smiled to take the sting out.

Declan picked up her hand, smoothed a thumb over her knuckles. "I apologize. I'm at work too much. I'm used to seeing what I want and expecting other people to fall in line. But no matter what, you'll always be here for Agnes." He shook his head. "Forget I brought up the rest."

They were silent another long moment. And yet, strangely, it wasn't uncomfortable. He wanted her. How could she ever forget that a man had said that to her? Plainly, flat out. *I want you.*

"I don't want to forget." Those words had caressed her soul. "But I do want to pretend."

He made the slightest inclination of his head to show he was listening. "Pretend how?"

He'd plainly stated what he wanted, like a businessman. *Here's the deal, here's what I'm offering. Take it or leave it.*

She wanted to be plain, too. But it was hard to ask for what she wanted. Maybe it was a female thing, that for so long women had been taught that you got what you wanted with subtlety or playing games, like the old saying about the way to a man's heart was through his stomach. As if making him good meals and catering to his every need was the way to make him love you. There was a whole new generation of women out there, and they were bold, asking for what they wanted, expecting to get it. But she wasn't that generation.

"I want to pretend that there's emotion, that it's more than just sex." She held his gaze, trying to be as bold as that younger generation. "I want an affair, something wild and crazy." She faltered there. Her words revealed so much. But if she did this, she wanted it all.

Even if it was a fantasy.

"I can do wild and crazy." His eyes darkened, as if he wanted the same thing.

She went for it. "I want to feel like we can't get enough of each other. Like when you look at me, you want to shove me up against the wall and do things to me." It was crazy, and she blushed so deeply that she felt the heat in her cheeks.

But his breath came faster, and she heard the thump of his heart. His eyes smoked and his gaze set her on fire.

"Yeah, I can do that." His voice was deep, harsh, edged with sexual desire. "I can definitely do that." His gaze was like a stroke over her body, as if he were imagining shoving her up against the wall, dying to get his hands on her.

Her blood raced through her, stimulating every nerve ending, her body going tight deep inside, getting ready for him. She became the woman she'd never been. Bold. Wild. Crazy.

"Do it now." Her whisper was barely out before he stood and grabbed her hand, pulling her out of the chair.

She had enough rational thought to grab Agnes's monitor.

He threw his door open, catching it before it slammed

against the wall, closing it softly behind her. They were both aware of responsibilities.

He bent swiftly, his hands on the back of her thighs, lifting her as he shoved her against the wall. She wrapped her arms and legs around him, fitting him tight to her body, and he took her mouth with a kiss so ferocious it was like an animal devouring her.

God yes, this was what she wanted, what she needed, what she craved.

The kiss was deep and openmouthed, their tongues together, darting and licking and sucking. He was rigid between her legs, and there was no doubt he wanted her.

She felt wild, as if she'd lived her whole life waiting for this moment.

Arms around his neck, she clutched the baby monitor in her hand. It was kinky and illicit and sexy. Finally, he pulled back, his eyes so dark they were like a mirror reflecting the wanton picture she made. "Is this what you want?"

She nodded, swallowed. "I want more."

His groan came out deep and masculine and untamed. She clutched him tightly as he carried her to the bed and came down on top of her. His hands went to the snap of her jeans. "Next time you need to wear a dress. Something easier for me to get into when I shove you up against the wall because you make me totally wild."

Oh God. This was everything she'd hoped for. "Maybe I shouldn't wear panties either."

His pupils went wide, and he growled like an animal, a sleek mountain lion deep in the woods.

"We don't have time for what I really want. But right now, I absolutely need to taste you. And I'll make you come so hard you'll barely keep the scream inside. But you're going to. As hard as it is. You're going to be so quiet it'll make you crazy." He yanked her jeans down, making her crazy with his touch and his words. "You can dig your fingernails into my shoulders because that's the only thing that'll keep your screams on the inside. And you're going to be thinking about what I'll do to you next time."

One leg of her jeans hung just above her knee, her panties around her thigh. He hadn't even fully undressed her before he crawled down her body, taking her in his mouth, before she could be nervous and embarrassed, before she could tell him to stop because... because...

Then she couldn't tell him anything at all. It was too good, like nothing she'd ever felt before, decadent and sexy with the sunlight heating her as it fell through the window. She went up on her elbows, besotted by the wicked sight of his head between her legs.

He cupped her bottom, angling her higher, her legs falling wider.

Words slipped out as the sensations rose and built and collided like atoms. "Never like this, God, my God, just like that, oh my God, I never, please, please, please." She didn't even know what she was saying.

Something was growing, expanding, screaming to get out. He put his fingers inside her, stroking deep and slow, while his tongue was wild and crazy against her, the feel of him almost more than she could handle. It was like an arrow straight down to her core, exploding like fireworks behind her eyelids. She wanted to scream the way he said she would, and she dug her nails into his shoulders, keeping it all inside, the pleasure rising like a tsunami, carrying her off, tossing her, throwing her, jumbling her.

He didn't stop until the sensations were so intense she tried to crawl away. She heard his voice from far, far off. "Is that what you wanted?"

She could barely breathe, her body a mass of aftershocks. But she managed, "I want more."

He looked up, a wicked grin curving his mouth. "Greedy little thing." Standing, planted between her splayed legs, his hands paused on his belt, letting her feel what he wanted. Then he unbuckled. "I can't get enough of you." His teeth were gritted." I want your mouth on me. I need it. You make me crazy."

If he was pretending, he was so very good at it. And she almost believed.

He unzipped, opened himself to her, and she felt her eyes go wide. He was long and thick and hard. And so very, very masculine. Her breath caught in her throat.

"Taste me," he begged. "I need it so bad. I'm gonna go crazy if you don't."

Taste him. The way he'd tasted her.

She had always been missionary with her husband. Sometimes he asked her to take him in her mouth and she had. But he never wanted to do it to her. And she couldn't say she'd really liked doing it to him.

Yet looking at Declan, her mouth watered.

Maybe it was the situation, the illicitness of it, the secrecy, sneaking off to his room while Agnes slept, the monitor beside her on the bed like a reminder. Even if the thing was muted and Agnes would never hear a sound. It was wicked and kinky, devilish and irresistible.

She wanted to be a woman a man begged to take him in her mouth.

She didn't even push her jeans off her leg, simply slid across the bed, then down on her knees in front of him. He was right there, eye level, a tiny drop on his crown evidence of how badly he wanted her. His scent filled her head, that musky, sexual perfume.

He breathed a filthy word that turned her on and made her crazy. It didn't matter if he was pretending or if this was real.

She wanted it. And she leaned forward for a tiny kiss right on the tip, tasting that drop, sweet and salty and decadent.

He groaned, he growled, then he said, "Take it," desperation in his words and his voice.

She believed. This was real. His desire was tangible. She could taste it.

She wrapped her lips around him, slid down on him.

And he was delicious. Before her eyes, his belly quivered with need. She was doing this to him. She made his knees weak, made him groan with desire.

She took him as deep as she could, until he touched her throat, until she felt him pulse against her lips. His growl was a rumble that filled the air, like the lion she'd imagined him to be. He dug his fingers in her hair, guided her movements, not thrusting, not forcing. Begging.

"Wrap your hand around me."

She curled her fingers around his base, squeezing, until he gave her another exquisite, seductive, tempting growl.

They found a rhythm together. He was like steel between her lips, his skin velvety soft, the throb of a vein on her tongue. She moved her hand in time with her mouth, and he grew harder, his muscles tensing, his breath a rapid puff between his lips.

"God, you're so good. So good. So damn good."

That's what she wanted, needed. To be *that* good.

He grunted and groaned and growled, his taste down her throat delicious and salty yet somehow sweet. But maybe that was her need and desire talking. This is what she wanted from a man, to make him groan, to make him beg. To make her willing to do all the things she'd never done.

His limbs started to tremble, a litany of dirty words along with her name falling from his lips, showing that he knew her, that she wasn't just a mouth or a woman on her knees. This was all about her and what she could do for him.

His voice was nothing more than a groan. "Come, Come."

It was a signal, warning her to back off if she wanted.

But she didn't want to. And as his body quaked, as she felt the pulse and throb against her lips, she held on. She took her hands away, gripping his thighs, letting him take over the rhythm, filling her the way he needed and wanted. His growl of release was powerful, yet oddly quiet, intimate. As intimate as the taste of him in her mouth.

He was everything she could ever want.

He grabbed her, holding her to him as he pulsed in her mouth. She took everything. Then she backed off, sucking on just his crown, using her hand to keep him going, even as his legs trembled so hard she thought he'd fall.

With one last groan, Declan reached down, hauled her up, held her tight as they tumbled to the bed together. Then he rolled until they faced each other. His eyes opened slowly, the fire still burning in them as he wrapped his big hand around her nape and pulled her in, his lips sealing hers.

That kiss was everything. That kiss said she wasn't just a nameless woman who'd taken him in her mouth. That kiss said she was special, beautiful, desirable. She was wanted. He kissed her long and deep, bringing the taste of herself into her mouth, taking the taste of himself into his. As if they'd shared everything.

Nothing had ever been more beautiful in her life.

"YOU'RE AMAZING," HE WHISPERED.

His body was still shaking on the inside.

He hadn't expected this intense need. He hadn't expected her to agree to all his demands. But she'd gone one step further and demanded more out of him.

Act like he'd never wanted another woman? Oh yeah, he could do that.

Act like he couldn't get enough of her? Oh yeah, he could definitely do that.

He wanted her again, wanted to slide deep inside her. Wanted to take her hard and fast, wanted to take her slow and sweet. Just wanted to take her. Over and over until he was sated and there was nothing of himself left.

Yeah, he could pretend all that. And so much more.

"YOU LOOK LIKE THE CAT THAT ATE THE CANARY," AGNES quipped.

Rose didn't react. She didn't even blush. What she and Declan had done in his room was too good for embarrassment. It was too good for regretting.

And it wasn't something she'd share with Agnes.

"Did you sleep well?" she asked.

Agnes winked. "You know I did."

She helped Agnes settle in the theater seat, her walker beside her, the aisle wide enough to accommodate it. There were thirty seats, three-quarters full as everyone waited for the movie.

Posters lined the walls, as well as stills and autographed photos of the stars. In the back, a popcorn machine belted out the scent of butter into the air and made her stomach rumble. Declan was getting them each a bag. They'd skipped dinner, still full from the tea. But the butter was doing a number on her. Or maybe that was the memory of Declan on his bed.

"This is the greatest love story ever told," Agnes said, beaming at Rose.

"What about *Gone with The Wind* or *Casablanca* or *An*

Affair to Remember?"

She told herself Agnes was talking about movies, not her and Declan. Although the gleam in Agnes's eyes could be saying something else.

"*Gone with the Wind?* He leaves her in the end." Agnes waved a hand flippantly.

"But you know they'll get back together, that he's going to forgive her."

"*Pffft.*" Agnes piffled into the air. "He's crazy if he takes her back. She's never going to change."

"Did you read all the sequels?"

Agnes piffled again. "Seriously? Those were other people's interpretations, not Margaret Mitchell's."

She was about to ask if Agnes had even read the other books, but Declan's return ended the discussion as he entered their row from the other side. Sitting next to Rose, he reached across to give Agnes her popcorn, his arm almost brushing Rose's breast. So close. Her skin heated.

"The best movie ever is *Le Mans*," he said with a straight face and a hot gleam in his eyes.

Both Rose and Agnes piffled.

"I bet neither of you has even seen the movie."

Newly bold, Rose said, "I bet there isn't even a romance in it."

He brought his thumb and index finger together. "A little bit."

Rose and Agnes piffled yet again.

"What about *Grand Prix?* That has a big romance."

"Anything with a race in the title isn't a romance," Rose drawled. Agnes sniggered and Declan harrumphed.

Then the lights went down, and the movie came up.

Beside her, Declan settled on the armrest between them, his sleeves rolled up, his bare skin against hers. He leaned close and as the opening credits rolled and the music rang out, he whispered, "I thought you were going to start wearing a dress from now on."

Rose went up in smoke.

DECLAN TOYED WITH ROSE THE ENTIRE MOVIE. HE SAID the seat was too small, so he raised the armrest between them, nestling thigh to thigh. It was sexy and hot and made it hard to even follow the movie. Luckily she already knew every scene.

He put his hand on her thigh. She was afraid Agnes would see so she crossed her legs, accidentally trapping his fingers.

He held her hand, occasionally leaning over to drop a kiss on her shoulder, or even worse, her ear, where the warmth of his breath made her tingle.

It was crazy. Yet he was doing everything to make her feel desired and special. He was like a candy store clerk laying all the goodies in front of her, teasing her. By the end of the movie, she was jittery with need.

They remained in their seats, letting the small theater crowd make their way out. Agnes clapped her hands as the lights came up, then waved enthusiastically at a couple from the tour who seemed as excited as Agnes.

"Wasn't that marvelous?" she said, her voice wistful, her gaze dreamy.

"I loved every moment," Declan drawled. "A more romantic movie has never been made."

Agnes leaned over Rose to bat at him, missing him by miles. "You're making fun of me."

He put his hand to his chest. "I would never make fun of you."

Her nose in the air, Agnes said, "I could do with a cup of tea and a crumpet with lots of jam."

"I'm a bit peckish, too," Rose agreed. "Even after the popcorn, I fancy a small salad."

"Your wish is my command." Declan's eyes ate her up like she was the treat he desperately wanted.

And he was the wish she'd made.

"Then, I suppose, you'll want to take your bath," he added, his gaze smoking.

Agnes had to see all that heat rising, and probably recognized the sexy byplay in their words and looks. "We better eat our food soon. We don't want Rose missing her bath." Her voice quivered with suppressed humor.

With the theater clearing out, Agnes pushed herself out of the chair, and Rose stood to help her, her hand under Agnes's elbow as she guided her into the aisle.

Then Agnes turned to Declan. "While Rose has her soak in the tub tonight, are you going to take me down to the game room to play cards?"

"Of course," he agreed readily. "I want Rose to be free to enjoy her new bath salts and scented soaps and rose petals and, of course, a glass of champagne."

Agnes let go of the walker long enough to clap her hands, grabbing the handles again before she toppled backward on the gentle slope of the aisle. "You bought her all that? You're a good boy, Declan, making sure Rose has all the luxuries. Because we don't have a bath at home." She put a hand to her chin as if she were considering the world's weightiest matters. "Perhaps at home you could occasionally see your way to letting Rose come up and use your bathtub. Just like you're doing now."

Agnes fluttered her eyelashes coquettishly. There was a wealth of meaning in her words that made Rose wonder if Agnes and Declan were plotting her seduction. Or was it she and Agnes plotting *Declan's* seduction?

He played along. "A marvelous idea. I've been telling Rose

she needs more alone time to keep her sanity around you, Agnes." He waggled his eyebrows playfully. "We all know how demanding you are."

Rose smiled. Agnes was the least demanding person she'd ever taken care of.

Agnes giggled. "He's right, dear. We must make sure you have some alone time."

The theater had emptied completely as they bantered.

And Declan's innuendos, added to his frisky touching during the movie, made her tingle with expectation and need.

What did he have planned for tonight after Agnes was in bed?

Was it over the top to stay wrapped in the fluffy hotel-supplied bathrobe rather than getting dressed again?

Rose had felt decadent as she climbed out of the scented water, having soaked for close to an hour, so long that she'd had to add more hot water. She was pleasantly languid from the heat, the champagne, the scents, and the relaxation.

The robe tightly belted, she opened the door and started to pad across the sitting room. Only to find Agnes and Declan already seated and observing her.

"Did you have a nice bath, dear?" Agnes smiled with a hint of guile. Then, without even waiting for Rose to answer, she yawned widely. "It's been such a long day. I'm so tired. And Declan beat me at every card game. He didn't even *try* to let me win." She moaned dramatically.

"As I recall," he scoffed, "you won at least one game. And when I tried to help you, you told me to buzz off."

"Only because you were cheating."

"I don't know how you could possibly cheat at that game. The cards are what they are."

"You tried to sneak the joker into your hand instead of playing it."

"I absolutely did not do that, Agnes."

"Stop bickering, you silly sausages," Rose said, making them all laugh.

As Agnes pushed herself off the couch and grabbed her walker, Declan said, "Is that my robe you're wearing?" He looked pointedly at the lapels Rose clutched to her breasts.

She pulled the robe tighter. "It's mine," she said in the primmest tone. Then she followed Agnes into their room and closed the door.

When she returned, after helping Agnes get ready for bed, she was still wearing the robe, almost in defiance. Declan had retrieved the bottle of champagne from the bathroom and poured two glasses. Rising from the sofa, he glided across the carpet as if he were a predator stalking his prey.

"I only lost that game with Agnes because I was distracted by thinking about you in my bathtub." He closed his eyes, breathed in deeply. "You smell so good."

"Now what was that about how you're supposed to haul me up against the wall and have your wicked way?" Her heart beat rapidly, wanting exactly that despite her flippant tone.

Declan shook his head, so close she could smell his aftershave and the sexy scent of man. "I'm saving that for tomorrow night."

She flicked her lapel. "You mean you can resist this fluffy robe with nothing underneath but skin?"

He smiled wickedly. "It's going to be *hard*," he said with definite emphasis." But I'll try my best."

She dipped her head slightly, looking up through her eyelashes. "Why?"

He cupped her cheek, then trailed his fingers across her throat to her shoulder and down her arm, leaving sparks in the wake of his touch. "I don't have the necessary protection for tonight. I'm planning a trip out to get something tomorrow."

Giving him a dumbfounded look, she forced him to bluntly say, "Condoms."

She giggled. "I didn't even think about that." She sobered immediately, wondering if she should tell him that she couldn't have children and he didn't need to protect her. Besides the fact that she was too old, even if she hadn't actually started menopause.

"I must admit I haven't been celibate while I was waiting to meet you."

She hadn't thought of the other things to be worried about. "Oh."

"Don't look so disappointed." The softness of his voice seduced her. "I plan to tease you mercilessly until you're crazy, and when we're alone tomorrow night, you'll jump me."

"How are you going to tease me?" He made her crazy just thinking about it.

Taking her hand, he swept up the two champagne glasses between his fingers and led her onto the balcony, pushing the table aside with his foot, and pulling the chairs next to each other.

She sat, and he wrapped the ties of her robe around his hand, pulling her closer. His smile was wicked and oh so sexy. "While we're out touring tomorrow, I might just lean in to whisper something filthy that I want to do to you. Or that I want you to do to me."

He was a different man in this moment. When she'd said she wanted to pretend, it gave him permission to let loose everything he held inside, all his tenseness, all his stress.

She was the same, feeling fifteen years younger, sexy, desirable, and a little wicked and dirty, too. She egged him on.

"What filthy things?" She was dying to know, but somewhat terrified as well.

Still holding the ties of her robe, he was so close she could see the thickness of his lashes. "I'm not going to tell you now. I don't want to give you any warning. I want to see how you react. I want to see your desire spark, your arousal heighten."

He should be sensing that right now. She had the urge to part the robe, let him see everything, test if he could resist.

But she loved this sexy foreplay. It made her feel special and desirable, beautiful and wanton.

"Am I supposed to whisper something back? Tell you what I'm dying for?"

He drank his champagne, his eyes dark with only a sliver of moonlight shining in their emerald depths. "I have a feeling you're going to walk very close to me, your hand grazing the front of my slacks as if you own me."

God, how he made her shiver.

"No one else will see. You'll shock even yourself, but you'll feel all those sexy tingles, because it's not the kind of thing you've done before. Because it'll make you feel bold and a little crazy. Someone different and completely sexy."

How did he know her so well? She was doing things she'd never done, feeling things she'd never felt, letting herself become a woman she'd never known. It was her bucket list. She'd thought she wanted to fall in love, but maybe what she needed was to let the desirable woman inside her loose, to do whatever she wanted without shame or fear.

"What if I said I wanted you to go down on your knees in front of me right now, untie my robe, and taste me like you did this afternoon?" Her voice felt tremulous, her heart beating erratically.

"I'd say you make me crazy." He leaned closer, the sizzle of champagne on his breath. "I'd tell you that you make me want to do more than taste you. That I want to pull you onto my lap and fill you up, make you come, make you scream."

She looked at him a long, long moment, the whisper of laughter floating up from the garden, the scent of flowers rising on the breeze. "This is what you meant about teasing. Because I'm so wet right now."

"And I'm so hard. That's exactly what I mean. I want you to go to sleep wet, thinking of me, of tomorrow night. I want you to wish you could touch yourself for a little relief. I want you to wish you could climb into my bed and take me in your mouth and wake me up just as I'm coming."

"Yes," she hissed on a breath. "And I wonder if you're going to be the one who screams."

He tugged on the ties of her robe, pulling her in, closer, closer. Then his lips touched hers, the sweetness of champagne filling her up, his taste making her crazy, his lips driving her wild, his tongue taking hers. Just when she thought he was going to give in and do everything she wanted him to, he pulled back, only a breath away, and whispered, "This is going to be so good. I promise."

She believed him.

"Now it's time for you to go to bed and dream about me." He dropped one last kiss on her lips. "You can sure as hell know I'll be dreaming about you."

That was the moment she knew she was in over her head.

Or that she'd get everything she'd ever wanted.

DECLAN WAS SO DIFFERENT THAN SHE'D ORIGINALLY thought. Where once he'd been a staid, stuffy businessman, now he was fun-loving and sexy.

True to his word, as they toured the ruins of Cong Abbey

the next day, he whispered naughty things when Agnes couldn't hear and wasn't looking.

"I'm so glad you're wearing a dress today."

"Well, you're lucky, because I only brought one."

He made more sexy, dirty promises. "I'm going to push you up against the wall and go down on my knees." He dropped his voice even lower. "And make you lose your mind." She already was losing her mind.

Her legs might have been cold in the dress if not for Declan's antics. The scent of him heated her, and she tingled in all the right places. As they watched a couple having their wedding photos taken, she was reminded of the night ahead.

They had more lovely weather, and the abbey ruins were stunning in their beautiful setting by the river, some parts more intact than others, perhaps because the thirteen-century abbey had been built over the charred remains of the original constructed in the seventh century. They walked by ancient graves, the stones still standing while the nearby walls crumbled. The abbey had been huge in its day, a signpost saying that at one time it had housed three thousand monks. Their fishing hut, in roofless decay, sat out over the river, its hearth still intact, giving her the image of monks fishing for their dinner in the dead of winter.

Beyond the abbey, they walked behind Agnes on the heritage trail which led through the town and out into the woods. From the trees arching overhead, they were serenaded by birdsong and scurrying squirrels. Declan linked pinkies with her and leaned in to nuzzle her ear, whispering his naughty desires. "I need your mouth on me."

She couldn't help laughing with joy at the sexiness of it all.

"What are you two doing back there?" Agnes called over her shoulder.

"Just commenting on the pretty birdsong," Declan said with singular innocence.

Agnes harrumphed, but Rose heard delight in the sound, too.

They passed over an ancient bridge, heading back into Cong village, and Agnes declared, "I'm a bit peckish," picking up the saying from Rose who'd gotten it from her mother.

"Me, too." Rose was hungry despite the big breakfast they'd had at the castle.

Declan continued his campaign of teasing over their pub lunch, taking the bench seat beside her instead of letting her sit next to Agnes. The pub was full of laughter and the yeasty scent of beer, and under the table, he stroked her thigh, gliding high up her leg beneath the dress.

She didn't think much about what to order, too entranced by his touch, and she ended up choosing a salad topped with black pudding, which was strangely spiced sausage with a slightly metallic taste, but still good.

"Here, try." She fed Declan a bite off her fork, realizing only afterward what a picture they made for Agnes.

Declan ate, closing his eyes and groaning softly. "Oh, that's good. Really good."

She couldn't be sure whether he was talking about the Irish specialty or the fact that she'd fed him off her fork.

The meal went on like that, touches under the table, sharing food. She included Agnes, who grimaced at the sausage.

Over Irish Crème Chocolate Trifle for dessert, Declan announced, "I'll be right back." He was out of his seat before Agnes could demand to know where he was going.

He left through the front door, returning fifteen minutes later.

"I thought you were *never* coming back," Agnes pouted.

"I had to find a gas station," Declan said. "How about a drive after lunch?"

Agnes clapped her hands, forgetting her pout. "Oh yes, please."

The little towns they passed through were pretty and quaint. The people of Ireland loved flower boxes, lining the windows of the houses and the sidewalks nestled against the buildings. The air seemed fresh and clean as if it had just rained, but there hadn't been a drop all day. And everywhere, the grass was green.

Agnes absolutely refused an afternoon rest. "I didn't come all the way to Ireland just to sleep all the time."

They drove on lovely country lanes, stopping at unexpected places, visited gardens in the middle of a pretty town square. The people were gracious, smiling. Life seemed to move at a slower, sweeter pace. There were old ladies on bicycles, and tiny cars that whipped into impossible parking places. They found a teahouse that served tea and crumpets, which was fast becoming a ritual. She would find a place to buy crumpets when she got home.

It was close to three o'clock when they pulled into a bigger town, and Declan patted Agnes's knee. "We're going to do something very special today. My big surprise."

"Oh goody." Agnes wriggled in her seat beside him.

They stopped outside a large building, a sign proclaiming it the town's community hall. It certainly seemed to be a hub of activity. Couples, small groups, women arm in arm climbed the big white steps to the open double doors.

Agnes put her hand over her mouth, her words muffled as she said, "Oh my Lord."

Declan laughed. "I found it for you, Agnes."

In the backseat, Rose asked, "What?" Then she saw the sign. *Bingo*. "How did you find this?" Her voice was full of wonder.

Declan laughed. "You can find anything on the internet."

Then he growled. "Except a parking spot. Everybody's trying to get into the bingo building."

Her heart melted. Bingo in Ireland. Who would have thought of it? But Declan had.

What an absolute sweetheart. Without even an argument, he'd given up all his work time for Agnes. And for her.

❧ 17 ❧

They waited in line to pay for their game boards, everyone around them greeting each other as if they were long-lost friends, despite the fact that they probably all lived in this same town.

Agnes wasn't the only one with a walker, and there were many canes, too. Bingo obviously was not a young person's game.

Now at the front of the line, Declan asked for three game boards and handed over the small amount of euros.

"From America," the woman gasped, as if never before had Americans attended bingo night. "However did you hear about us?"

Agnes beamed. "Declan looked it up on the internet," she said as if the internet was the most marvelous invention of the last two centuries. And maybe it was. It kept people connected in a way they never could before. You no longer had to take a flight across an ocean to see relatives in Europe. All you had to do was make a video call.

"Declan," the woman repeated, her tight white curls springing with excitement. Her blue eyes, only slightly rheumy, glittered with zeal. "That's an Irish name. Are you visiting family?"

Declan shook his head. "Just on a holiday. I've never been to Ireland before."

She tucked her chin in, looking at him over the rims of her glasses. "You must have had Irish parents or grandparents."

"Great-grandparents," he supplied.

"Welcome," she said on a huge sigh as if she'd prayed he was Irish somewhere down the line. Then she handed over the boards. "Good luck to you. Take a seat anywhere that suits you."

A stage stood at one end of the auditorium, as if community plays or concerts were performed here. Round tables that seated six filled the floorspace, and up on the stage, the bingo cage was ready for the games.

"Yoohoo." The lady ran after them, flapping papers. "Since you're new with us, I forgot to tell you that we play four different games. She handed a sheet to Declan and tapped each of the grids pictured. "It's not just down or across or diagonal. We make designs and you just fill in where the white squares are. William, he's our bingo caller, will tell you which game we're playing. And over there we have tea and coffee and sandwiches." She pointed to a long table against the wall. "The coffee is only decaffeinated. We don't have regular."

She rushed back to her check-in table, the line having grown while she instructed them.

"The Irish are such lovely, hospitable people," Agnes said.

"They mostly certainly are," Rose agreed. "Let's get you seated."

"I'll get the sandwiches and tea," Declan offered.

She smiled her thanks as she settled Agnes at an empty table. They must be early because the tables hadn't filled up yet. With Agnes perched on chair, Rose rolled the walker to a row of them along the side of the room.

She slipped into the seat next to Agnes as the little lady said, "I'm so happy I think I'm going to cry. Declan is such a good boy. I thought he was going to be working the whole time we were here. Or maybe he's working in the evenings after I've gone to bed." She looked at Rose, a sparkle in her eyes. "Unless the two of you stay up talking."

It was all Rose could do not to let heat creep into her face. "It's easier for him to make calls while you're sleeping. Because of the time difference."

Agnes winked, as if she knew everything.

Rose could only hope she hadn't been loud when Declan took her to the moon.

He returned with sandwiches, decaf coffee for himself and Rose, and a cup of tea for Agnes. Instead of sitting next Agnes, he tapped a chairback. "You sit here," he instructed Rose. "I want to be in the middle."

What did he have in store for her?

Agnes chattered constantly as their table filled up and introductions were made, telling everyone they were American.

"How exciting," said an elderly woman with green eyes and hair dyed red as Maureen O'Hara's in *The Quiet Man*. She said something to Declan in what Rose could only assume was Irish. At his blank look, she added, "Declan Delaney, that's such an Irish name. Don't you speak the Irish?"

Declan, with a smile, shook his head. "I was born in the U.S."

She pursed her lips. "When did your folks emigrate?"

With his Irish name, everyone wanted to hear his story. "My great-grandparents came over before the First World

War. When I was born, my father wanted to make sure I had a first name that was as Irish as my last."

"Wonderful. And how did you find us?"

Agnes went through the story of how Declan had scoured the internet.

Cloda—Rose hoped she had the pronunciation right—turned to Agnes. "Your son is the most amazing man. It comes from his Irish roots. He takes such good care of you."

Rose opened her mouth. "Oh, he's—" But Declan squeezed her thigh to stop her.

Agnes finished for her. "He's an amazing boy. I said I wanted to see where *The Quiet Man* was filmed, and he immediately booked us flights. No questions asked." She reached past Rose to pat Declan's hand.

Though there had been a bit of argument in the beginning.

The table filled up, more explanations, more laughter, more Irish, and more amazement that Declan didn't understand. It was an all-Irish event except for them, and everyone was so welcoming. They were the center of attention as word went round.

A handsome elderly gentleman approached the table to introduce himself, taking Agnes's hand in his. "What a lovely lady. We are so happy that you've joined us all the way from America."

Agnes simpered and giggled.

The cacophony of voices rose in the auditorium, echoing off the high ceiling. The man, white-haired and no more than five feet, reminded her of Michaleen in the movie, who'd taken Maureen O'Hara and John Wayne on their courting ride.

Then William, the bingo caller, banged the gong sitting on the table beside the bingo cage.

Everyone rushed to their seats, *rushed* being relative, as

William cranked the cage's handle. It was obvious the gong meant sit or you'd miss the first number. He reached inside and called out, "*B* sixteen."

The room was utterly silent as each person scoured their board for the number. Agnes leaned close to Declan and whispered, "Do I have it?"

He pointed to her board, where she set a chip on the number.

William whirled the cage once more, reached in, called out the number. "*O* seventy-one."

As the game continued, sometimes Agnes found the numbers, sometimes Declan helped. But he had an eagle eye on his own board. Even Rose found it a little difficult to figure out where all the numbers were until she'd memorized the board.

Two tables over, a couple of ladies whispered manically to each other, and a man called out, "Could we please have quiet in the room. Some of us can't hear William."

The room hushed again. This was serious bingo. William rolled his cage, pulled out a ball, spewed out the number, repeated it, and gave folks a few seconds to look over their board. The process was done over and over again.

While Declan helped Agnes as well as managing his own board, his hand slid to Rose's thigh. He leaned close, laughing softly, his breath warm and sensual against her hair. "You missed *N* thirty-one."

She elbowed him. "You're throwing me off my game."

Agnes leaned across Declan. "We need silence in the hall, you two." Luckily, it was during the cage rolling and no one heard her.

With Declan's hand on her leg and his arm so close, his body heat was a distraction. She kept missing numbers. He used every excuse to lean in, his warm, sexy breath against her ear. Sometimes he pointed out her number, others he whispered things like, "I want you to think about what I'll do to you when we get back to our castle." As if he were a marauding knight and she his captured lady.

She shivered with desire. Finally, someone shouted out, "Bingo." And almost on top of him, a woman cried out, too. "Bingo."

"Is it whoever calls out first?" Agnes asked red-haired Cloda seated next to her.

"When it's this close, they split the pot."

William checked the numbers on their boards and declared them both winners, handing over a stack of euros to each.

He stepped up to his microphone again. "Let's start the new game with number two on your sheets." He smiled, a grin splitting his craggy face. "But before I roll the cage, I'd like to introduce our American friends." He waved a hand into the audience, indicating their table. "Please introduce yourselves. We don't often get visitors, unless they're family."

Agnes was beside herself, standing up so quickly she almost tottered over before Declan grabbed her hand. Her voice boomed in the hall. "I'm Agnes and I'm so delighted to be here. We're staying in Cong because I wanted to see the birthplace of *The Quiet Man*. Everyone has been so wonderful. And the best part is tonight and meeting all of you." She took a breath. "And this is Declan and right next to him is Rose. They brought me here, all the way from San Jose, California, which is near San Francisco."

"Do You Know the Way to San Jose?" A woman sang out the song title in a beautiful soprano.

When Agnes sat again, everybody clapped. Then William rolled the cage and the game began again.

And so did Declan's game, touching, whispering, making her crazy, even as he gave Agnes hints if she couldn't find a number on her card. It was more difficult this time since they were using a pattern instead of straight lines.

But Agnes punched the air and yelled, "Yippee." Declan called out for her, "She means she has bingo."

Agnes bounced up and down in her chair. "Bingo, bingo, bingo."

Everyone cheered with her, including Cloda, and the gentleman who'd kissed Agnes's hand. William took her card, checked it, and declared, "She's a winner."

Rose was sure they'd have let her win even if she'd gotten one of the numbers wrong.

The pot was ten Euros, and Agnes didn't have to split.

Holding her winnings to her chest, she spoke in a teary voice. "This is the best day of my entire life." Then she smiled. "At least since the last best day of my life."

Everyone in the room raised their hands in a thunderous applause.

It just might be the best day of Rose's life, too. And a prelude to the best night.

THE TEA AND SANDWICHES IN THE BINGO HALL HAD sufficed for dinner, and when they returned to the castle, Agnes wanted to stroll in the garden. "Then I'll be sleepy and ready to hit the hay."

Declan leaned close to Rose. "And then you can take your bath."

That's exactly what she needed. After getting Agnes ready for bed, she paraded in her robe through the sitting room, where Declan sat with his feet propped on the coffee table, and closed the bathroom door behind her. Running her bath, she sprinkled in rose-scented salts and bubble bath, then scattered the rose petals across the water and lit one of the candles.

The glass of champagne Declan had poured sat on the tub's edge, the iced champagne bucket standing on the floor beside it. He'd made it all so romantic.

Sinking beneath the water, she relished the scent, the heat, the silky bath salts against her skin, and the taste of champagne on her tongue. The tub had every convenience, even a shelf to hold her glass within easy reach.

She closed her eyes and lay back against the rim, sighing over the luxury.

The door opened. She didn't shriek or gather bubbles to cover herself.

He'd changed into a hotel robe. Her skin tingled against the heat of the water.

After setting Agnes's monitor on the counter, he grabbed the champagne out of its bucket and poured another glass. "You don't mind if I join you, do you?" he asked casually.

She smiled, but she was breathless. "Not at all. The tub is made for two."

This was another dream come true, another need fulfilled, another tick mark on her bucket list.

Sliding his glass next to hers on the shelf, he unbelted his robe, slowly, as if he were stripping down for her. She could have wept for the beauty of his body. The other times had been fast, half-clothed, but this was agonizingly slow and teasing.

He was fit, not an ounce of spare flesh, a dusting of hair on his chest that arrowed down, and she followed the straight line of that arrow. He was already hard. She wanted to touch him.

"It's only going to get worse if you look at me like that." His voice came out in a low growl.

"Look at you like what?" she said innocently, her eyebrows raised in mock surprise.

"As if you want to lick me like a popsicle."

Climbing in, he sank down, facing her. She pulled her knees up to give him room, but he settled his legs on either side of her and reached beneath the water to wrap his big hands around her feet, snugging her toes against him. "There, that's better." His voice was almost a purr. "Just the way I want you."

She wriggled her toes until he groaned and she could see the full, hard length of him.

Picking up his glass, he saluted her. "Cheers."

She drank, loving the sizzle of the champagne in her throat, the bubbles going to her head. "Now, what was it you were going to do to me?"

"I'm going to make you sigh with pleasure." He grinned. "Then I'm going to make you scream." He set his glass back on the shelf. "Then I'm going to make you beg for more." Leaning forward, he took her glass and set it aside, too. "And I'm starting right now."

The water swirled as he rose over her, letting her feel him bob between her legs. Hands under her armpits, he shoved her higher against the back of the tub, until her breasts peaked above the water.

"So beautiful," he said, his head bent, his breath hot on her already overheated skin. "I need to taste every inch of you." He looked up, his eyes burning. "And I'll start here."

He lowered his head, taking her nipple in his mouth, tonguing her breast until her body felt like a live wire. He pressed harder between her legs, intensifying every sensation. She moaned when he sucked harder, as if there were a direct line between her breasts and the very center of her.

He turned then, slowly, shifting in the water until she was

on top. Pulling her legs up to straddle his hips, she felt him pulse between her thighs.

He brought her down close, until her breasts brushed his chest. "I've dreamed about you, don't you know?"

She shook her head. Where he was concerned, she didn't know anything for sure.

"Long before you propositioned me."

She gasped, pulled back. "I didn't proposition you."

He grinned, his eyes hot and bright.

Who was this playful man she could never have guessed existed? Her heart answered. This was the man she could fall in love with.

She knew how dangerous the thought was. But she'd rather fall in love and get hurt than never know what loving him was like.

"You're right," she said. "I propositioned you when I fell into your arms and started blubbering."

He laughed outright. "I'm a sucker for a blubbering woman." He ran his hands down her sides to her bottom, hitching her closer, until she could feel the length of him everywhere she needed him.

"It's a weakness of mine," he whispered. "*You're* a weakness of mine."

She reveled in his words

"You're too hard to resist."

"I think you're the one who's hard."

She wriggled on him, and he pulled her down for a hard, sweet kiss filled with so much promise that she was breathless.

❧ 18 ❧

The kiss was slow and sweet and delicious, a lingering swirl of tongues and lips, sizzling with the taste of champagne, hot with banked desire.

"I miss kissing," she whispered against his mouth.

She couldn't remember the last time she'd kissed as more than a brief prelude to sex, kissing just for the taste of it, the feel of it, the beauty of it. It must have been in the early days of her marriage. Maybe even before they were married, when they were young and desperately in love, before jobs and the lack of money and barrenness consumed them.

He hooked his hand around her nape. "Kiss me until the water goes cold."

She smiled softly. "Or until the champagne bubbles go flat."

He laughed, the rumble of it vibrating against her breasts. "I can think of a lot of things to do before the champagne goes flat." He licked the seam of her lips. "And there's always another bottle in the fridge."

They kissed, sweet pecks leading to open mouths and tangled tongues, then backing off to catch their breath and start all over again. She stretched out on top of him, her knees to his sides, the heat and hardness of him between her legs teasing her with what was to come. She lost herself to his touch, his fingers gliding over her body, never lighting anywhere for long, but stoking the fire.

This was her fantasy, to lay in his arms for an hour. The sex would come later, and it would be sweet, but this was another item for her bucket list.

Finally, the water cooled, bringing a chill to her skin.

He gazed at her with the heat of desire in his eyes. "We either need more hot water." He pulled her down for another sweet kiss on the mouth. "Or warm ourselves up in bed. What's your vote?"

"Bed," she said, her voice husky.

He helped her up, wrapped them both in a towel as he dried her back, her arms, her thighs. They stepped onto the mat, and he pulled the plug, the water draining away.

As he bent his knees to dry her calves, she suddenly felt self-conscious. She'd never stood naked in front of a man other than her husband. Declan was new and different, and this was a critical time when he could judge her.

And he was her boss. Agnes's friend.

He stood, naked and beautiful like a Roman statue. "Don't."

She couldn't say anything.

"Don't get nervous." He read her mind, her body language, the look in her eyes. "You're beautiful, and what we're doing is perfect. Don't think. Just enjoy." He handed her the towel. "Dry me off," he murmured, seducing her with a soft tone.

He held her gaze as she dabbed water droplets off his chest, his scent musky with male arousal. She dried his stomach, reached around him to swipe the towel across his back. Slowly, she went down on her haunches, toweled his muscular thighs, his toned calves. Then she dragged the towel back up to his center, dried every drop as he stood before her, proud and erect. Her mouth watered, and she leaned in to lick a pearl of moisture from the very tip, a decadent, wicked, delicious taste.

He exhaled, a long sigh of pure pleasure. Then, as if he couldn't take the lingering touches or soft caresses a moment longer, he hauled her up in his arms. Wrapping her legs around him, she dropped the towel on the floor as he grabbed Agnes's monitor and carried Rose into the bedroom.

He moved slowly, giving her time to think, time to say no. Time to get nervous all over again.

Leaving the monitor on the side table, he tugged the covers aside and laid her on the bed, leaning over her, her legs still spread around him.

"You are so beautiful." He trailed a finger around her breast, down her belly, to the mound of her sex.

She tried not to think about her body's flaws.

This was supposed to fantasy, wish fulfillment. And she wanted to pretend she was as perfect as he was.

"You're magnificent," she told him. He was thick and hard and ready. She dragged her heels up his calves, locking her ankles.

If she was going to take a lover, there was no better choice than him. "Didn't you promised to make me scream with pleasure?"

His grin was wicked enough to send shivers coursing through her. "I'm going to make you faint with pleasure you've never experienced before."

She laughed. "My, you are cocky."

He palmed himself in a deliciously sexy gesture. "Oh yeah, I'm cocky."

Then he came down on top of her.

H<small>E COULDN'T REMEMBER THE LAST TIME HE'D ENJOYED A</small> woman the way he enjoyed Rose. He didn't have to pretend with her. She wasn't some young thing wanting to scratch an itch with an older man, looking at him with dollar signs in her eyes and estimating the size of his bank account. She wasn't out for what she could get from him.

He wanted to taste her, kiss her, caress her, sink inside her. He wanted only to give her pleasure.

She made him feel young again, carefree, lighthearted. All the things he'd never truly been.

He took her mouth in a long kiss, needing more despite the delicious kisses in the tub. He wanted more of her lips, her taste, until he needed to taste her everywhere. Stuffing a pillow beneath her head, he started down her body, kissing, licking, nipping, bent on giving her the long, slow build to exquisite pleasure that he'd promised.

"Now to make you scream," he murmured as he pressed his hips between her legs. He wanted to make her come over and over before he took his own pleasure. "I can wait a very long time. I have immense control. And I'm going to make you come until you can't think anymore."

"I'll hold you to that." Then she moaned as he plumped her breast in his hand and took her in his mouth.

She arched. "Oh my God, I can feel that straight down."

"Didn't you know there's a nerve that goes from here—" He trailed a finger from her breast to her sex. "Right down to here?"

She smiled with a snort of laughter. "That is so not true." Then she gasped as he took her other breast in his mouth, caressing the underside in a slow path down her ribs, over her belly, to the springy curls between her legs.

He liked that she didn't wax, that she was neatly trimmed

but still all woman. He palmed her, but didn't slip inside. She was moist against his skin. He kissed her breasts, licked and sucked, while he gently massaged between her legs with the heel of his hand.

He looked up to find her eyes closed, the pillow bunched tightly in her fingers.

She was all his in this moment. When had he ever felt like this, so taken by her scent, the softness of her skin, the sweetness of her taste? It was more than sex with a hot woman. She made him tremble inside. She made him powerful yet gentled him at the same time. She filled him with desire but made him want to give just as much.

"Should I put my mouth where my hand is?"

She groaned deep in her throat. "Yes. Please, yes."

Lifting her head, she watched him kiss his way down her torso, her belly. Her skin was warm and tinged with pink, as if she weren't used to being a man's total focus, her pleasure his only goal. But she wanted it.

That was the power he felt. That was his need.

He slipped between her spread thighs, her arousal perfuming the air, but he didn't go for the gold immediately.

Rose wasn't a woman to be rushed, she was a woman to savor. He was pretty sure she hadn't had a lot of savoring in her love life. And he wanted to give her that.

He slipped his tongue along the seam of her sex, relishing her taste. When she moaned, he went deeper, found the heart of sensation. She arched into him, flooding him with her dew, and suddenly he needed all of her. Cupping her bottom in his hands, he lifted her, opening her fully.

And she was utter sweetness against his mouth.

OH GOD, HIS MOUTH WAS GLORIOUS. ROSE BASKED IN THE sensations.

She gripped the pillow in both hands and rose to meet him, matching the rhythm of his tongue and lips on her. There could be nothing more sensual, and she let herself go in a way she never had.

Maybe because he was so new, so unlike her husband, so different from the Declan she thought she knew.

Maybe because she wanted the experience, to store up memories, to tick one more thing off her bucket list. Somehow it was even better than the first time, as if they'd been wild and crazy and rushing everything. But now he took his time, building her up, up, up. She was there, ready to come, then he'd back off, the sensation slipping just beyond her grasp. Only to have him start all over again, taking her higher this time. He took her to the brink over and over, pulled back, then pushed her higher, ever closer to the cliff edge.

Until finally he slid two fingers inside, filling her, finding that perfect spot she'd only ever found on her own. He stroked her slowly, not fast, not hard, but relentlessly.

Her legs trembled, then her whole body, and she surged against his mouth, curling his hair around her fingers, holding him tight, waiting, striving, needing. Until it hit, a huge wave rolling her under with its intensity, then shooting her out again.

She bit her lip because she couldn't scream, even in the privacy of his room.

Yet trying to hold it in made the sensations go on and on, her body contracting with pleasure until it became almost more than she could handle. She yanked on his hair without thinking, pulling him up. She hadn't even realized she was watching him down between her legs, and yet now, when she closed her eyes, the sight was burned against her lids, his tousled hair, his nose and mouth buried against her, and, when he looked at her, that purely wicked glint.

He climbed up her body, pulled her into his arms, kissed her deeply. Her taste on his lips and tongue called to her. The kiss was long and sweet while his hands were on her again, sliding into the slickness between her legs.

She loved the kissing, the taste. She loved the feel of his finger on her. He was taking her there again, building her up with slow, exacting circles. Her body jerked, throbbed.

Now was when he should have entered her, but he played, taking her up again in increments. It took her longer to climax this time, but it came harder, almost a surprise, like the prize at the bottom of the Cracker Jack you thought you'd never find.

He didn't stop, kept her coming, his mouth devouring her cries.

"Please," she whimpered. "I want you inside me."

He dropped a kiss on her mouth, pulled back, his eyes blazing. "I'll make you come again and again before I let go."

He reached to the side table where he'd left a condom packet beside Agnes's monitor.

Seeing it, she felt a shaft of embarrassment, maybe even a little shame. But in the next moment, all she felt was the thrill as he tore open the packet.

He placed the condom precisely, rolled it down slowly. He was so big, so hard, so thick. But she was no virgin and she wanted him.

Instead of coming down on top of her, he stayed on his haunches and pulled her to him, draping her legs along his hips.

"We need just the right angle." He grabbed a pillow, shoving it beneath her bottom.

She didn't want to think about how many times he'd done this before.

"That's so much better." He gave her a sexy, devilish grin, then his features tensed in concentration as he filled her slowly.

She hadn't felt a man inside her for so long she'd feared it might hurt. But she was so wet, he slid easily.

"Oh my God." It was so good, so perfect.

As he stroked over that special spot, her body spasmed.

He groaned. "Oh yeah." His voice had the same breathy quality as hers.

He barely moved, just a subtle caress inside her, but God, he induced madness. She wanted to look at him, but she couldn't, her eyes squeezing shut, as she reveled in his possession. "So good, so good," she chanted, unable to stop herself.

Then he put his thumb on her, not just doubling the pleasure, but ratcheting it up on a logarithmic scale. Sensation blasted through her, the slow moves inside her somehow better than fast and hard. And then she simply exploded.

She cried out, couldn't control it. In the same moment, as her body clamped down on him, he fell on top of her, taking her hard, fast, and deep, just the way her body craved. He kept her riding the edge of bliss, as she laughed, maybe even cried.

When it was over, he rose above her, sliding slowly over that same spot. "I knew this would be perfect." And he started all over again, that relentless stroke inside her, his thumb caressing her, the cataclysmic sensations, the pleasure screaming through her.

This time when he leaned over, thrusting hard and deep, he didn't stop, riding the wave of her pleasure, letting it take him over, grunting his release against her hair. Until he was holding her, whispering deliciously filthy words in her ear, about how perfect she was, how good she felt.

This moment was all she could ever want.

Until the next moment, when she'd want it all again.

🌿 19 🌿

Declan idly stroked his fingers over her warm skin, a sheet over them as they cooled.

He'd wanted to make her come again, yet the tight clench of her body forced him over the edge. He'd felt the moment she climaxed the second time, and he couldn't hold back, until he'd emptied everything he was as a man straight into her.

It had been beyond anything he'd known.

"Well," she said in a soft breath. "I haven't felt like that for a very long time."

"You divorced three years ago?" In the dark and the quiet, he didn't mind asking personal questions. "And you haven't dated anyone else?"

She shook her head against him. "Three years. And no, I didn't date. There was Mom to take care of. And after Mom, I didn't feel like dating." He was sure she would have had chances. "But I've never felt like this before."

"I'm so glad I could be of service."

The words were flippant, but he didn't feel flippant. She was special. He'd had women, but being with Rose was more than just "having her." He'd been besotted with his wife, but he couldn't say the sex had ever been like this. Not amazing, not breathtaking, never to the point where he lost his control and lost his mind. Maybe love meant the sex didn't have to be great, as if emotion made up for what the physical lacked. He wouldn't deny he'd had feelings for his wife. He just couldn't find them now, not with Rose in his arms. Not after the way she'd dragged him into bliss right along with her.

"And I do mean *never*." She nuzzled her nose against his chest. "Maybe I'm old enough now that I can let myself go in a way I never could when I was younger."

He wondered if age was the magic ingredient. "How long were you married?"

"Almost thirty years."

Jesus. He couldn't imagine it. "You must've gotten married very young."

She nodded, her silky hair caressing him. "We had to get married. I was pregnant."

He stroked her arm, her shoulder, then up her beneath her hair, deciding what to ask or if he should ask at all. And need won out. "I thought you didn't have any kids."

"I don't." She sighed. "I lost the baby."

"I'm sorry." Pain for her stabbed him in the heart.

Her shoulder lifted beneath his fingers as he stroked her. "We were young." Her voice was soft with memory. "We were in love. We thought we could make it. And we thought there would be more babies."

"But there weren't."

"Just miscarriages."

He saw how truly hard her life had been, in ways he'd never imagined. The anguish, the desperation. "I'm so sorry."

"I came to terms with it a long time ago. If I'd known in the beginning that I'd never have children, I might have done things differently."

He wanted to know everything about her. "Like what?"

"I would have gone to nursing school. As it was, I just got a certificate."

And she could never make as much money. "Don't a lot of people go to school and become mothers as well?"

"Yes." Her voice grew fainter. "I should have. But I needed the money and the overtime. We wanted a house for the kids and to one day buy a shop for my husband. He was a mechanic, and he wanted his own business. But, well..." She trailed off, finally adding, "None of that happened."

"Is that why you got divorced, because he could never start his own business?"

She was silent a long moment while he continued the slow caress up and down her arm. "It was partly that. The man he worked for was older, and he always said he'd let my husband have the shop when he was gone. But he died without a will, and his son didn't care about any deals his father had made. My husband was out of a job when the son sold the shop. I had to take care my mom. And..." She shrugged, the rest of the story apparent. Her husband grew bitter and walked out. Or something close to it.

"You must think I'm a failure," she whispered.

He tipped her chin, forcing her to look at him. "I don't think that all. I just want to know you better." He shouldn't want to. The relationship was wrong since she worked for him. It made him a sleazebag boss. Yet he couldn't let her go.

She gave him another long look. "Why?"

He could have said it was because they'd had sex and she was in his bed. He couldn't remember wanting to know more about the women he'd slept with. He didn't know if he'd even wanted to know more about his wife. She was an object. He could admit that now, as distasteful as it was to think he could have been like that. She was like a trinket he craved. When he got her, he didn't really know what to do with her.

Except to have a child. Then he discovered he couldn't even do that.

So who was the bigger failure here?

He gave her the only answer he had. "Because I like you." And she was special.

She didn't smile as she looked at him. "I like you, too." She blinked, as if she had to think a moment. "Tell me more about you, if we're getting to know each other."

He'd asked her, and she deserved the same. "What do you want to know?"

"What do you want to tell me?"

In keeping with the quiet of the room, he spoke softly. "Since you told me about your marriage, I'll tell you about mine." It was probably what she'd wanted to ask anyway. "Or has Agnes told you everything?"

Tipping her head to look at him, she fluttered her eyelashes. "Agnes would never reveal *all* your secrets."

He laughed. "Right. Agnes gave you her version, which isn't necessarily the true version." Although truth is based on perspective. "She probably told you Giselle cheated on me."

She raised both eyebrows. "Giselle?"

He smiled without humor. "She was exotic, right down to her name."

"Tell me about her."

He wanted to, though usually his wife, his marriage, and his divorce were off limits. "She was younger, twenty-five, and I was pushing forty. I'd never been married, and she wasn't like any other woman I'd ever met. She was fun-loving, sexy." He stopped with the descriptions, realizing he couldn't tell the woman in his arms how sexy his ex-wife had been. "She was a good Catholic girl. And we could only go so far. So I married her."

She puffed out a breath. "You married her just to have sex with her?"

She'd told him the truth, and he could do no less. "It was more complicated than that. I thought I loved her. I would have married her anyway. But the sex speeded things up. And I wanted a family. You think you've got time, but I wasn't getting any younger."

"But you didn't have any kids," she said, echoing his words to her.

"It didn't happen. We had tests, and it turned out to be me who was the problem." He didn't know how much circumstance changed the outcome of his marriage, that if he'd been able to father a child, things might have been different. "Maybe I didn't have enough money for her. Or she didn't like the prenup. Or she thought that since we couldn't have kids, I'd throw her out. I don't know. Things just changed after that."

"Disappointment can do that to you." The gentle understanding in her words caressed his soul.

"It eventually became clear that she was sneaking around with someone else. Then she left me. She got the same settlement whether she left or I divorced her. It was spelled out in the prenup, and she took the deal. It turned out she'd been seeing a business associate of mine, and at the time, he had the bigger bank account. She had a baby, and I'm pretty sure he didn't make her sign a prenup. Maybe that was my first mistake."

"Or maybe she was just a gold digger."

He chuckled, the laughter squelching the other uncomfortable emotions inside him. "Agnes has been talking."

"Agnes loves you very much. And she was affronted on your behalf."

"She didn't need to be. I'd already figured out that I was just a paycheck to my wife long before we parted ways. It doesn't hurt."

Liar. She didn't say it, but he heard her think it. Maybe he was a liar.

"Before it got that far, why didn't you just adopt?"

"Why didn't you adopt?" he tossed back at her.

She laughed, a terrible, sad sound. "We didn't have enough money."

He was an idiot. "I'm sorry. That was insensitive."

But she added, "My husband wouldn't have adopted anyway. He didn't want a child that wasn't his own flesh and blood. He thought you'd never know what you'd end up with if the seed wasn't your own." She laughed again, a little less sadly this time. "Although I don't think it matters. Things can get messed up anyway."

"Giselle didn't want to adopt," he admitted. "It came to me later that she didn't think an adopted child would keep me as committed to her."

He tightened his hold on her as they digested each other's history.

"How do you feel about not being a father?"

"I have my work. I enjoy it. I don't feel I'm lacking something essential. Maybe it's like the old saying about not missing what you never had." It was also something he didn't let himself think about. "And you?"

"I know a lot of women will go to any lengths, fertility treatments and so on. And I was tired and depressed after the miscarriages. But finally we both seemed to accept it. And we had a decent life. At least until the whole thing with the shop. My husband just seemed to lose himself." She shifted, snuggling closer. "But really, I was okay without kids in the end."

"Until your mother got sick."

She nodded, her hair soft on his skin. "Until my mother. But Agnes fills that need now. She's very special to me."

He stroked her arm, soothing her. "You and Agnes are meant to be together. That's not going to change."

"Are you sure?" she asked without looking at him, as if gazing into his eyes might reveal a truth she didn't want to know.

"It will only change if you want it to."

"But this," she said softly. "What we just did."

He heard the part she didn't say. What about when it was over? "It will never change what you have with Agnes."

She nestled against him. It felt so comfortable, so right, in a way he'd never known. No matter what happened between them, he wouldn't take her away from Agnes. He hoped they would always be friends. Even when this ended.

All good things had to end. Right?

Even as he had the thought, there was a rustle from Agnes on the monitor.

Rose jerked. "Agnes needs me." She reached over him, her breasts caressing his chest, stirring his body all over again.

Picking up the monitor, she pushed the talk button. "Agnes, I'll be right there. Don't get out of bed yet."

"I'll wait for you, dear."

She scrambled off the bed, searching for her robe, remembering it was in the bathroom. He should have brought it out with him.

But then he hadn't been thinking about when their night would end.

As she came out, holding the robe tight, he had the wistful thought to ask her to come back, to sleep with him. But that was impossible. Agnes needed her far more than he did.

She whispered, as if Agnes might overhear, "Thank you. That was amazing." She kissed him gently, sweetly.

The barest touch of her lips made him want more, and he wrapped his hand around her nape, held her there, deepening the kiss for a long, sizzling moment.

Until he had to let her go.

Pulling away, she smiled. Then she ran out his door.

He realized that by the very nature of their relationship, he would always have to let her go. And one day, that would be permanently.

Under his ribs, there was a kernel of discomfort. It wasn't an ache or a pain. It was just... uncomfortable. Like a tiny pebble in his shoe. He knew it was there, but it wasn't bad enough to hunker down, take off the shoe, and shake it out.

At least not yet.

🦋

As she rushed through the door, Agnes said, "Did you have a nice bath, dear?"

God. She'd had the best bath ever, the glorious kisses, his touch as he dried her off, the long, slow caresses, his lips on her, his taste in her mouth, his kiss on her body, the feel of him deep inside her.

And she'd learned she was capable of multiple orgasms.

Had she wasted the last thirty years? Just imagine if she'd come like that every day. Or every other day. Or even every week. She started the multiplication in her head, stopped before she made herself crazy.

"It was nice," she said softly. "Now let's get you to the bathroom."

"You can sleep in his bed," Agnes said as Rose helped her to the walker.

She didn't twitch a single muscle as she bore the weight of Agnes's words.

She could ignore it. She could acknowledge it. She could flat-out lie.

She went for half measures. "Sweetheart, I'm here for you and only you."

Agnes patted her cheek. "You're such a dear girl. If I'd had a daughter, I would want her to be exactly like you."

Rose felt a growing warmth around her heart. "You're so like my mother."

They smiled at each other in the dim light of the bedside table. She'd fallen in love with Agnes, who was sweet, caring, and kind. And very, very funny.

She clearly saw the danger.

She loved a woman who would leave her sooner rather than later and was falling for a man she'd eventually have to leave.

20

The day was dreary, though not actually raining. Despite the unusual and amazing weather they'd been having, they took their umbrellas. Nothing would stop Rose and Agnes from enjoying themselves.

Declan didn't mind being their designated driver. He'd stopped thinking about work. It would all be there when he got back.

On the agenda for the day was a visit to Kylemore Abbey, a monastery for Benedictine nuns. But since Lettergesh Beach was only fifteen minutes past the abbey, they drove there first. It was the site of the horse race in *The Quiet Man*.

"I don't recognize it," Agnes admitted. "But I'm glad I saw it."

The beach was blustery and cool and deserted, and Declan was sure the sands had shifted and the dunes had moved in the seventy years since John Wayne had ridden his horse here. But Agnes was satisfied with a few pictures.

They backtracked to Kylemore.

The abbey had started out as a private home, built by a rich English doctor, then owned by a duke and duchess. The seventy-room house, in Declan's mind, qualified as a castle. It overlooked a picturesque lake, along with a neo-gothic church the doctor had built in memory of his wife. The restored walled gardens, a stream running through, grew an amazing array of blooms, vines, vegetables, herbs, and ferns.

They'd toured the house first, which was open to the public on the ground floor, the nuns utilizing the rest, then strolled to the church and the mausoleum where the doctor and his wife were buried. After that, they'd taken a shuttle to the Victorian gardens.

"I can walk," Agnes had argued. "It's only a mile." There was a trail through the woodlands.

"But if you walk, you might be too tired to stroll through the gardens themselves," Rose said logically.

Agnes had grumbled, but finally agreed.

She surveyed the formal gardens. "Can you imagine how marvelous it would have been to attend school here?"

The abbey had been a boarding school and a local day school until 2010. The gardens weren't restored until the 1990s, so not too many students in the abbey school's ninety-year history had enjoyed what they saw now. Declan decided not to remind Agnes of that.

"The view," Rose said. "How could anyone ever study?"

As luck would have it, the clouds parted and the sun came out. The gardens encompassed six acres, and it was a good thing they'd taken the shuttle or Agnes wouldn't have made it through. As it was, she took frequent rests on her walker, using the time to gaze at the surrounding beauty. Rose had brought snacks to keep the wolf from the door, as Agnes put it, and they ate biscuits as they walked.

Before they left the abbey, they stopped at the gift shop for souvenirs.

"Oh my goodness." Agnes gasped at the array of chocolates made by the abbey nuns.

There were large dark chocolate and white chocolate sheep that looked puffy enough to count if you couldn't fall asleep. Boxes of small milk chocolate sheep sported a white chocolate one added in for fun. Tables were stacked with truffles and chocolate bars and chocolate sheep on sticks that you swirled in warm milk to make hot chocolate. Shelves were filled with jars of mixes for brown bread, fruit scones, and blueberry muffins, along with pots of various jams, Irish Whiskey marmalade, lemon curd, honey, and an array of chutneys. There were displays of handmade soaps and creams and candles and pottery, everything made by the nuns at Kylemore Abbey.

Agnes opened her purse. "Rose and I really must have a hot chocolate sheep each. And you, Declan—" She beamed him a smile. "—need the Irish whiskey marmalade."

"I'll get it for you," he said.

She waved him away. "These are presents for you and Rose."

"But you don't have any euros."

She pursed her lips like an old maid. "Rose took care of getting us euros before we left home."

He looked at Rose, who shrugged.

"Thank you. That's sweet." Rose smiled at her. "We can have our hot chocolate tonight."

Agnes made her purchases, and while she wasn't looking, Declan bought a box of chocolate sheep, some truffles, a jar of scone mix as well as lemon curd they could eat back home. And soap for Rose's bath.

"Would you like lunch at the abbey café?" he asked.

"Do they have fish and chips?"

Rose looked at the menu as they passed. "No. But they have a lamb pastie."

"I need fish and chips," Agnes insisted.

"But you had fish and chips in Dublin."

Agnes rolled her eyes like one of the girls she would have taught in school years ago. Girls had been rolling their eyes for eons. "You can never have too much fish and chips."

They put her walker in the car and went in search of a chip shop. They found one in a charming town with quaint stores, cute houses, and the lyrical accents of locals. Agnes was bouncing up and down as they parked a few doors from the chip shop where tourists walked out carrying fish wrapped in newspaper.

"Just like in the olden days," Rose said.

"You mean like when I was a child," Agnes drawled.

At the door of the shop, they discovered there was no indoor seating.

"We can eat over on those picnic benches." Agnes pointed to a park across the street with red benches. The Irish loved color, from the brightly painted doors of their houses to their fire hydrants to their phone boxes. They seemed to have more of those than you found in the U.S.

Declan helped Agnes onto the bench. "I'll get the fish and chips."

But she patted the seat beside her. "Why don't you let Rose do that?"

He gave her a look. If she wanted to send Rose to buy the fish, her mind was brewing something. "I'm perfectly capable," he said.

She huffed at him. "I want to talk to you, Declan." She put a hand to the side of her mouth and whispered loudly, "A private conversation."

With the sudden tenseness that crossed Rose's face, he got a big clue what the private conversation would be about.

Something to do with last night. And Agnes had already gotten to Rose about it.

He didn't want to talk about last night. He didn't want to ruin the memory by explaining what they'd done, or having to quantify or qualify it, or dredging up his feelings or Rose's. He wanted to savor it. And he wanted to dream about the next time. Because there would be a next time. No matter what Agnes had to say.

Yet they'd need to have this conversation at some point. He reached into his back pocket for his wallet and pulled out some euros, handing them to Rose.

"Thank you," she said softly. "I'll get two orders, and we can all share."

"That's delightful, dear," Agnes chirped. "Be sure to get malt vinegar for the chips."

"Of course." Rose smiled. Then she looked at him, her eyes speaking volumes, telling keep his trap shut.

He sat beside Agnes as Rose jogged across the road and disappeared into the chip shop.

"All that fatty fish and greasy chips are bad for your cholesterol," he said, an obvious gambit to forestall Agnes.

"I'm eighty-seven years old. I don't have a lot longer to enjoy fish and chips in Ireland. A little extra cholesterol won't hurt me."

He laughed. "All right. Have the fish and chips."

Agnes grinned happily. "I do love that girl, you know."

"Rose?" he said idly, though he knew who Agnes meant.

"Yes, Rose. She's really grown on me. I don't know what I'd do without her." She turned to him. "You aren't going to get rid of her, are you?"

He choked on his own breath. "Why the hell would I get rid of her?"

She shrugged like a teenager. Soon she'd roll her eyes again. "I know what you men are like when you're done with your playthings."

"Plaything?" The word stabbed him in the solar plexus.

"She's not a toy, Declan, to be discarded when you get tired."

"I have no intention of discarding her." He decided not to deal with what was happening between him and Rose, but with Agnes and Rose only. "She's here for you, Agnes. As long as you love her, and you need her, she'll always be here."

Something misted in Agnes's eyes before it faded away. "Thank you, Declan, because I'm happier than I've been since Marvin passed."

He laid his hand over hers on the table. "That's all I want, Agnes, for you to be happy. And Rose makes you happy. I would never send her away."

"But if she gets hurt and things get awkward, she might leave."

"I won't let anything be awkward." He gave her the best he could. "I'll never intentionally hurt Rose." He had no control over her feelings, but he'd do his best not to hurt her. "She loves you. She's not leaving you. Wild horses couldn't drag her away."

Her lip trembled. "Are you sure?"

He nodded solemnly. "Not wild horses or wild dogs or wild hippopotamuses," he said, hoping to make her smile. "She's here to stay. I promise."

Whatever happened, they would each nurse their individual wounds in private, never for Agnes to see. They both knew it had to end. But his intention was to make this the most pleasurable experience Rose had ever known, ensuring she'd have no regrets.

Agnes beamed her big smile and reached into the pocket of her coat. Removing a folded piece of paper, she spread it on the picnic bench. "You need to take Rose here. It's in just a few days, and we'll still be here."

He leaned over to read the flyer, saying the words out loud. "Dinner and dancing under the stars at Burkefurd Castle." He looked at Agnes, a knot in his chest. "I don't dance."

"But you eat. It's dinner. And none of you young people know how to dance these days. Just put your arms around Rose and shuffle around the floor while they play the music. Even you can do that."

He wanted to laugh, but there was just something wrong about what she was asking. "And what will you do, roll your walker around the dance floor?"

She beamed that smile again, lighting up her face. "I won't go. This is for you and Rose."

He snorted. "Fat chance. She's never going to let you stay alone in the room."

She puffed up, her back straightening. "I can take care of myself."

He didn't snort again, but he stared her down. "What if you have a fall?"

"I have my walker. I won't fall."

"If you remember to use your walker."

She huffed and pursed her lips. "I always use my walker. And I don't fall."

"May I remind you that we hired Rose because you had a fall?"

She narrowed her eyes at him militantly. "And you will recall that I didn't break a single bone. I didn't need to go to the hospital. I don't fall, I bounce."

"She won't put you in a situation where you bounce."

She smiled. It was pure Dr. Evil. "You're going to convince her."

He shook his head. "I'm not even convincing myself."

She tapped the flyer. "You two deserve some fun instead of hanging around an old lady all the time. You need young-people time."

He and Rose were already having their "young-people time." And it was awesome. They didn't need dinner and dancing, not at Agnes's expense. "This trip is for you. Not us." Where the hell had she seen that flyer?

She set her jaw in a stubborn line. When Agnes got something in her mind, getting it out was like digging for a splinter. "If this trip is for me, you have to do what I want. And I want you two to go to this party. It's right in the castle. You don't even have to drive. You can call me every fifteen minutes. I bet that walkie-talkie would even work."

He didn't believe the baby monitor would reach from their suite to the ballroom. "We can't do this unless you attend, too." That was a brainstorm, insist Agnes go with them. And when she refused, none of them would go.

She glared with that stubborn face again. "Then find someone to stay with me," she snapped.

She was impossible. "We don't know anyone in Ireland."

"We can pay someone who works here. Or maybe there's someone in the village."

"You want a stranger staying with you?"

Agnes ignored him. "There's that pretty maid who turns down the bed. Let's ask her."

He changed tactics. "Why do you want us to go for dinner and dancing so badly?"

She put her hand on his arm, squeezing earnestly. "Because Rose never gets to do anything fun. She took care of her mother for five years. Then she was scrambling to find a job. Now she's taking care of me. When was the last time that girl had fun?"

Last night. He didn't say that. It was a different kind of fun. But Agnes was echoing what he'd said to Rose on the balcony a few nights ago. She needed time for herself. She needed to do something fun.

Maybe Agnes was right. Rose deserved to dress up. She deserved a fabulous meal and a night of dancing. Even if he couldn't dance.

Across the street, Rose left the chip shop, box of newspaper-wrapped fish in hand. She waited for a car to pass, then ran across the road. She was kind and sweet and generous. She was still young. She deserved to have fun. And not just in his bed or his bathtub. She was more than just a roll in the hay.

"All right," he said to Agnes as he watched Rose, the scent of fish and chips already making his mouth water. Or maybe Rose made his mouth water. "We'll see if we can find somebody to stay with you while we're out."

Agnes wriggled happily on the bench, her hand up for a high five.

Now he just had to convince Rose.

"IT'S OUT OF THE QUESTION," ROSE HISSED. THEY SAT ON the balcony while Agnes took a nap before dinner.

"No, it's not." Declan wasn't listening to her.

Rational talk hadn't worked with Agnes either. Rose had listened to the whole plan while they ate their fish and chips. Then again on the drive back. She'd said she'd think about it. She couldn't fight Agnes. Which meant she had to get Declan alone and convince him it was a crazy idea.

She wasn't leaving Agnes with someone she didn't even know.

"While you were helping Agnes," Declan said, "I called the concierge. They have a service for this very thing."

She growled at him, glaring. "It's a babysitting service. It's completely different from taking care of an elderly adult."

"I asked. I've got it covered."

In reality he was the boss and he could do whatever he wanted. But he was still trying to convince her.

"Didn't you tell me you had hospice volunteers who sat with your mother when you went shopping?"

"They had training. And there was no way I could take my mother with me. I didn't just flit off for a night of fun on the town."

"I checked. Their people are trained, too." He had an answer for everything.

"I don't know why you want to do this."

"Agnes convinced me you deserve to have some fun on this vacation. She's happy at the idea of us going out for dinner and dancing."

Didn't he see that Agnes was matchmaking?

And there were her feelings about it. She tried to deny how badly she wanted to throw her arms around him and say yes, yes, yes. She wanted to spend a special evening with him that was outside his bed. It was frightening how badly she wanted to go. It showed how deep she was in this relationship. Too deep. Over-her-head deep.

"I have to consider Agnes's safety first."

"I totally agree. But this is safe. We can call the room every half hour. Or every fifteen minutes, if that will make you feel more comfortable."

"That's not going to be possible," she scoffed.

He turned everything around on her. "Are you afraid to spend an evening alone with me? Without Agnes? Without sex?"

She shivered and hoped he didn't see. "Of course I'm not afraid."

"I think you are," he said softly, almost teasing her, definitely challenging.

He had all the answers. He could get her to do anything he wanted. Because *she* wanted it, too.

"If you're not afraid of an evening with me, and I've

already taken care of making sure that Agnes is looked after, there's no reason to say no."

She didn't know why he was pushing so hard. She was already sleeping with him. What else did he want?

And she asked, "Why?"

"Because I want to dine with you. I want to talk with you. I want to hold you in my arms and dance with you." He paused a long moment, letting that sink in. "Then I want to come back here and make love to you."

Her heart jumped. She didn't know whether he meant to say those exact words. Or if making love and having sex were synonymous. It was just terminology.

But the moment he said it, she knew she'd do it. There was no fighting him or Agnes. Or herself.

She gave him the simple answer, the only answer. "Okay." Then she crossed her arms over her chest and stared him down. "But I don't have a single thing to wear to an event like this."

He grinned, a devilish, wicked, beautiful, sexy grin. "Then we'll have to go shopping."

21

They headed to the shops the next morning.

"Shopping." Agnes clapped her hands delightedly when Rose told her. "I'm so glad you've decided to go to the ball," she said like Cinderella's fairy godmother.

Except that Declan was doing the buying. Rose didn't feel guilty about it. In the face of Agnes's happiness, she couldn't regret anything.

She kept telling herself this was as much for Agnes as it was for her.

Except that she couldn't get the image out of her head, she and Declan dressed to the nines, feasting on gourmet food, and dancing the night away.

Then the inevitable fall when her prince turned back into her boss.

Declan had asked the concierge where they might find a good dress shop, and they'd driven twenty kilometers to a larger town. It boasted a main thoroughfare of handsome shops and had the added benefit of being close to the Ross Errilly Friary, a medieval site on their list to visit.

Ireland surely had malls like they did in the U.S., but this town, with its quaint shops, was better. The mannequins in the windows might be adorned in slightly outdated dresses, but then Rose was slightly outdated herself.

Half an hour later, Agnes and Declan were seated in over-stuffed chairs, a pot of tea and a plate of scones on a table between them. It seemed old-fashioned and decadent to be served so sweetly while the sales lady, somewhere in her sixties with hair styled like a 1940s movie star, brought dress after dress for Rose to try on.

"For a fancy event like the one at Burkefurd Castle, we need something classic." She waved her hand across an array of dresses hanging over her arm.

Declan raised an eyebrow as if to say, *See, we're going to an amazing event.*

Parading in each new dress, she felt like a bride modeling her trousseau for her mother. The groom wasn't supposed to be there.

It was like a fashion show, and the cocktail dresses felt elegant swirling around her legs as she twirled for Declan and Agnes.

This one was sleeveless, tight in the bodice, a belted waist, and a full skirt.

Agnes clapped her hands. As she had with every dress Rose tried on. "That's perfect." Her eyes were aglow. "Emerald green like the Emerald Isle."

Declan slowly shook his head. And Rose had to admit it wasn't quite right. The emerald was beautiful, but the dress resembled something Beaver Cleaver's mom would have worn while vacuuming. All she needed were the pearls.

But the next dress one was exquisite. The sleeveless black velvet flared slightly just below her breasts, the soft folds draping her curves. It was topped by a short jacket of gray and blue that perfectly accented the black velvet.

"Oh my." Agnes was breathless.

The look on Declan's face told her he was dying to see her in it. And dying to strip her out of it, too.

She was terrified to look at the price tag.

"That's lovely," the sales lady said in her high, sweet Irish voice. "It's classic and will never go out of style. But—" she patted another armload of dresses. "—you never know what will turn out to be perfection once it's on. You should try them all. Then make your decision."

Declan agreed with the saleslady, his eyes smoking. "Definitely. We should try the others."

Agnes reached for a scone. "The girl is looking a bit peckish, Declan. She needs a scone and a cup of tea."

"How remiss of me," the saleslady tittered, flustered because she hadn't carried scones into the dressing room. "I'll hang these up and get you a couple of scones right away."

Rose wondered if the woman was worried about crumbs or grease on the dresses, but after a cup of tea and a scone with jam, she wiped her fingers thoroughly. Then she tried on three more dresses, entertaining Agnes while Declan made her turn and twirl and pose before him.

She might fear for the future. She might fear for her heart.

But she loved every moment of her fashion show.

THEY SAT ON THE BALCONY, THE SCENT OF ROSES WAFTING up from the garden. It was Declan's favorite spot. They'd made love after Agnes went to bed, then he'd carried Rose out here, seating her on his lap.

After dinner, they'd ordered hot milk, and Rose and Agnes had swirled their sheep from the abbey until the milk turned chocolaty. Agnes had been enchanted. And even more so when Declan presented them with the assortment of goodies, including more scented soap for Rose's bath. Their delight with their gifts made him happy.

Tonight Rose bathed alone while he'd entertained Agnes with checkers down in the lounge. She talked to everyone who entered, curious about whatever game they chose to play. He hadn't seen her so carefree, so open, so happy in years

The trip had done wonders for her. Then again it was the attention Rose showered on her. Her loving care, her concern, her ability to laugh with Agnes over anything had given the elderly lady a new lease on life.

He'd made the right choice. He would never regret it, no matter what happened between Rose and him. She was the best thing he'd ever done for Agnes.

"You're amazing and gorgeous." He pushed the hair back from her brow, the feel of her skin warm and smooth beneath his fingertips.

She wrapped her arm around his neck. "Thank you for the dresses. You didn't have to buy three."

"I couldn't decide which one I wanted you to wear." He shrugged. "So I had to get them all." She'd been uncomfortable, but he wanted to shower her with gifts. He knew deep in his gut, though Rose had never said anything, that she was a woman unused to gifts. She didn't know luxury. She'd always been a hard worker, giving up many of the things she'd wanted out of life.

A few dresses were the least he could do for her. With them came the promise of more dates back home when she would wear those dresses for him.

This thing between them wasn't over. Not yet.

"They're too extravagant. Where am I going to wear them?"

With any other woman, it would have been assumed he'd

take her out to dinner, to soirees, to the opera or the ballet. But Rose had no expectations.

He gave her a few. "I sometimes attend events. Those dresses will be perfect for any of them."

"Events?" She looked at him like the proverbial deer in the headlights. "What am I supposed to do at an *event*?" The word held terror.

"Usually they're fundraisers. Or business engagements. Or the occasional symphony or show."

In the light falling through the window behind them, her eyes widened. "I'm not equipped for any of those things. I wouldn't even know what to talk about."

He smiled, softly on the inside, bigger on the outside. He had so many things to show her. "At the ballet or the symphony, you don't have to say anything."

"What about intermissions?"

"You'll be with me. You don't have to talk if you don't want to. Not at the dinner parties either, or any events I go to."

There was more fear than shock in her eyes. Her mind had glazed over the fact that he wanted to take her with him and gone straight to wondering what she'd say to his associates. At least she wasn't flat-out refusing.

"Mostly we just eat and drink, wander around and mingle. I'll introduce you, they may ask you a question or two, move on, no big deal."

"What if they ask if I'm sleeping with you?"

He laughed outright, the sound carrying into the night. "No one's going to ask if we're sleeping together." They'd simply assume they were. And he didn't mind. "If they ask what you do, you just say you take care of my Aunt Agnes."

"That's sort of like lying."

He shrugged. "If you feel that way, then tell them your Agnes's caregiver. I guarantee they won't care."

"But if they ask why I'm not taking care of Agnes right at that moment?"

He put his fingers to her lips. "You worry too much."

His business associates wouldn't ask a single question, or even talk to her. The wives, on the other hand, might talk about themselves, or the weather, or the garden, or the trouble they had with the help or the kids.

He made another promise. He was making a lot of them. "If you're uncomfortable, we'll get the hell out. All you have to do is tap my hand and look at me with that same terror in your eyes that I see right now, and we're outta there."

Finally she laughed. "I can't keep up with you. But I love the dresses. And I'm grateful."

At least she didn't ask him why he wanted to do this. Why he was turning an affair into a relationship when he remembered damn well what had happened the last time he'd taken an employee into his bed?

He didn't have an answer. At least not one he wanted to examine.

THEIR DAYS PASSED WITH TOURING AND EATING AND having fun with Agnes. And the evenings were spent making love with Declan.

She couldn't get over the three dresses. Or the fact that he wanted to take her to "events." It was probably just talk, so she didn't worry. She couldn't imagine he'd follow through when they got home.

The night of the dinner dance arrived. Rose had spent the last two hours getting ready, a shower, washing her hair, applying makeup, slipping into the black velvet dress.

When Declan, seated on the couch with Agnes, ate her up

with his gaze, Rose felt utterly beautiful like never before in her life.

He was snazzy in a dark suit he'd brought with him, as if he'd expected to escort Agnes to a fancy dinner some night.

The woman who showed up at the door was little more than a girl, twenty at most. She introduced herself. "Hallo, I'm Orla." Then she looked past Rose. "I'm here for Agnes."

From the sofa, Agnes waved exuberantly. "It's so good to meet you, dear. Come and sit down. Do you know how to play Skip-Bo?"

The girl skipped into the room and threw herself on the sofa. "I've never heard of it. But I can learn. Surely you can teach me. "

Agnes giggled. "Oh yes, I can teach you."

She would never remember the rules of the card game, but she'd make them up as she went along. And she'd have Orla wrapped around her little finger.

The girl was sweet, and her excitement made Rose feel a little better.

"Declan," she said. "Would you remind Agnes about the Skip-Bo rules while I have a little talk with Orla?"

Orla immediately stood, rushing to Rose's side.

"There's just a few things I need to tell you." She led Orla into the bedroom where she went over an exhaustive list, the main item being that she should never leave Agnes alone until she was in bed. "Keep the baby monitor right by your side and go in at the first sound. Because Agnes won't wait."

Nodding eagerly, Orla repeated every instruction Rose gave her.

Ten minutes later, after another check of her hair and makeup, Rose and Declan made their way downstairs to the party.

In the elevator, he leaned close, his warm breath against her ear, exciting her even before the evening started.

"You're delectable in that dress. I don't think I've ever seen your knees before." He chuckled softly, a burst of warmth against her hair sending a shiver through her. "Except when you're naked in my bed."

Despite being alone in the elevator, she blushed.

The dinner was in the castle's ballroom. It had been decked out with fairy lights and the rugs removed to make a dance floor. The tall French doors overlooked the patio which had been lit with torches and heaters for those who wanted to dance outside. The band softly played standards and ballads from the 1940s and 1950s, appropriate for the general age group.

Once the waiter had seated them, taken their drink orders, and whisked away, she leaned close. "These people might be older than us, but I bet they can outdance us."

There were elegant couples and groups, the men in tuxes, the women in gorgeous floor-length gowns.

Declan laughed. She loved how much more often he laughed now.

"I have to admit all I can do is shuffle."

She grinned. "Me, too."

He kissed her swiftly, deliciously on the lips.

The table was intimate, with only their place settings, a candle, and a vase of flowers. Most of the tables were full, couples, foursomes, and some groups of six, eight, or ten. It was a festive affair, the tablecloths in pastel colors with matching napkins, crystal stemware, bone china, and real silverware. She could see her reflection in the knife.

As inappropriate as it might be, she set her phone by her place setting. It was on vibrate, but she'd hear the buzz if Orla called her.

"This was the great hall where they used to have all the parties and dinners and banquets." Then he added when she gave him a look, "I did some reading about the castle."

"Are you going to give me the whole history?"

He laughed. God, yes, she loved his laugh. "You have to do your own reading."

The waiter returned with their drinks and to tell them about the three-course prix fixe menu. She was quick to pick out the lobster bisque to start, rack of lamb, and bread pudding with whiskey-butterscotch sauce for dessert.

Declan ordered something different for every course.

When the waiter was gone, he said, "Now we can share."

"My fork might accidentally stab your hand if you try to take my lamb."

He chuckled. "Sleight-of-hand. You might not even see me until it's too late."

That could have been a metaphor for their relationship. He'd tiptoed into her heart before she'd noticed. His sweetness and caring for Agnes, his loyalty to his parents, his hidden depths of humor and fun, things she'd never expected about him. And then there was his sexy playful nature that came out in the bedroom.

It was terrifying how easily she fell under his spell. And it could be terribly painful in the end.

"All right." She tried to be smooth, to play along despite the fears rolling around inside her. "I suppose I'll have to knuckle under and let you have just one bite of my lamb."

Declan leaned close, which wasn't hard with the small size of the table. "Only one bite? What if I give you more than one bite of mine?" Oh yes, they were talking about more than a bite of roast beef or lamb.

She remembered her bucket list. She wanted to fall in love. But she hadn't qualified it, and now there were so many questions. Did that love have to last? Did it have to be returned? Did she need to hear the words?

She was already falling, and she feared the landing would be very hard.

She could stop it now. She could protect herself. She wouldn't come out unscathed, but maybe it would hurt a lot less.

But oh God, she didn't want to stop. She wanted him. She wanted to savor every moment. Maybe she was stupid, but she just couldn't let go, not yet, even if this thing between them only lasted until they flew home.

She just had to make sure she didn't lose Agnes in the process.

She dropped her voice to a sexy note. "What if I like yours so much better that I just took it all?"

His smile was wickedly delicious. "I'd have to succumb and let you have every bite you wanted. But once you're done, I'll need to have all of yours. And I'm going to savor every taste."

The banter was sexy and decadent. When you're young, you somehow think that sex is only for the young. And when you're middle-aged and old enough to have your very own AARP card, you tell yourself that sex doesn't matter anymore.

But the nights with Declan had shown her how very much it mattered, and how very good it could be.

And she needed more.

"Are we talking about food?" She gave him a long, hot look. "Or sex?" she ended very softly.

"Darling." He kissed her breathless. "We're talking about both. We must indulge all our senses. First, there's champagne." He raised his glass to toast her.

The taste was clean and sparkling, the bubbles going to her head. "Are you trying to get me drunk?"

"Believe me, I want you well aware of every moment while I ravish you."

She laughed. She was drunk, but it wasn't champagne. It was his closeness, his outdoorsy, sexy male scent, and the way he looked at her, as if he could eat her up. As if she were better than roast beef or a sweet dessert. As if she were a delicacy he wanted to savor for hours.

The table might have gone up in smoke if their waiter hadn't arrived with their soup. He gave her phone one quick disapproving glance, but said nothing. She wanted to explain, but with a look from Declan, she decided she didn't need to explain.

"Oh my God." She moaned after her first spoon of lobster bisque. Dipping another spoonful, she held it over her palm and offered it to him. His fingers were a light stroke along the back of her hand, a sensual touch that made her pulse race. His gaze flared hot as he sipped from the spoon, as if he were tasting her rather than the bisque.

What more could a middle-aged woman want than a sexy man eating out of her hand? What more could *any* woman want than this moment with Declan?

"That tastes as good as you do," he murmured.

She blushed despite everything they'd done together.

"Now you've got to taste mine." He held out a spoon of asparagus soup.

She closed her eyes, tipped her chin up, breathed deeply after she swallowed. "Oh my. That is so good." Then she looked at him, her lips parted as if she were waiting for more.

"You're such a tease," he said softly.

She loved teasing him. She loved the sounds he made when she kissed him, touched him, licked him.

Who would have thought Declan Delaney was such a sensual man?

❧ 22 ❧

Rose melted beneath Declan's hot gaze and looked away before she spontaneously combusted. It was only then she realized people were watching.

He followed her glance. "We're not exactly with the younger generation." His voice dipped. "And you're shocking them."

"Me?" She put a hand to her chest. "All I did was enjoy your soup."

"It was the way you enjoyed it. With such relish, tipping your chin so everyone could see the beautiful column of your throat." He leaned in, lowering his voice. "Most of the patrons here will need to ravish their wives once they get back to the rooms."

"You do love that word *ravish*. It's old-fashioned."

"I'm an old-fashioned guy."

It was as if eating a meal had turned into foreplay.

They fed each other morsels of meat, her lamb, his roast beef. He cleaned away a drop of gravy from her lip with his thumb. She lost herself in his dark gaze, his eyes a seductive blaze, undressing her as if he wanted her for his main course.

He was as mouthwatering as his beef. And he encouraged her to chew the rest of the meat off her rack of lamb. "Other people are doing it."

"That doesn't mean I should."

But there was a lot meat she couldn't get with her knife and fork. And an elegantly dressed lady delicately held a chop between the thumb and forefinger of each hand.

"You can't waste anything," Declan cajoled.

"I can take it in a doggy bag."

He chuckled. "You're afraid people will point at you."

She shook her head, trying to appear prim. "We're not at a rib joint."

But she took up the challenge when she felt the lick of the hot, hungry look in his eyes.

Holding a chop, she chewed gingerly, trying to preserve her lipstick. Declan sat back to watch her, thoughts of the sensual things he planned to do to her running through his head. Oh yes, she could see his dirty mind working.

She was glad for the show she was giving him, as if it were a prelude to a striptease. When she was done with the last chop, he took her hand before she could reach for her napkin and licked her thumb and forefinger clean, first one hand, then the other. It was so blatantly sexual. As if he were staking a claim for everyone to see, advertising exactly what he'd do to her later tonight. Heat rose off him in waves.

She didn't look at anyone in the room. She didn't want the fire to die down.

She wanted to relish every moment as if it were the last she'd ever have.

SHE WAS BEAUTIFUL. AND DESPITE THE THINGS SHE allowed herself to do with him, she was shy, as if it were all new to her. He enjoyed offering her delights she'd never dreamed of.

Over dessert, he stole bites of her bread pudding while she laughed and slapped at him playfully. He teased her with tastes of his lemon pudding cake.

Had he ever felt like this before? He wasn't a playful man, but he wanted to play with her. He was a man for whom work was everything, and yet he gave up hours of work to spend time with her. He was not a man who thought about the future with a woman—at least not since his wife left—yet he wondered what a future with Rose would be like.

"I'm pretty sure I like your bread pudding better than my pudding cake." He stole another bite, making her laugh, though he had to admit his cake was good.

"If I had a fork instead of a spoon, I'd have to stab your hand."

"Didn't you threaten that when I wanted some of your lamb?"

She moved her bowl and almost turned her back as she ate, warding him off.

He met a lot of people in his daily dealings, many of them beautiful women. He met them at social functions he felt obligated to attend. It was part of what he did as a businessman, another place where deals were made. But no one ever seemed truly real. Not as real as Rose.

"How about I switch desserts with you?"

When she laughed, her laughter was genuine, a part of her.

Except for his family and Agnes, he wasn't around people who knew what real laughter was.

Maybe he was just as guilty as them, wearing the face he was supposed to, the consummate businessman looking for the next opportunity.

"Order your own," she told him.

He leaned in, smiling against her hair, breathing her in. "I'd rather con you into giving me yours."

"So that's it, you're just a con man." There was such a light in her eyes as she turned to him, such a sweetness.

But she made him think. Was he a con man? There was always an angle, always the element of working things to his advantage.

Had he been like that with his wife? He'd been her boss first. But had he ever truly been himself? He'd never thought of it before, that maybe he hadn't given everything he could.

"If I could con you into my bed," he whispered, "you know I would."

She snorted softly. "You already have."

"Was that a con?" he asked with a rumble in his belly.

She was serious a moment before a sweet smile curved her lips again. "If anything, I conned you, by falling into your lap and crying my eyes out."

Yet he answered seriously. "Nothing was ever a con between us."

The waiter took their empty dessert bowls and returned a couple of minutes later with two Irish coffees.

She sipped. "That's deliciously decadent."

Declan couldn't help himself. "Being with you is deliciously decadent."

She blushed, and he wanted nothing more than to take her back up to their room and make sweet, perfect love to her.

But just as much, he wanted to hold her in his arms as they danced, feel her body against his as they swayed with the music.

Yes, she was different, what he felt was different.

And he didn't want it to end.

DANCING WITH DECLAN WAS LIKE FLOATING ON A CLOUD, his arms around her warm and strong.

Declan Delaney was so much more than his money. Money was just a way to take care of Agnes, to make his parents' lives easier. He wasn't dictatorial. He was decisive. He wasn't heartless. He was just guarded after his wife left him. He wasn't uncaring. He just hid his feelings behind a wall.

The music was sweet and slow, a tune she recognized but whose name she couldn't remember. She closed her eyes and swayed against him to the song's rhythm, savoring the strength of him, the hardness of his muscles, the sweetness of his arms around her. This was what she'd come all the way to Ireland to find, the bliss of being in Declan's arms.

Couples danced around them, several who'd obviously danced together for years, their steps smooth, their feet gliding across the dance floor in perfect tune with each other's moves.

But she treasured this, the slow slide of Declan's body against hers as he swayed.

It was like making love.

The tune changed, the tempo picked up, and couples switched to a dance like something out of the old movie, *Grease*. Rose, who had no idea of the steps, danced around like she was good at it, grabbing Declan's hands and pulling him into her rhythm. She lost her breath, collapsing against him, and it was almost as sweet as the slow dance. The music changed again, and they danced until she felt drunk on his closeness.

Finally they fell into their seats, Rose grabbing her water-glass and guzzling. Laughing, she slouched in her chair. "I'm getting too old for this."

"You're not too old for anything."

She felt the heat of his thoughts, of the things he'd do to her later tonight, the heat of her own desire.

There had never been a more perfect night in her life.

Then she saw her phone screen.

And her perfect night dissolved into a nightmare.

"I'M SO SORRY, SIR, SO SORRY." ORLA WAS WRINGING HER hands as they entered the suite. "She's in the bedroom."

Rose rushed to Agnes, her heart beating wildly.

She heard Orla explaining to Declan. "We've called the doctor. She moved so fast. I heard a rustle on the monitor, but before I got into the room, she was already out of bed."

Declan fired off questions. Had she done this, had she done that, why didn't she do this?

The bedside lamp illuminated Agnes's pale face. In the light, Rose made out the small bandage on her head, blood soaking through it.

She felt sick. Crazy. Scared. Guilty. She should never have left Agnes alone.

"How are you doing?"

Though Agnes's eyes were closed, she wasn't asleep, her breathing edgy rather than rhythmic and smooth. "I'm fine, dear." She touched her head. "I'm used to banging my noggin."

"You were supposed to bounce." Rose didn't peel back the bandage. The doctor was on his way, and she'd leave it for him. "Do you have a headache?"

Agnes shook her head. "No. I'm fine. I'm just a silly sausage."

"You most certainly are." But Rose couldn't smile.

In the quiet, she heard Orla's voice. "The way she fell, I

think she tripped over her walker. I don't think she even tried to use it."

Declan's answer was an angry rumble, though Rose couldn't make out the words.

"I'm glad you're okay." Though she wasn't as assured as Agnes seemed to be. "You didn't use your walker?"

"Of course I did. I just don't know what happened." Agnes opened her eyes. "It was all so fast." She lowered her voice. "I had to go and I couldn't wait."

It wouldn't do any good to remind Agnes that she absolutely needed to wait. Or that she at least needed to grab her walker. "You scared Orla."

Agnes sighed. "That poor girl. I had to go and I didn't want to bother her."

"That's what she's here for. So you can bother her."

But Agnes was of a different generation whose paramount rule was never to be a bother to anyone.

This incident didn't bode well for the new caregivers Declan wanted to bring in for Rose's breaks. Agnes would be just like this, not wanting to bother them.

"Since you have a crack on your head, the doctor needs to look at you."

"Do we really?" Agnes's voice took on a whiny edge.

"Yes, we do," Rose said sternly.

She'd made a huge mistake leaving Agnes. But she wouldn't let it happen again.

THE DOCTOR MADE A HOUSE CALL FROM THE VILLAGE. Since the hotel had provided the temporary caregiver, they'd insisted on doing whatever they could, even paying the doctor's bill.

After his first few minutes of fear, frustration, and anger, Declan realized the accident hadn't been Orla's fault. Agnes simply forgot. She thought she could do anything, maybe even that she was invincible. Orla left when the doctor arrived, still wringing her hands, still apologizing, tears still blurring her eyes even though Declan told her she wasn't to blame.

A gray-haired gentleman with a soft voice and a pleasant bedside manner, the first thing the doctor asked was, "How are you feeling, dear?"

"I'm in good shape for the shape I'm in," Agnes quipped, bringing a smile to his craggy features. They all had a laugh. Except Rose.

"Let's just look at you."

He asked her questions, her name, her age, her birthday, and so on, all to make sure she wasn't disoriented. Agnes answered everything. Then he poked and prodded, checked her from her shoulders down to her toes. He made her sit up, helped her stand, had her take a few steps. Then he sat her on the edge of the bed and combed through her hair, testing her scalp.

"Now let's see that cut."

Agnes winced as he removed the bandage. "Good, you've stopped bleeding." Opening his bag, he cleaned the wound, testing it as he worked. "You don't even need stitches."

"Oh goody. I don't like stitches."

Declan liked the way the doctor talked to Agnes, not to them, as if she was capable of answering everything herself.

"Head wounds bleed a lot, so it can be scary. But luckily your cut is very minor." He ended with a butterfly bandage over the injury.

Declan wasn't exactly sure how Agnes had managed to cut her forehead, on the bedside table or the bed itself. It was hard to say. There were drops of blood on both.

The doctor stood. "I don't feel that anything's broken."

He smoothed a hand over Agnes's forehead. "And there's no concussion."

It was then that Rose finally spoke, her voice sharp. "Can you really know that? Shouldn't we take her to the hospital, do an X-ray or a CAT scan?"

Still looking at Agnes, the doctor said, "That's not necessary. It's just a bump on your head. You might have some bruising, but it's nothing more than a flesh wound." He smiled. "Our skin isn't as resilient as we get older."

"But Doctor," Rose insisted. "We're in a foreign country. We really want to make sure."

Declan moved to her side to put his arm around her, but she flinched away.

"Agnes is fine," he told her. "Like the doctor said, it's just a bump."

She turned on him, her teeth gritted. "At home, we would have put her in the hospital overnight."

"I don't want to go to the hospital, Rose."

Rose tipped her head at Agnes. And Declan realized she'd called Rose by her name instead of *dear*.

The doctor smiled, unbothered by the fact that his judgement had been called into question. "I've had a bit of experience, and I assure you this is very minor. But—" He shook his finger at Agnes. "You need to wait for someone to help before you go running around in the night. And you need to use your walker."

"I remembered it," Agnes said emphatically.

The doctor gave her a knowing look. "No getting out of bed in the middle of the night all by yourself, do you hear?" He shot her a mock glare.

"Of course not, Doctor," Agnes said with absolute seriousness.

He tweaked her nose. "After all, we're not spring chickens anymore, are we?"

"Speak for yourself," Agnes huffed, a telltale twinkle in her eye.

She would recover. Just like all as the other times she'd fallen, gone to the hospital, had the X-rays and the CAT scans, only to find there was nothing more than a few bruises and cuts or scrapes.

Like Agnes said, she bounced.

Rose was an entirely different matter. She'd hovered by Agnes's bedside while the doctor checked his patient, a slightly manic look glazing her eyes, one that had been growing since the moment she saw the missed call on her phone. Her face had turned bloodless as she feared the worst.

She felt guilty for every moment with him that she'd now decided had been stolen from Agnes.

It wasn't even a crazy notion. While she was gone, the very thing she feared had happened.

He understood why she hadn't brought in other caregivers to look after Agnes while she took a break. Rose didn't trust anyone else to take care of Agnes.

And now he was afraid she wouldn't even trust herself.

ROSE STILL FELT SICK AFTER THE DOCTOR LEFT, NOT JUST her stomach but her whole body. So many things could have happened. Agnes could have had a concussion. She might have broken her hip, or her arm or her wrist or twisted her ankle.

All the things that could gone wrong roiled in her belly like a basket of writhing snakes.

God. All those nights with Declan, on the balcony, in his bathtub, in his bed. Eating and dancing away like nothing could happen, like she didn't have responsibilities.

And Agnes had fallen.

As much as she'd enjoyed the things she'd done with Declan, she absolutely could not risk Agnes again. Besides, the relationship was going to end anyway. Better to end it now before there was any more damage.

Declan was looking at her, willing her to meet his gaze. Rose didn't.

"Here, Agnes, let me help you," she said. "Do you need the bathroom before we get you back in bed?"

Was she really okay? Was the doctor right? Rose would have felt so much better with at least an X-ray. But she'd been overruled.

"That would be good, dear."

She helped Agnes to the bathroom, then got her settled once more.

Declan moved to the other side of the bed, leaning over Agnes. "I'm glad you're all right. You scared us."

She flapped a hand at him. "It was a lot of bother about nothing."

He kissed her forehead and whispered, "Goodnight."

Then he turned to Rose. "I'd like to talk to you."

She couldn't talk. She couldn't even look at Declan. She knew what he'd say, that it was nothing serious, thank goodness, that there was no reason she couldn't climb into his bed and do all the things he'd promised.

But she couldn't. She wouldn't.

"Agnes needs to sleep. We can talk in the morning."

She would never forgive herself if anything else happened to Agnes.

❧ 23 ❧

The hotel manager stopped by the next morning, apologetic and wanting to know how Agnes was doing. Orla dropped in as well, still tearful and sorry. Declan assured them both that Agnes was fine.

But Rose and Declan didn't talk in the morning. They didn't talk over the next few days.

Rose made sure they weren't alone to talk.

A bruise purpled Agnes's forehead, but they toured the Irish countryside, ate in pubs or fancy lunchrooms or bought sandwiches for a picnic. They took walks and visited gardens and strolled through castle ruins or abbeys or churches or woodlands. They used the castle pool, too, doing exercises while Declan swam.

The weather continued to be amazing. Rose's mother must have been looking down from above, keeping the rain mostly at bay. Dark clouds sometimes scudded across the sky, dumped a few minutes of rain, but then everything cleared up, and on they went with their holiday.

In the evenings, they played games in the lounge.

"I'm fine, dear. You must have your bath. I know how much you love them." Agnes was insistent.

Rose couldn't enjoy even that. She couldn't risk Declan invading her space, climbing in with her, seducing her. What if something happened?

Declan would feel guilty, too, if it did.

There were no more champagne nights on the balcony. No more decadent dinners. No more bouts in his bed. After she helped Agnes, Rose opened her e-reader. She didn't go out to the sitting room, afraid Declan might ask her to stay, afraid she might say yes.

Until Agnes muttered in the dark one night, "You're rustling too much, dear. Do you think you could read in the sitting room? I just can't get to sleep."

Rose hadn't been rustling, except to soundlessly swipe a page. She wondered if Agnes was matchmaking again. As if nothing had happened.

On the other hand, it was time to have it out with Declan, tell him to stop touching her at every opportunity, a hand on her elbow, his fingertips at the base of her spine, tucking her hair behind her ear. He drove her crazy. It had to stop. She hadn't signed on to be a playmate. She'd been hired as Agnes's caregiver.

She'd forgotten her duty for a little while. But Agnes's accident reminded her.

Besides, the affair was destined to end anyway.

"All right. But promise to call out if you need me." In the dim light of the e-reader, she saw Agnes flap her hand.

"I'm a little tired of being reminded all the time." Her tone was peevish.

"I'm not leaving until you promise."

She let out an annoyed sigh. "I promise."

In her pajamas, though they covered everything, Rose debated changing into her clothes. The thick robe won and she pulled it on. She wouldn't get within a mile of him anyway.

Baby monitor in hand, she closed the door softly behind her.

And there he was, out on the balcony, a glass of whiskey on the table beside him, a champagne flute next to it as if he'd been waiting for her.

As if he and Agnes had schemed.

Obviously having heard the door close, Declan turned before she had a chance to retreat.

She was trapped. They'd have it out over champagne. She should have done this before.

Stepping through the French doors, she took the chair beside him, and asked even before she touched the champagne, "Did you and Agnes plan this?"

"Plan what?" His tone was irritatingly mild.

She waved at the champagne. "This friendly drink. How did you know I'd come out here?"

"I pour a glass of champagne for you every night. And when you don't come, I pour it down the drain."

Guilt washed through her. "Don't try to make me feel guilty."

He laughed softly. "You're doing a very good job of it on your own."

He had a point. She was so very good at guilt trips. But she wasn't giving in. "I'm not feeling guilty," she lied. "I'm making sure Agnes is safe."

"But you're afraid to be alone with me in case I try to lure you into my bed." The light of the moon in his eyes made him so enticing. "And you're afraid you'll say yes."

They needed to have it out so he'd stop saying things like that. "I know Agnes's fall was an accident. But it made me realize that what was happening between you and I was becoming excessive. I should never have agreed to a night as if we were dating. This is just sex."

He grinned wickedly. "So that means if we don't go out to dinner or dancing or dating, we can still have sex."

He thought it was a joke, damn him. "That isn't what I meant."

She'd said yes to dinner and dancing and the dresses because she was becoming obsessed with him. She'd started believing things could actually be more than "just sex." She wanted to make love every night, wake up in his arms in the morning, go to his events, hang on his arm, steep herself in his scent.

But her duty was to Agnes. She could do all the things for Agnes that she'd never done for her mother. She could take her places, laugh with her, make sure Agnes enjoyed every moment she had left.

"That part of our relationship is over," she said without a quiver of anguish or desire. At least not in her voice.

"What if I don't want it to be over?"

She couldn't answer the question directly, because, oh God, how his words made her heart beat faster. "What happened to Agnes was a wake-up call for both of us." She shrugged, trying to make it nonchalant. "We had a good time. But we both know this won't last forever, especially once we get home. It's better to be done with it now and get back to making Agnes our priority."

He looked at her until her bones started to melt and her belly quaked. Then he trailed a finger along the seam of her lips and cupped her cheek. She tried not to jerk back, not to show the effect his touch had on her. She couldn't let him know what he did to her.

"It doesn't have to be over now." His voice was anything but mild. "And not when we're home either."

She wanted to ask if that meant they'd have a real relationship, or if they'd be lovers in secret. If he would be hers for a few weeks until he got tired of her or a pretty young thing caught his eye. But she was afraid of the answer.

Because they didn't have forever.

Maybe if Agnes hadn't fallen, she could have gone on deluding herself. But she'd had all these nights to dream, and she wanted far more than he did. Her emotions were too involved. If she didn't stop, she was going to fall for him irrevocably.

And when it ended, she wasn't sure she'd be able to stay with Agnes. Like a sixteen-year-old with her first crush, she would die inside seeing him every day and knowing he was out of her reach.

It had to be cut off now. No matter how he tried to convince her.

HE WAS LOSING HER. EVERY MOMENT WALKED HER FURTHER away from him. She was too full of guilt, but there was no way he could make her see that. People immersed in their own guilt couldn't see there wasn't always a cause and effect.

But he had to try because... Just because.

"Agnes didn't fall because we took a night off."

"I know." She answered too quickly, the bite in her words filling the air.

"She could have had a fall back home."

She'd been staring into the garden, but she turned her head. "She's not going to have a fall. I'm with her. I'll make sure she's safe."

He had an idea that she would find achingly hard. "Did your mother ever have a fall?"

She fixed him with a glare that could have flayed flesh from his bones, and he saw the truth no matter what she said.

"Only a couple of times." Her teeth clamped together. She wore the guilt of those falls like a hair shirt. And she was trying to make up for it with Agnes.

"Then you know it can't be helped. Sometimes accidents happen. They move one way while you're moving the other, so fast you can't catch them."

The grinding of her teeth was so loud, she could have been chewing on rocks. "My mother was an entirely different situation." Her words came out fast, as if she were speaking at double the speed. "She had Alzheimer's. But Agnes listens to me. She knows not to get out of bed."

He wondered if it was right to point out the obvious, that she'd told Agnes to wait for Orla and Agnes hadn't. That fact could make Rose dig in her heels. But it could also make her think, try to justify, then eventually come back to reality, instead of the horror she'd created in her head.

"If she listens to you and stays in bed, there's no reason why you and I can't..." He paused, pondering the best words. "There's no reason we can't keep on the way we were. We have the monitor. As soon as you hear her, you can go to her like you did before."

She stared at him, her eyes dark, unreadable.

He was digging a deeper hole moment by moment, but he said the only thing he had left. "Come to bed with me." He held out his hand. "We need each other tonight."

Still that implacable, immovable, impenetrable stare. What was she thinking?

She cut him in half when she said, "It's too late for that."

Then she walked out on him.

A GENTLE SNORE PUFFED FROM AGNES'S LIPS.

Rose fluffed her pillow, tucked it under her head, tried to sleep.

But who could sleep after that?

She'd wanted to say yes so badly. She wanted to climb onto his lap, wrap her arms around him, kiss him deep and long and hard until he put his hands under her robe and took her right there.

She wanted any crumb he offered.

It was pathetic. It was dangerous. It was out of the question.

She opened her eyes, stared at Agnes in her bed. Agnes was all she needed. Agnes was a way to make up for all the things she'd done wrong with her mother. Agnes was her redemption.

She should never have climbed into Declan's bed. She should never have started that bucket list.

At home, it would be so much easier to keep him at arm's length. Then he'd find someone else to invite into his bed. And forget about her.

She couldn't care about that.

"OH MY." AGNES'S VOICE WAS WISTFUL AND SAD. "DON'T you just hate the end of a trip?"

"Yeah. I hate the end of a trip." Declan's voice rumbled through the car.

"Can we drive through Cong to see the statue one more time?"

Declan laughed softly. "Yes, we can see the statue one more time."

Rose loved his laugh. She'd had the best moments of her life in Ireland, ones she would never forget. But like all holidays, you had to go back to your life, and everything became just a memory and photos on your phone.

Agnes had to get out. "Can you take my picture, please?"

It was too much trouble to get the walker out of the trunk for a quick photo, so Declan helped her get in position by the statue and stepped away. Rose took the picture.

Agnes held out her hand to Declan. "One with you, too."

As Rose snapped the photo, her heart felt like splinters in her chest.

"Would you like me to take one with you in it?" The British voice surprised her. She turned to find a petite lady standing beside her, an umbrella hooked over her arm. Once, she might have been over five feet, but now she was of an age where she barely reached Rose's shoulder.

"Yes, please, take a picture. Thank you," Agnes called.

Rose handed over her phone. "Thank you so much."

She would have stood on Agnes's other side, but somehow Declan moved between them, his arm around her.

It felt so good, so warm, so comforting.

It was a lie.

They smiled, and Rose feared her face would crack.

The lady seemed to skip over. "Such a wonderful family. It's not often you see the kids take Mom on a trip like this."

Rose opened her mouth to say they weren't a family at all, that they never would be.

But Agnes wrapped her arms around their waists, hugging them as the lady tapped the phone again for a close up.

"They're the best." Agnes beamed at the little woman. They could have been twins.

"Thank you." Rose took her phone, and Agnes waved as they helped her back in the car.

It wasn't the first time they'd been mistaken for a family.

It wasn't the first time Rose wished they could be that family.

But they weren't.

They made it to Dublin in time for tea. Their flight out was tomorrow. They had one more evening to enjoy, but it poured with rain, as if Dublin were punishing them for leaving.

They ate in the hotel. There hadn't been an available suite for this last night so they had two separate rooms. Rose was glad. She had to break from Declan, from the beautiful sight of him, from how badly she wanted to throw herself at him.

The day finally over, she settled, thinking Agnes had fallen asleep, when words flowed across the darkened room. "You're in love with him, aren't you?"

Rose felt the mattress give way beneath her as she fell down, down, down. Like Alice falling into the rabbit hole. She spoke before she hit bottom. "No, Agnes. I'm too old to fall in love again."

"You're never too old, dear. If I'd met a man after Marvin died, I would've fallen in love again. I just didn't meet that man. But you met Declan."

"Agnes, go to sleep. We have to get up early in the morning."

Agnes sighed. "You might not be able to admit it to me, but you should at least admit it to yourself." She was silent long enough for Rose to think she'd truly fallen asleep. Until she added, very softly, even for Agnes who was never very soft, "You just have to decide what you want to do about it, dear."

❧ 24 ❧

He wished they had more time.

They were up early to check out and get to the airport, but from the moment Declan woke, a sense of heaviness lay on him. He couldn't remember feeling this same loss at the end of a vacation, but then he hadn't been on holiday since his divorce. Vacations were something you did with a partner or a friend or family.

In the first-class class lounge, they were served mimosas and a variety of treats, having arrived far earlier than their flight was due to board.

"I'm old," Agnes had said. "I don't want to feel rushed."

They all agreed it was a good idea not to rush Agnes.

Beside him, she stood up. "Since we're going to be on the plane all day, I'd like to stretch my legs."

Rose stood also. "That's a good idea."

Agnes waved her hand. "No, no, you look after our carry-ons, dear. Declan will take me."

He was in for it now. Agnes wanted a private conversation, and she wasn't subtle. But he did her bidding.

"It will be like our strolls through the castle garden," he

reminded her. And reminded himself about his nights with Rose, in the big tub, on the balcony, in his bed.

He missed those nights. Back home, they would haunt him.

The concourse was crowded with business people, tourists on their way back home, backpackers, traveling families. But Declan took his time with Agnes. He had the fleeting thought that the luxury of being old was that you didn't have to rush anymore, that life could be enjoyed at a slower pace.

"Thank you, Declan." Agnes patted his hand.

"You're welcome. But for what?"

"For this wonderful holiday. For making Rose so happy."

There was the reason for this little stroll. "You don't have to thank me."

Agnes took the reins of the conversation. "I'm sorry I ruined everything by having that silly fall."

"We were scared." He squeezed her age-spotted hand, her skin paper-thin. "But you're fine. It was just a bump, and you'll heal." He gently touched the bandage on her forehead, a yellowing bruise spreading out from beneath it. "It wasn't even a blip in our vacation. We did all the things we wanted, right?" He wanted to get her off whatever track she was headed along.

"I'm fine," she assured him. "But it ruined things between you and Rose."

The end had been inevitable. He just wasn't ready for it. "It's all good, Agnes. Rose and I are friends."

She looked up at him, her gaze too knowing. "You're not fine. You're falling in love with her. Then I go and fall and suddenly it all ends."

He spluttered trying to get his words out. "I'm not falling in love." And while he denied being in love, he wouldn't denigrate what they'd done. It was better not to refer to it at all.

"We're friends, Agnes. And we'll be good friends when we get home."

"I have eyes, my dear boy. Rose makes you laugh. You were a different person while you were with her here in Ireland."

He sighed. And he denied. "I'm on vacation, Agnes. Of course I laugh more. We're all enjoying ourselves."

She stopped and shook her crooked finger. "That's my point. You weren't on vacation. You were going to work. But Rose changed you."

He still wanted to deny, yet it was becoming harder. "I gave up some of my work time to drive you around." But that made it sound like he was blaming Agnes. "Not that I minded. It was my pleasure. But that's all it was."

"You're making excuses."

He stopped, trying to sidetrack her. "You must be getting tired. Should we rest?"

Rushing passengers cut a path around them as if they were the eye of the storm.

"You're changing the subject."

"We didn't have a subject."

"All right, let's sit." She turned, cutting people off as she headed to a couple of empty seats.

When they were settled, she started in on him again. "This holiday has made me realize that you work too much. How can you enjoy life when you're working all the time?"

He looked at his watch. "We should head back. We don't want to rush to the gate."

But tenacious was Agnes's middle name. "I don't want you to be a lonely old man when you get to be my age, with no children in the family who are willing to take care of you."

He grinned, again trying for a little redirection. "I'll hire a sweet young thing like Rose to take care of me."

Agnes ignored his attempt at humor. "But you could have

243

Rose now. She made you happy for a little while. And she can make you happy all the time."

He didn't want to think about being happy with Rose. He didn't want to admit how lighthearted he'd felt. As if he were a different man, not himself at all, maybe a younger man. Or just young at heart.

"I'm happy. My work is satisfying. I attend events and functions with people all the time. You might not realize this, but I'm rarely alone."

"You might not be alone, but you're lonely. They're acquaintances. You can't even call them friends."

Her vehemence stunned him. "You don't know anything about my life when I'm at work."

"I know you haven't been the same since your divorce."

"It has nothing to do with my divorce. I'm fine." His words came out sharper than he intended.

"I want you to be more than fine. I want you to be happy."

"Define happy," he snapped before he thought better of it.

She defined it for him. "Happiness is the way you were with Rose. Laughing. Buying her dresses. Playing bingo with her."

Why did her words hurt? "Bingo was for you."

"You played with both of us. And you had fun. She made you happy." Her face collapsed into a frown. "But I had my fall, and you stopped laughing, you stopped smiling. I feel terrible for that."

The harshness drained out of him. He picked up Agnes's hand, stroked the papery skin. "Nothing is your fault. Accidents happens. But you're fine. Rose is fine. I'm fine. We're all fine."

She squeezed his hand lightly, and her eyes turned misty with tears that didn't fall. "I want you to be together. You're meant for each other. I really thought it was going to happen."

He rubbed her hand. "I know that's what you want, sweetheart. But this isn't a fairytale romance novel. People don't fall in love because you want them to."

She blinked once. "Can you tell me you don't feel something for her, Declan? I saw the way you looked at her."

He couldn't lie to her. Even if he could lie to himself. "I care about her. But that doesn't mean I'm in love with her or that we'll grow old together. As much as I'd like to do that for you, I can't."

She sighed with all the sorrow a childless, eighty-seven-year-old widow could feel. "I'm so sorry for you, my dear boy."

"That doesn't mean Rose and I won't be here for you. We'll always try to keep you happy."

Yes," she said so softly he almost didn't hear. "I'll be happy. But neither of you will be."

THEY'D RETURNED FROM IRELAND THREE WEEKS AGO.

Rose told herself they were getting back to normal. It was almost as if those idyllic days with Declan had never taken place. Except for the times her body ached for him late at night, when she couldn't fight off the memories. Maybe that's why they called it the witching hour.

Otherwise, she was fine. She and Agnes had their routines. They played games, they went shopping, strolled the Rose Garden, took long walks, at least as long as Agnes could handle. They cleaned up the weeds at Rose's house that had sprouted in their absence. They spent a lovely day at the Filoli estate out in Woodside, walking among the flowers and drinking tea. They'd visited the Legion of Honor in San Francisco to see all the statues and masters' paintings.

And Rose continued her work in Declan's garden. Gardening was a lifetime vocation.

Today, however, was too hot for Agnes, and while she napped, Rose found a weed patch she'd missed in the backyard. As long as she toiled in the garden or played games with Agnes or drove her to interesting sites, Rose didn't think about Declan.

She was concentrating so hard that she didn't hear him until his shadow fell across the flowers just beyond her patch of weeds.

Tenting her hand over her eyes, she could finally see him.

He was as beautiful as ever. As sexy. As tall and handsome. And just as perfect.

But she was over that now. It was only the nights that weakened her. She never thought of him during the day.

"Shouldn't you be at work? It's the middle of the day." She tried to be conversational.

He hadn't been down to dinner since they'd returned. He hadn't sat out on the porch with her and talked. They'd become strangers.

And wasn't that what she'd asked for?

"I needed to pick something up." He gazed down at her inscrutably. "I can hire a gardener. You don't have to do all this work."

She sat back on her haunches, still shading her eyes. "Please don't. I love it out here. And Agnes does, too. It makes us both happy."

"All right," he said without any inflection or even a facial expression. "I appreciate your efforts. Everything is flourishing under your care."

"You're welcome. I thought I'd take Agnes to Costco tomorrow. We can pick up some new flowers, plant them back here." She waved her hand over the geraniums and impatiens that had grown leggy. She wasn't asking for permission. She would pay for the flowers herself. She just needed to talk and hold his flat expression at bay.

She wondered if he ever thought of their nights together.

"I'm sure Agnes would love that. What will you get?"

"Whatever they have left. It's late in the season."

"Sounds good."

She missed their talks. After everything they'd done to each other in that big bed in Burkefurd Castle, she would have thought they could talk about anything now.

Sex screwed up everything.

Falling in unrequited love made it even worse.

"Agnes invited me for your special shrimp scampi tonight." He'd partially turned away, as if he couldn't leave fast enough, or he hoped she'd rescind Agnes's offer.

But it would be rude to uninvite him. And dinner with Declan would make Agnes happy. "It's just frozen shrimp so we have more than enough."

He was still half turned. "Thank you. I look forward to it. I won't be back until six, if that's not too late?"

She shook her head. "That's fine."

She could handle his coldness. They'd have dinner with Agnes as a go-between. They wouldn't even have to talk to each other.

As she watched him walk away, she thought of all the hopeless dreams she'd have during the witching hour.

HE HAD WORK TO DO, PLACES TO GO, PEOPLE TO MEET, deals to make, papers to sign.

So why was he at the garden center looking over the array of flowers and shrubs?

Of course it was his garden, so really the flowers were for him, right? Not a gift for Rose, just a job he was handing her. *Please plant my flowers.*

That thought made him feel slightly more... normal.

He'd seen her immediately as he unlocked his flat door, the sight of her in the garden like a jolt to his heart. She looked like a little girl making mud pies. And he thought of Agnes's words. Did he really want to be alone when he was her age? Did he want to spend the next thirty years doing the same things he did now, what he'd been doing since the divorce, just work and work functions?

It was an unanswerable question.

He was so busy he didn't have time to be lonely. But he was alone. He'd never thought about it before Rose. But after returning from Ireland, he'd thought about it a lot. As much as he'd thought about Rose.

He wanted to buy the flowers to make her smile, to see her happy. Other than his parents and Agnes, it had been a long time since he'd thought about making someone happy.

That made Rose different from every other woman.

He chose the ones with the brightest blooms, petunias and marigolds and pansies and impatiens. Then he saw it, a blue hydrangea, her favorite. He bought that, too. When he got the flats and tubs to the car, they filled the trunk.

At his office he parked far out in the lot, under a big shade tree so that Rose's flowers wouldn't wilt. But before it was even five, and before he'd finished all his work, he started to worry about the flowers. Maybe it was too hot in the trunk even in the shade. He couldn't bring Rose dead flowers. He checked them twice, and they were fine, and he laughed at himself for being ridiculous. But he couldn't stop worrying about those damn flowers.

He couldn't stop thinking about her.

He couldn't stop imagining himself at eighty-seven years

old, or sixty-seven, or even fifty-seven, and being alone without Rose. But that's where he was headed. Alone. Maybe, possibly, probably even lonely. Without her.

If he'd never had Rose, he might have been okay. Just like he was okay about being childless because it never happened.

He'd always been about work, even when he was in junior high with a paper route and in high school delivering pizzas. He worked hard to make things better, but when they were better, he hadn't stopped. It had been his wife's biggest complaint. He enjoyed his work. But in Ireland, with Rose, he'd learned there were other things to enjoy. Maybe, too, it was just his time of life, middle-age. He'd been forty when he married, not as well established, *getting* there but not *there*. Back then he couldn't see there was a different way to look at life.

Was he an old dog who couldn't learn new tricks?

His relationships had always been short-term, with the exception of his marriage. Before and after though, nothing had lasted long enough to be called a relationship. Rose hadn't asked for long-term. But she was a long-term woman. She'd had one love over her entire life. That was the absolute definition of long term.

He didn't know if he could give her that.

But he could give her more than two weeks in an Irish castle. He could give her more than one evening of dancing. He could give her more than a few nights in his bed. Every day he could give her the next day, and the next one.

He pulled into the driveway, hoping she would still be in the garden. She wasn't. She and Agnes would be in the kitchen preparing shrimp scampi for him.

He left the blue hydrangea on the back porch where she would see it in the morning. Then he carried the flats of flowers to the garden, setting them down in the shade so they wouldn't wilt.

He stood there a long moment, looking at all she'd done out here, the changes she'd made, the beauty she'd added, the love she'd given to every single plant. Rose had made his garden flourish. She'd made Agnes flourish. She'd made him flourish as well.

Now he just needed to know if Rose would let him help her flourish, too.

❧ 25 ❧

"What on earth is he doing out there?" Agnes stood by the French door of her bedroom, looking into the backyard.

Rose followed the line of her gaze to find Declan bending down to set something on the ground.

Then she saw what he'd held. "Flowers," she whispered, her voice full of wonder.

"Will you look at that?" Agnes pointed.

And Rose saw the blue hydrangea under the porch overhang.

"He bought you a blue hydrangea."

"He didn't buy it for me," she said immediately. "It's for the garden."

Agnes snorted. "Get a grip."

Rose laughed. Agnes could always make her laugh, especially when she sounded like a teenager rather than an octogenarian.

He'd obviously bought the flowers because she planned to do some shopping at Costco. But she wanted to believe he'd bought the blue hydrangea because she loved them.

She wasn't, however, about to put any ideas in Agnes's head that weren't already there. "When exactly did you invite him for dinner?"

Agnes waved a hand errantly. "Oh, I don't know. Maybe when you were in the bathroom." She'd obviously used speed-dial to extend the invitation.

She was still matchmaking.

Even if there was nothing to matchmake.

Except that Declan was leaving presents in the garden.

She was still ruminating half an hour later while Agnes sat at the kitchen table watching her prepare the shrimp scampi. According to Agnes, it was Declan's favorite, though he'd never said that when she made it before.

At the knock on the door, Agnes called out, "I'll get it," and jumped up, at least as much as Agnes could jump.

Rose could have answered it much more quickly, but she let Agnes do as much on her own as she wanted. As long as she was safe. It didn't matter if Declan waited a few more minutes.

Over the stove fan, she heard their voices. "Rose absolutely loves the blue hydrangea you bought her." That brought a smile to Rose's lips. Agnes was so obvious.

Declan's answer was inaudible.

Agnes went on. "She's making your favorite shrimp scampi in return."

She was laying it on a thick even for Agnes. Shrimp scampi had been on the menu before the blue hydrangea showed up on the porch, even before Agnes had invited Declan to dinner.

She didn't want to hope. She didn't even want to *think* about hope.

She was making a good life with Agnes. She was happy making Agnes happy.

He'd showered and changed into khakis, his blond hair still damp and glistening. And he was achingly handsome.

But she was happy with her life as it was. She didn't want to change it again.

He held out a bottle, saying, "Champagne," unnecessarily.

"Thank you." It was same label he'd bought her in Ireland. Was he trying to seduce her with memories? "And thank you for getting the flowers."

"You're welcome."

She didn't mention the blue hydrangea. "Have a seat." She waved a hand at the table Agnes had set. "It's almost ready."

"Shall I open the champagne for you?" he offered when she expected him to just sit and leave her to cook.

She was flustered, nervous, even a little crazy since they'd spent barely five minutes together since they'd returned from Ireland. And here he was taking up too much space in the kitchen and offering champagne.

She couldn't stop asking herself what it all meant.

The cork popped.

What if he wanted to start their affair again? Or what if the flowers and champagne didn't mean anything at all?

He reached past her, close, too close, as he retrieved the champagne glasses.

He smelled too good after his shower. Suddenly she was back in Ireland, where there was just the feel of him, the scent of him, the taste of him.

She was too old to moon over a man, wasn't she?

The champagne fizzed as he poured in tandem with the crackle and pop of the shrimp in the pan.

Then he was close again, handing her a glass. "To quench your thirst while you cook." Oh God, that voice, low and seductive, as if he were saying so much more.

Her mouth watered for more than shrimp and champagne, and she gave him a strained smile as she took the glass.

253

"Sit." The word came out like a command. "It'll be done in a minute."

He smiled as if he knew what he was doing to her, as if he intended every sensation that flooded her body.

She served the scampi over black rice, something she'd recently discovered, and set both plates in front of Declan and Agnes with a smile. Then she plated her own and sat, unfolding her napkin over her lap.

Agnes raised her glass. "Together again, just like in Ireland," she toasted.

Rose almost choked, and Declan smiled his sexy, wicked smile. "I second that."

Rose did not make a third.

"Delicious as usual." His politeness was overwhelming. "Thank you for inviting me."

Because he was looking at her, Rose said, "Agnes invited you."

It was rude, but she wanted him to know she hadn't asked for this dinner date.

Then again, maybe he was the one pushing. Maybe he wanted her back in his bed.

"I invited myself. I missed your scampi and the company of two beautiful ladies."

Agnes tittered at the compliment.

He definitely wanted something. She'd have to get him alone and tell him in no uncertain terms that it wasn't happening. She was too old to be a sex buddy. That wasn't her generation.

Agnes watched the two of them like they were a spectacle at the Colosseum.

"I've got a plan I want to run by you both," Declan said. Just looking at him made her heart race. "My parents haven't seen Agnes in ages. I thought I'd fly them up here, especially since it's hot down in Palm Springs now. They'll get a break from the heat, and we can all do some sightseeing."

"Oh my." Agnes sighed her delight. "We could get out the Royal Albert china and make scones with lemon curd and some of that Irish whiskey marmalade. Like the high tea we had in Ireland."

They still had the scone mix and lemon curd that Declan bought at Kylemore Abbey, plus the marmalade Agnes had given him. And Rose had found crumpets, at Trader Joe's, no less.

But now she could only stare at him, wondering what game he was playing.

He went on as if he couldn't feel her laser-pointed glare. "In the fall, when the weather is cooler, I'd like to fly the three of us down there to visit my parents in their own habitat. It's something we should do once a quarter, up here when it's too hot down there, and vice versa. Now that we know how well Agnes travels, it would be good to keep everyone in touch."

Rose was speechless.

Agnes was bubbling over with excitement, fizzing as high as champagne poured too quickly. "Oh, I would love that, please, please, please, Declan. That's the most marvelous idea ever. I'll even sit in a wheelchair so we can get through security faster."

Declan chuckled.

Rose sat stupefied. It was almost as if he were making her part of his family. But all he really needed was for her to take care of Agnes. And to fill his bed when he required it.

"What do you think?" he asked her point blank.

She didn't want to give him the idea that they could be sex buddies. "That would be amazing for Agnes and your parents. They're such good friends. They should keep in touch."

He went for point blank again. "What about you?"

"Of course I'll come. Agnes will need me."

Agnes beamed at her. "I can't do anything without you, dear."

She patted Agnes's hand. "Thank you for needing me."

"You'll like the Palm Springs area when it's not so hot," he assured them. "We can take the tram up Mount San Jacinto and also visit Joshua Tree National Park. It's an amazing place."

Why was he pushing? And why did he have to do it in front of Agnes? "You don't have to convince me. I've already said I'd be happy to help Agnes."

"The trip could be good for you, too."

He was definitely offering something. "I'm sure *Agnes* and I," she stressed," will have a marvelous time."

He stayed after dinner, even after the champagne was finished. He stayed for coffee and for card games. He stayed and he stayed. Until Rose realized he wasn't going to leave until Agnes was in bed.

"Declan certainly is friendly tonight," Agnes said as Rose helped her into her nightie.

"He's being friendly to you."

"And to you, dear." She beamed like a lighted Christmas tree.

Rose harrumphed exactly like Agnes would.

When she was tucked in bed, the little lady said, "You better go out and face the music." Her eyes twinkled like the star on the top of that same Christmas tree.

Rose kissed her good night, stroked a hand down her arm. "Don't get your hopes up about anything except getting to see Declan's parents."

DECLAN HAD RETRIEVED ANOTHER BOTTLE OF CHAMPAGNE, which he held up as she returned to the parlor.

"I shouldn't have any more." She needed her wits about her.

"The three of us finished that bottle hours ago." He poured despite her protests. "Shall we sit outside?"

She thought of Burkefurd Castle and the balcony overlooking the garden. She'd even thought of planting roses in Declan's front yard, right next to the porch so they could smell them at night.

Despite the inner voice shouting about self-preservation, she followed him out to the porch. The evening was cooling down after the warm day, the stars sparkled in the sky, and the air was sweet.

She drank the champagne because it tasted good. And because the first two sips gave her the courage to say, "What game are you playing, Declan?"

She didn't expect him to give her the unvarnished truth. Whatever he wanted, he would couch in soft euphemisms, words intended to gentle and persuade her.

But he surprised her. "I made a mistake letting you get away in Ireland. And it was a mistake letting you keep your distance since we've been home. In Ireland I made it sound like I just wanted a fling." He shrugged, giving her a wry smile. "Maybe that's all I did want then."

He looked at her. She looked at the garden, unable to meet his eyes.

"But that feels like a lifetime ago." His voice was soft, his words mesmerizing.

"It was only three weeks," she said bluntly.

He dropped down to a whisper, his tone like the gentle brush of his fingers across her skin. "I've missed you, Rose."

He made her want to cry, he made her want to throw herself in his arms.

"I miss holding you, touching you, kissing you, making love to you."

She had to close her eyes. If she looked at him, she'd be lost.

"But I miss our talks the most. I miss sitting on the balcony with you. I miss sitting on this porch with you. I miss our dinners and all the games we played with Agnes. I just plain miss you."

She wanted to fall into everything he said, to believe it meant they had a future. And she finally had to ask him, "What are you really trying to say?"

She needed him to spell it out. She didn't want to assume only to find he meant something entirely different.

"I want to be with you. Not just for a few hours while Agnes is asleep. I don't want you to have to sneak back into your room. I don't want this thing between us to be furtive. I want to see if I can do it right this time."

He looked so earnest, so serious, so driven. She wanted to touch him, lay her hand on his cheek. "For how long?" she asked without touching him.

"I want to believe it could be forever."

"But you don't know if you can do forever."

He shook his head. "Do you know if you can do forever?"

The absolute truth? She didn't. And she shook her head.

"Maybe we can try. Maybe we can be together without limits, without a time period hanging over us. We can just *be*."

There were still so many problems. "What about Agnes? I can't leave her alone at night."

"It's possible to have someone stay with her at night. And you can be with her during the day. It's not unreasonable."

It wasn't unreasonable. It was normal. But... "I'm afraid of leaving her alone with someone else."

"So am I. But you can't be with her all the time. We already agreed you need a break sometimes."

Not that she'd done anything about it since they'd returned. "What if something happens? I'm not sure I can risk it." She'd felt so sick in Ireland when Agnes fell. Just like she had when her mother fell.

"You know you need time for yourself. Just like you needed it with your mother. Everyone does. And we can protect Agnes with good people."

Did she really think she was the only one who could do it right? Maybe she did. Maybe she was arrogant. Maybe she needed to start trusting others. Maybe it would actually be good for Agnes, too.

"We can make this work," he said gently, as if he could see her weakening. "We can make *us* work."

He was so much more sure of things than she was.

Yet she was the one with love on her bucket list.

He seemed to be offering her everything she could ever want. She just had to reach out and take it, without fear.

But Rose was a very fearful person. "Even without Agnes in the mix, I'm not sure I have the courage," she admitted. "I was married for thirty years. And things were far from perfect. But I stayed because I was afraid of what my life would be like without him. That it could be worse. That I'd never meet another man, never have another relationship, never fall in love again, that I'd be alone for the rest of my life, that I'd turn fifty and suddenly become more invisible than I already was."

"But he left you." His voice was soft, as if he wanted to avoid hurting her. Yet the truth had to be said.

She nodded. "I loved my mother very much. I still miss her. But maybe—" If she was totally honest with herself. "Maybe moving in to help her was like running back home, a place I could stay if things went bad. And they did go bad. But was it all my husband? Or was it me?" She shook her head. "I don't know. But I'm afraid of making another mistake." Her eyes stung with all her fears.

Maybe here was the true reason she wouldn't talk to him after Agnes's fall. Fear. If *she* ended things between them, then she wouldn't hurt so badly. Except that strategy hadn't worked.

"Don't think for one minute that I'm not afraid, too. I'm afraid for Agnes. I'm afraid this thing between us can't work. We all have fears."

He reached out, she thought to take her hand, but instead he refilled their champagne, as if he wanted to touch her but didn't know how.

"I told you about my wife," he said. "But I made the divorce sound like her fault, that she was a gold digger who only wanted my money and a baby to cement our marriage." He shook his head, a sad, thoughtful move. "But I never gave her the time she needed. When we were first married, she remained as my secretary. We were together almost every moment. It was exciting and wonderful and I felt like a new man. But then I thought, I have enough money, why do I make my wife work? Once we had a baby, she'd stop anyway. And we thought the baby would happen at any time."

He looked at the road as a car passed, sighed heavily, drank another swallow of champagne.

Then he spoke again. "So I sent her off to redecorate our house for the perfect family we wanted to have. When she came to me with paint samples or curtain fabrics, I told her I had my job and she had hers, that I didn't need to step on her toes." His sigh was mournful as he rediscovered the demise of his relationship. "I told myself I was giving her carte blanche to do all the things she wanted without having to come to me for permission. But really all I did was work my usual long hours and shut her out. When the babies didn't come, I blamed her, as if she wasn't holding up her end of the bargain.

But we got tested and we found out it was me who couldn't have kids. I thought what the hell am I going to do now? How can I make her happy? And somewhere along the way, I stopped trying to make her happy because I didn't know how."

She reached out for him then, a simple touch on his hand. "I'm so sorry. But she still cheated on you. She got pregnant by another man. You can't take all the blame."

He shrugged as if it didn't hurt anymore, when she knew it had to be tearing him apart. "Yes, she cheated. But I have to look at why, what she needed out of that marriage that she wasn't getting. At the office, she had all my attention. She was my right hand. We were a team. And all of a sudden I sent her off to take care of the house as if I didn't need her anymore."

"It wasn't all your fault, Declan," she tried to soothe him.

He looked at her for a long moment, a look that trickled along her nerve endings. It wasn't bad, it was almost exciting, as if he were really seeing her, really listening.

Finally, he said, "I can say the same for you. It's not all your fault."

"I suppose that's true. I wasn't happy. Not for a long time. I think mostly that was because I never went after my dreams of being a nurse. Maybe I was afraid of failing at that, too. And I blamed him, yes." She nodded to herself. "Because I felt like I had to support him. He wanted to own that garage, so we had to save money to make sure he could keep it running, and for future improvements he knew he'd have to make. But when it was taken away from him unjustly, he gave up. And I blamed him for that."

"We should never give up our dreams for someone else."

She breathed in deeply, nodding. "It was my biggest regret."

"I thought your mother was your biggest regret."

She snorted out a laugh, sad and rueful at the same time. "She is my biggest guilt. There were so many things I didn't do for her."

"You took care of her for five years. You lost your husband in large part because you moved into her house. You did everything you could for her."

She moved her head gently side to side, breathing in, thinking as she stared at the railing. "Did I? There were the years before it got so bad. But I didn't have time for her. I was always so busy."

"You were busy making money to fund the garage your husband wasn't even guaranteed he'd get."

She clucked her tongue. "You're throwing my words back at me."

He laughed softly, nodded, then sobered. "Sometimes we can't see past the moment, that we'll have time to fix things. You probably believed that when you'd saved enough money, you'd be free to spend time with her."

"Just like you thought you'd have time to spend with your wife once the baby came."

He breathed out a sigh. "Just like that. Then we realize we're out of time and we won't get the thing we were working so hard for."

"You're right," she agreed.

"I realize something else. I used my divorce as an excuse not to try again."

And she thought that maybe she was using her guilt over her mother and her fear for Agnes as excuses against accepting Declan, a way to keep her heart safe.

"I told myself it was all because of the unequal relationship, me the older boss, her the younger employee. So even though I was attracted to you from the moment you stepped into my office—"

"You were?" Her heart tripped all over itself.

He picked up her hand, kissed her knuckles. "I couldn't stop thinking about you."

Her cheeks heated.

"But I was afraid. I told myself you were an employee and off limits."

"But you changed your mind in Ireland?"

"I saw you with Agnes. How caring you were. Then you cried in my arms, and there was no going back." He rubbed his lips over the back of her hand, setting off sparks. "Let's not allow our fears to stop us." He squeezed her fingers gently. "Do you want to be with me?"

The question required only a yes or no answer. But she couldn't seem to get the word out.

He kissed her fingertips. "I want to be with you. Let's not make this another regret. Let's not tell ourselves we'll be okay if it doesn't work. Let's just say we'll absolutely make it work."

He was a can-do, will-do kind a guy. She was still afraid to try. But in this moment, with everything he offered, she was even more afraid *not* to try. "Yes," she said softly, clearly, emphatically. "Do you know what was on my bucket list?"

He shook his head.

"To fall in love. But even to myself, I couldn't admit I wanted to fall in love with you."

His eyes turned a hot emerald green. "And did you?"

She could have nodded without saying the words, but she let go of the fear. "I'm totally in love with you."

He grinned, for the first time since they'd sat on the porch. "And I totally love you."

"Is that why you bought the blue hydrangea?"

He nodded. "I bought it because you love blue hydrangeas. And I want to see you growing in my garden." He raised her hand to his lips. "Let's start our no-fear pact right now. Let me make love to you." He stopped her when she opened her mouth as if he knew what she'd say. "We've got

Agnes's monitor. We'll hear if she needs you. And tomorrow we'll work out everything else. But right now, we need each other. Even if I have to make love to you on Agnes's parlor floor so you'll be close enough to run to her if she needs you."

She laughed, a truly joyous sound even if it was soft. "Making love in Agnes's parlor. Now that would be kinky and wicked."

"And sexy as all get out," he finished for her. He stood, held out his hand.

She took it with her whole heart, letting him lead her into the house. And into their future.

EPILOGUE

"Come back to bed," Declan growled.

"I'd love to," Rose said, already belting her robe around her waist. "But we promised Agnes we'd take her to Gilroy Gardens today."

He groaned. "That doesn't mean we have to take her at..." He cracked one eye open to look at the clock. "Eight o'clock. On a Saturday, no less. The place doesn't even open until eleven."

She laughed at him. "You wouldn't be so tired if you hadn't insisted on having your wicked way with me at three o'clock in the morning."

He growled again, and slipped his hand beneath the covers. "I'm ready to do it again. Aren't you?"

She danced away from him as he lunged across the bed. "I'll be ready again tonight. After a fun day. Then you can rest assured I'm the one who'll attack you."

He flopped back on the king-size mattress, throwing his arms wide. "Susanna will be with Agnes until nine."

Rose had moved her meager belongings into Declan's flat

three weeks ago. Right after that glorious night when they'd made wicked love on Agnes's parlor floor. Very quietly, too.

Agnes now had two nighttime caregivers, Ana and Susanna, who stayed from nine at night to nine in the morning. Agnes was entranced with the rhythm of their names. They helped her get undressed and into bed, watched over her all night, then dressed and showered her in the morning.

When the girls arrived, they were usually watching TV or a movie—they'd binged the rest of *The Walking Dead*—and Rose stayed until Agnes was ready for bed. Declan always came in to say good night, unless they were attending one of his business galas. Rose had been to two events with him, wearing the beautiful dresses he'd purchased for her in Ireland. And the parties hadn't been anywhere near as terrifying as she'd thought.

Rose was usually down before nine in the morning, making Agnes's breakfast. Three days a week, she and Agnes went to the swim center for water exercises, and Declan usually met them there to swim laps. Blue, another caregiver, came in for a couple of hours every other day so Rose could go for a hike. It was a perfect arrangement. The girls had fallen in love with Agnes just as Rose had, and together they were all part of Agnes's silly sausage club.

Every weekend she and Declan took Agnes somewhere special. Today it was Gilroy Gardens, after which they'd head over to the coast and stop at a fabulous seafood restaurant that always had a queue. If the weather was nice, they could sit at the very top picnic bench and see the ocean over the sand.

"Get up, lazybones." She swatted his thigh. "We have to get to the restaurant by three-thirty or the line will be out the door. And Agnes will be very upset that she had to wait."

Declan growled again then launched himself at Rose, capturing her around the waist and carrying her into the huge bathroom. Where she let him have his wicked way with her in the shower. She could never resist his wicked ways.

She'd never been happier.

Later that morning, Agnes echoed her thought as they strolled through the trees of Gilroy Gardens. "I've never been happier." She clapped her hands in delight.

Then she pulled Declan to the most amazing tree Rose had ever seen.

"Tell us all about it." Agnes pointed to the placard, and Rose read.

"This one's the Basket Tree." The hollow trunk was a tall, loosely woven basket of diamond shapes you could see right through, the tree's leafy branches growing out the top. "It was originally six sycamore trees planted in a circle and grafted together. All the fancy trees came from The Tree Circus over in Scotts Valley," she told them. "The man who built Gilroy Gardens saved the trees, digging them up and trucking them over here. It's our job to find them all somewhere in the park. There's the Needle and Thread Tree, the Two Leg Tree, the Four-Legged Giant, the Zig Zag." And on and on.

Agnes clapped her hands again before grabbing the handles of her walker. "I visited The Tree Circus. Marvin and I loved all those weird sites. The Tree Circus became part of that prehistoric world where those massive dinosaurs poked right up out of the trees as you drove along Highway 17 to the beach. And there was Santa's Village." She made a face, fluttering her eyelashes. "Yes, it was all kid stuff, but Marvin and I loved every moment. Then we'd go out to the Boardwalk and ride the Giant Dipper. They had that old steam train somewhere around there, too, that you could ride into the mountains."

"I was sorry to see Santa's Village torn down," Declan said. "And to lose all the dinosaurs. But I didn't know they'd moved the trees."

"Nobody values history anymore," Agnes grumbled.

Rose wouldn't exactly call them historical monuments. "I remember The Lost World and Santa's Village, but I never actually went there."

Driving over Highway 17 in her dad's old station wagon, they always stopped for breakfast at the Denny's in Scotts Valley. But they never went to The Lost World or Santa's Village because her brother, who was five years older, said that was all for babies. Besides, her parents wanted to spend the day at the beach and on the rides at the Boardwalk. It had truly been a wonderful time.

Rose still called her brother. She hadn't told him yet about Declan. She had no idea whether he'd be happy for her, or even angrier than he already was.

She wound her arm around Agnes's shoulders. "You know, I think that old steam train is at a place called Roaring Camp in Felton."

Agnes fairly bounced on her toes. "Oh my dear, I haven't been there in years and years and years." Agnes might not always remember what she had for breakfast or what they'd done yesterday, but the distant past was alive and well for her. "Do you think it's still running?"

Declan was already tapping on his phone. "We're in luck, ladies. Roaring Camp is still open and the trains are still running." He looked at them with a glint in his eye. "Why don't we go there next weekend when my parents are visiting?"

Agnes bounced so hard, her curls jumped. "Oh yes, please, please, please."

Rose had everything on her bucket list. And even more. She'd fallen in love with a wonderful man. In Agnes, she experienced the joy of feeling like she had her mother back with her. Declan had helped her see that she'd done everything she could for her mother, had, in fact, done more than most. But she could still learn from her regrets, from all the time she'd lost when she could have been taking her mother to fun and exciting places and making her last cognizant years happy. With Agnes, she'd been granted a redo.

Who would have thought a trip to Ireland could give her so many second chances?

DECLAN'S HEART RESONATED WITH AGNES'S WORDS. HE'D never been happier in his life.

After the enjoyable day at Gilroy Gardens where they'd discovered all the circus trees, they made it to the coast by three-thirty. But still there was a line outside the seafood place known for its fabulous cioppino.

"What do you want, Agnes?" He knew full well what she'd say.

"Fish and chips," she crowed.

And Rose said exactly what he knew she'd say. "I'll share with you, Agnes."

"You two are so stuck in your ways." But his heart felt light, the smile on his face unbeatable. "You both go out back and pick a table. I'll wait in line and order." You ordered at the counter, got your seat, and put a number on the table for the server to deliver your food.

After twenty minutes in line, he carried their drinks onto the back patio that led up to the top of the sand dune. Rose had opened the big umbrella to shade Agnes from the sun, and overhead the seagulls swarmed, several brave ones dropping down to stalk the aisleway in case anyone dropped a bit of fish or didn't throw out their trash.

The food arrived far faster than it had taken to order it.

Agnes cooed at the sight. "Oh my, it's piping hot."

Steam rose off the fish and from his cioppino.

While Rose divided the fish and chips between two plates, Declan dropped something into his soup that neither of them noticed.

Agnes moaned and groaned over the battered delight. "I'll eat with my fingers." She nibbled proudly, and Rose, smiling, did the same.

Declan did his own share of moaning and groaning, giving Rose a wicked smile whenever he caught her eye.

"My oh my, this is the most delicious cioppino I've ever tasted in my life," he said, imitating Agnes. It was full of mussels and clams and prawns, crab and white fish and even squid. "I'll finish up this last spoonful," he told them as he tossed a crab claw on the discard plate beside his bowl.

He ate until the spoon made a clink on the ceramic, and he lifted it out of the soup. "What's this I found in my bowl?"

Rose and Agnes craned to see.

"It looks like a ring," Agnes chirped.

Rose just stared at the ring on his spoon.

Declan plucked it off, still dripping with the tomato broth, and swished it in his water glass. Okay, maybe the soup wasn't the best idea, but then he couldn't imagine sticking a diamond ring in Rose's coleslaw hoping she'd see it before she bit into it.

"Now that it's washed off, I do believe it's a ring." He held it out to Rose. "Maybe it belongs to you."

"Are you asking her to marry you, Declan?" Agnes fluttered her eyelashes.

Declan nodded, his gaze on Rose's beautiful, stunned features. "I am."

"Then ask her properly." Agnes pointed. "Get down on one knee. That's what Marvin did."

Maybe he should have done this at home, or at least somewhere more private. He should have known Agnes would put her two cents in.

But he did exactly what she told him to, going down on one knee beside Rose, a seagull waddling close to stare at him with beady eyes.

"This ring is not for you," he told it. Then he took Rose's hand. "It's not the most romantic spot. Maybe I should have taken you somewhere with white tablecloths and flickering candles. But will you marry me, Rose Christopher?"

She bit her bottom lip and tears glistened in her eyes.

"It's the most romantic proposal I've ever heard." Agnes clapped her hands to her cheeks.

And Rose whispered, "I will."

Declan slipped the ring on her finger, then stood and pulled her into his arms amid a round of applause.

He whispered in her ear, "Do you know what was on my bucket list?"

She shook her head.

"A long and happy life with you. I love you more than anything in the world."

Rose wound her arms around his neck. "And I love you, Declan Delaney."

Agnes sighed with delight. She'd gotten everything she'd hoped and prayed for the two people she loved most in the world.

Once Again, a later-in-life series that will whisk you away to fabulous foreign locales where love always gets a second chance.
Look for the next *Once Again* novel, **Under the Northern Lights**, a Christmas story.

ABOUT THE AUTHOR

NY Times and USA Today bestselling author Jennifer Skully is a lover of contemporary romance, bringing you poignant tales peopled with hilarious characters that will make you laugh and make you cry. Look for Jennifer's series written with Bella Andre, starting with *Breathless in Love*, The Maverick Billionaires Book 1. Writing as Jasmine Haynes, Jennifer authors classy, sensual romance tales about real issues such as growing older, facing divorce, starting over. Her books have passion and heart and humor and happy endings, even if they aren't always traditional. She also writes gritty, paranormal mysteries in the Max Starr series. Having penned stories since the moment she learned to write, Jennifer now lives in the Redwoods of Northern California with her husband and their adorable nuisance of a cat who totally runs the household.

Learn more about Jennifer/Jasmine and join her newsletter for free books, exclusive contests and excerpts, plus updates on sales and new releases at **http://bit.ly/SkullyNews**

Somebody's Wife

The Jackson Brothers: 3-Book Bundle

Castle Inc

The Fortune Hunter | Show and Tell

Fair Game

Open Invitation

Invitation to Seduction | Invitation to Pleasure

Invitation to Passion

Open Invitation: 3-Book Bundle

Wives & Neighbors

Wives & Neighbors: The Complete Story

Prescott Twins

Double the Pleasure | Skin Deep

Prescott Twins Complete Set

Lessons After Hours

Past Midnight | What Happens After Dark

The Principal's Office | The Naughty Corner

The Lesson Plan

Stand-alone

Take Your Pleasure | Take Your Pick

Take Your Pleasure Take Your Pick Duo

Anthology: Beauty or the Bitch & Free Fall

Made in the USA
Middletown, DE
24 November 2023